Wenlock

Whispers

By

Bill Stenlake

Wenlock Whispers Copyright © 2019 William (Bill) Stenlake

Wenlock Whispers is the 3rd and last in the Wenlock series. It is not a trilogy but there are links between the three books.

Wenlock Whispers by Bill Stenlake
All rights reserved. No part of this book may be reproduced, distributed or transmitted in any form, by any means without the prior consent of the author.

All characters in this publication are fictitious and any resemblance to persons, living or dead is purely coincidental. Some places named in the book exist and are real and some do not exist and are not real. The placement of all things geographical is relevant to this story only and as such should be deemed fictional.

Book Cover Photo: © FlairImages/Dreamstime.com

Other books by Bill Stenlake:
- HOLLOW MILL
- THE KEEPER
- KENAN'S LEGACY
- CORNERSTONE
- THE GRAND MASTER
- DETECTIVE BRAMLEY BOOK 1
- RANDOLPH
- VOICES IN MY HEAD
- LOWARTH TOLL
- THE CORIDAE KEY
- BRAMLEY BOOK 2
- THE MANNACHS
- DIMENSIONS
- THE ROOTS
- A PAIR OF SHORTS
- THE WATCHER
- THE KEEPER TRILOGY
- IT'S DARK IN WENLOCK
- RODDY JOHNSTONE
- IT'S MURDER IN WENLOCK

Wenlock Whispers By Bill Stenlake

These are my definitions:

Whisper: To speak in a very quiet way, this can only be heard by someone next to you.

Whispers: The act of speaking in a very quiet way, this only is heard by someone next to you.

A Whisper: Something that is said quietly to other people, that you don't want others to hear you say.

A Whisper: Something said to another that may only be a rumour, therefore it is unsubstantiated.

Whispers: More than one thing, most likely unsubstantiated, that are said about others or events, by one or many.

Whisperer: The person who is whispering.

Wenlock Whispers may be one of these, or a mix of these, even all of these. Perhaps it is none of these. That is for you to decide.

Chapter 1 Edmund

Edmund is sitting with his back against a tree. He does this a lot, especially towards the end of the day, when his chores have all been done. He has a feeling inside him that something is about to happen. He isn't wrong about that, but when it does; it still catches him slightly unawares and makes him jump.

'Fighters will come. You must not be there when they do.'

He hears the soft voice next to his ear saying this, but he knows from experience that when he turns, there will be no one there. It has happened before. Also he knows that what is whispered to him will not be the complete story. He has to fill in the blanks, so to speak, but he has never been wrong with how he has interpreted the whisper, to describe the threat.

He just lets the thoughts come into his head over the next few minutes. He wonders sometimes if it is the whisperer who gives him these thoughts, as he doesn't know how else he comes up with the conclusions he does.

He has got this together, well the little that has come to him this time. He is ready to go to warn Edgar and Edith, when he hears another whisper in his ear. This has not happened before. Never has he had two warnings so close together. Never on the same month, let alone the same day just a few minutes apart.

'Much water will come, and floods too.'

He settles back against the tree to wait for the blanks to fill in on this one. There is little more that comes through to him, but what he does find himself doing, is linking the two whispers together. He thinks about this and wonders if because he isn't going to be there anyway because of the fighters, then he doesn't need to be told that. He doesn't get any further, so he gets up this time to deliver the warnings.

Now Edmund is sitting with his back against another tree, waiting for the prophecies to materialise.

It is dark, very dark. There isn't even a decent sized visible moon this night. It is barely more than a slither and it does nothing to illuminate the night sky. It is also quiet, very quiet. There isn't a single sound from any source. On top of that there is no wind at all, not even a wisp. And did I mention the fact that it is not the warmest of nights? It is not freezing, but it is close to that.

So all they can do is wait, wait for what is to come.

Everything stays the same, until maybe half the way through the night. Eyes are starting to get heavy, with the need to close them for sleep. Others have already succumbed to this and their light breathing can just be heard. Any louder and they would have to be woken to reduce the risk of being heard, and hearing things for that matter. Who is to say who the breathing belongs to?

It would be so much more comfortable if only they were back in their houses, well huts is what they really are. They are built of wood and thatched with straw. The central fire would burn throughout the night and keep them all warm, certainly warmer than they are at this precise moment. But here they are, away from their houses. They are away from their small settlement. They are just inside the tree line, up on the escarpment. They are about four hundred yards from where they would normally be asleep and warm at this time of night. So why aren't they at home on this night?

Well initially that is down to Edmund. Edmund is ten years old, but he is wiser beyond his years. Either that; or he has a sixth sense that guides him and his family away from potential conflicts. They can be conflicts with the weather on one hand and conflicts with people on the other. He has a history of it; well he has had for the past three years. So when Edmund tells his father and mother,

Edgar and Edith, that he has heard about an impending danger, they do more than just listen; they act. They act every time these days, because of what happened the first time Edmund heard something and told them. He told them something and they did nothing about it. That act cost them. It very nearly cost them their lives. In fact it would have done, if Edmund had not told them something else, to get them out of that particular tight spot.

Edmund has never played on the fact that they now react to what he says. He can honestly say he has been tempted to, as he has that kind of mischievous temperament, but he has always managed to pull back, even if it is at the very last second.

But the reason they are where they are this night, makes Edgar and Edith suspect that he might be playing with them. The reason they think this, is because Edmund has said that he has received two whispers, rather than the normal one, warning of two different threats. The problem is that neither threat looked plausible to them. So they very nearly chose to ignore Edmund on this occasion. In fact they would have done so, if he hadn't started gathering his things and put them by the door, before approaching them both and giving them a hug and a kiss. He had tears running down his cheeks as he said he would miss them after they died. He didn't actually say they would die if they stayed there, but his actions and emotions told them he knew they would die. It was hard for them to ignore him and so they relented and went with him up onto the escarpment. That is where Edmund said they would be safer. That was worrying too, because he only said safer, not safe.

The first threat was that their settlement would be attacked by people they had not encountered before. Fighting men would come and destroy everything and everyone in their path. The second threat was that there would be a great flood and the settlement would be washed away.

Edgar and Edith had questions about both threats. Why would fighting men come here and destroy everything? There is nothing to destroy, other than the Abbey a few miles away. And with regards to there going to be a great flood; well that is unheard of. There has not been anything like that in living memory, or any memory that has been passed down for that matter. The days have been sunny and warm for the time of year and the nights have been cold. The skies have been clear for weeks. Why would there be a flood this night?

So here they are on the escarpment, waiting for who knows what to happen. Edgar has built a small shelter for the three of them. Edmund thought this was a good idea. Edgar's brother and his family have also come up with them, but they haven't built a shelter. They only go so far in their belief of Edmund's prophecies. The other two families in their settlement have opted to stay where they are.

The silence in the night air is suddenly disturbed rudely, by the sounds of men shouting, roaring even. Everyone is wide awake in an instant. Everyone except for Edmund has stood up and is looking in the direction of the settlement. That is the direction this roaring is coming from. Then they see the first glow, coming from that direction too. They know what is causing that.

Edmund is still sitting with his back to the tree.

'You are not safe. Go to the cave.'

Edmund for some reason knows there will be nothing more to fill in on this warning. He can also feel the fear rising in him. He gets to his feet and goes over to Edgar. He tugs on his clothes, to get his attention.

'We have to go. We are not safe. We have to go to the cave.'

'What cave?'

'The one I found on the far side of the escarpment; the one with the hidden entrance.'

'But they are burning our huts.'

'Yes, but we are not in them. We must go now. We must hurry. They are coming to look for us.'

Edmund doesn't know where that last bit came from, but he really believes it to be true. Edgar and Edith get ready to follow, but Edgar's brother does not think that the fighters are going to come up there. He says he won't move.

'You will have to lead us' Edgar says to his son.

Edmund turns and leads them away from their shelter. As he does so, he sees his uncle and his family take over the shelter that Edgar has built. He knows he will never see them again. He also doesn't want them to tell the fighters where he has gone. He leads Edgar and Edith away from there, but not in the direction they need to go, to find his cave. He waits until he is well out of sight and sound of them, before turning in the right direction. It takes him ten minutes to lead them to the cave. All the way there, until they drop over the far edge of the escarpment, they can hear the sounds of the fighting men behind them in the distance. At times they think that distance might be closing.

Chapter 2 Edmund

Just as they start to make their descent, another sound comes to their ears, the sounds of dogs barking. We are not talking about yappy dogs barking here; we are talking about serious barking, big dogs barking; big dogs with a serious agenda, barking. That sound is far from welcome news.

Edmund starts down the slope. If, and it is still if, these dogs have picked up their scent from the settlement, they will easily be able to follow that scent up to where they had pitched the shelter. They will easily come across his uncle and the others still in the shelter. His uncle, no doubt, will have heard what they have heard just now. Edmund is guessing that they will now be panicking and wishing they had left when he did. But there is nothing he can do about that now. He has no way of changing that, or helping them for that matter. They won't know which way he had gone once out of their sight; that was why he didn't leave in the direction he was really heading for.

Anyway, if these fighters have tracking dogs, then Edmund and his parents are not much better off than his uncle and family. The dogs will soon track them down too. Their scent leading away from the shelter they built, will be just as easy to follow as the original scent from the settlement.

Edmund knows there is no point in changing his plans at this stage, despite the dogs and the fighters being so close on their tails. And strangely enough he doesn't feel panic, or the need to worry unduly about the outcome of their current dilemma. Part of the reason for that is that he hasn't heard a whisper. He knows that isn't something that he can be certain he would hear, but inside he thinks that something will intervene to protect them.

The entrance to the cave is hard to find, if you don't know where it is. The dogs will find it sure enough, but finding it and accessing the cave are two different tasks. Edmund has been here before. Edmund has played in this cave. Edmund has experimented in this cave too, playing games. Planning a game in his head, a game where he is hiding from people. True, he didn't think he would be hiding to save his life and the lives of his family, but nonetheless it will stand them in good stead for this threat, hopefully.

There is no doubt that the sounds are closer than they were. They are drifting over the top of the edge and down to where they are now, approaching the cave. If Edmund was to guess where they were coming from, he would say the place where they left his uncle. He hasn't the time to think about that right now.

He pulls the moss away from in front of the cave. He has matted a lot of it onto a set of sticks. Quickly he gets Edith followed by Edgar, to crawl in. The opening isn't large, but they easily crawl through. He tells them to keep going further in. They will have to crawl for about twelve feet, before the cave opens up enough for them to at least sit and wait for him to guide them deeper. While they do that, Edmund busies himself with the task of covering the entrance up again, from the inside.

Just before he pulls the moss cover up to put in place behind him, he feels something on his face. He looks up at the skies and is puzzled. The skies are clear. There are no clouds, at least none that he can see, but there are raindrops falling onto his face. Within a matter of seconds, the drops have gone from the odd one or two that alerted him, to a constant volley of drops. In a few seconds more, the heavens open and it starts pouring with rain. It starts battering down, with the drops bouncing off his face and the ground around him.

He realises that he has wasted more than enough time, precious seconds, looking up into the skies. He pulls the moss back into place, as he crawls backwards into the cave. He ties the corners onto the crude hooks he has made for this purpose when playing his game. He then crawls back a foot or so and starts to grab the rocks he has stockpiled in the small alcove just inside the cave. He fills in the entrance to the cave quickly, so that the gap is filled. He then pulls the bigger rocks out of the alcove and slots them into place. They each have their own position in the entrance, so that he can do it quickly. Maybe all along this moment was what he has played his game for.

With the rocks in place, he moves backwards deeper into the cave, towards his parents. The rocks he has just placed are tightly in place and slotted together in a way that is impossible to push out from within, or push or pull out from outside. He can hear the rain falling as he moves backwards. It sounds as if it is falling harder than before, harder than he can ever remember it falling. It has rained a couple of time while he has played in here before, but nothing like this hard.

He doesn't think of it at this moment, it only comes to him later, but this heavy rain will do a tremendous job of wiping out the trail of their scent. It is a shame that it hadn't started to fall just a few minutes earlier, but then it may not have changed things much.

Edmund joins his parents and then squeezes past them. They can go deeper in the cave on their hands and knees. They don't have to crawl now. They turn a corner a few yards further in. Edmund whispers back to them that he is going to stop. It is pitch black in there and there is nothing that they can see. Edmund is six feet beyond the corner when he stops. He can feel his mother's hand on his foot. He stands up, feeling above him to make sure he has the right place. He has. He knows that because his hands don't have anything to stop them going up through the gap. He knows the gap is big enough for him to easily fit through, as he has been through it before. He only hopes it will be big enough for Edgar and Edith too.

He tells them he is going up as he does so. He tells them to carefully follow him through. Once he is up he moves to one side. Edith comes up next. She is up with him with ease. He tells her to move along a bit, to make room for Edgar to come up too. It is harder for him to get through the gap, but he does it without too much difficulty. Once he is through, Edmund gets him to help him with his plug for the gap. Again he has used a frame made of wood tied together. To this frame has fixed some thinnish flat rocks. The frame is wider than the gap they have come up through. In the dark, they slot the frame into place. Edmund then takes the stout wooden poles he has prepared and wedges them into place. One end slots over the edge of the frame, while the other end is wedged against the passage ceiling. The gap has been filled successfully and it wouldn't be easy to break through it. Well Edmund thinks it is well plugged and not easy to find. When he fitted it originally, he just slotted it in from below. It fits snugly with the rest of the passage ceiling and without a strong light it wouldn't be easy to spot, if you didn't know it was there.

Satisfied he has done what he needs to, he tells Edgar to move over to where Edith is waiting. Edmund carefully manoeuvres over the hatch and follows him along. The space they are now in opens out. It is about six feet across. It is nearly high enough to be able to stand up, but not quite. It goes no further than this.

He continues to talk in a whisper. The one thing he has no idea of, is how far their voices might carry. He tells his concern about this and they talk in a very low whisper. They can't hear any noise carrying through to them from the outside. They can't hear the rain, if it is still raining; it is.

Edmund has previously brought piles of dry leaves in his cave, to make the floor more comfortable to sit on while he was in there. They make a good cushion against the cold of the stone floor, as they sit in there waiting for who knows how long. He has also had the foresight to put a container with water in. It isn't exactly fresh, but as they stay in there over the next two days, it is better than having nothing to drink.

They have no idea of the passage of time. Initially they are on edge, that at any minute they will be discovered in their hideaway. That feeling soon leaves them, when no one comes in the first hour or so. The rain has done a good job of obscuring their scent, while actually the fighters have given up the hunt very shortly after the rain had begun, when the dogs couldn't help them. They were only just leaving where they found Edmund's uncle, when the rain came down. They thought they had found everyone they needed to by then. They left the escarpment to find shelter. Edmund and his parents weren't to know this at the time. They had no way of knowing what was going on in the outside world.

Their cave maintains a steady temperature. It is neither warm nor cold. They have little difficulty staying in there. The only problem they know they have; is when they will have to decide to risk leaving the place. Obviously they can't stay in there forever.

The water has run out quite a while before they decide that they need to leave their hiding place. It isn't a time they have looked forward to with much enthusiasm. But if the rains have washed away their scent, then at least they are unlikely to be in too much danger, just emerging from the cave.

They retrace their steps, leaving everything ready, just as they found it on entering. Edmund is at the front, as he knows the order of the stones covering the mouth of the cave. He also knows where the ties are for the mossed frame over the entrance.

They know even as they approach the entrance that it is still raining outside. They can hear it bouncing off the ground the other side of the stones. What they didn't know at that time was that it hadn't stopped for a second while they have been hiding in the cave.

The water is literally running down the side of the escarpment when they emerge. They only take long enough to gather water in their hands and have a well-deserved drink, before they return to the cave for shelter. This time they only pull the moss cover into place and stay in the first section of the passage, where they can kneel. They assume that no one will be out there looking for them in this weather. In that they are correct.

Chapter 3 Edmund

By the end of the next day, it is the lack of food more than anything else that makes up their minds to leave the safety of the cave. There is that and the fact that at last the rain has stopped falling. Initially it let up a little, but after a few more hours it relents and finally stops. They wait a further hour or so, in case their attackers are just waiting for this time to resume their hunt. There isn't a single sound coming to their ears that spells out any danger. The sounds they are hoping not to hear, being dogs and men roaring.

Even so, they look at Edmund to see if he thinks it is safe for them to leave. The only thing he has to judge that on; is that he hasn't heard any more whispers since the first warnings. Nevertheless, he concentrates and also even tries to contact the whisperer to get something confirmed. Of course he has no way of knowing how to contact the whisperer in the first place, but that doesn't stop him trying. Whether his thoughts get through is something he will never know. He doesn't get a reply, or a whisper of warning.

They have to move now, while there is still going to be light for another couple of hours. Who knows how long it will take to get food and what state the settlement will be in. They fear the worst of course. They are right to as well.

They make their way out of the cave and slowly up to the top of the slope. The ground is wet, very wet. On the flat it would have been soft, but there isn't much soil between the surface and the rock underneath. Even so, it is slippery in places. When they reach the top, the ground is about the same there, except there is water lying everywhere. Edgar walks ahead of the other two, as they make their way to where they had pitched their temporary shelter. When they find it, there is little left except the makings on the ground, swishing around in puddles. But they don't think this was caused by anything other than the apparent excessive amount of rain that appears to have fallen over the past three days. There is no sign of his Uncle or the others.

They quickly move on from there and make their way, by an indirect route, back to the settlement. As they had feared, there is little left for them when they get there. Their huts have been wilfully destroyed by force and then by fire. There is nothing left, other than the charred remains of the few huts that had stood proudly there before. There is little evidence of any possessions they might have left there, in their own huts or the others. There is evidence however of the other people who had occupied these. There is also plenty of surface water around there. It is about six inches deep as they slosh around, inspecting the remnants of their former abode.

Edgar is worried though. If there is this much water laying on the ground here, then how much will there be on the lower ground, down by the stream. One thing is for sure and that is that there is no source of food to be had here. Anything they might have stored away for lean times has either been destroyed or washed away.

At least they had taken the means of catching fish and hunting with them when they had left. Edgar decides that catching fish is more likely to be possible in the current conditions. The need to find food overrules the need to bury the dead, or what is left of them. Their charred bodies aren't going anywhere soon, so they will leave it until they have caught something to keep the hunger at bay, before they come back to give them a decent burial.

They leave the settlement and make for the stream, except when they come into view of it, there is far more than a stream rushing down towards the river, a few miles away. The stream that had been maybe six feet across most of the time; is now ten times wider than that and who knows how deep. The water is flowing extremely fast and Edgar knows that if any of them make the mistake of slipping into the water, then they would be washed away before anyone could even blink, let alone try to do something to try to save them. The view in front of him makes him think. If this is what the stream has swollen to, then the river must be massively swollen, with who knows how many streams like this running into it.

That has put paid to the thought of fishing for their food supply. There wouldn't be a chance in a thousand that he would be able to catch any fish in waters running this fast and with the stream this wide. He thinks now about his chances hunting, but he is worried about that too. Despite the waters being so high and what would appear to be a lot of the lower ground flooded by flood waters, they have not seen a single piece of wildlife since they left the cave, not one.

Edgar doesn't know what to make of that at this moment. The answer doesn't come to him for quite a while. It is after they have moved off from the settlement and rather than follow the flow of the stream down to the river, they decide to move to higher ground. Part of the reasoning for this is that they don't know how much more water is yet to come down the stream. Often the stream will swell more than a day after any rain has stopped. The rain has only just stopped this afternoon, so if there is still more to flow down the streams, then there is the likelihood that the stream is still going to get bigger, deeper and wider. If they follow the course of the stream down, then they might find themselves in trouble. They might even get trapped by the rising waters, not only of this stream, but by the others that join this one on the way down to the big river. No it doesn't make sense to go down at this stage. What they need to do is to go up; back up to the level they were at before.

They decide not to go to exactly the same place though. Although it is unlikely to get more flooded than it is already up there, there is also nothing there for them to forage or hunt. Food is a priority, well after their safety of course.

The only problem with the direction they choose; is that it means they will be more open, visible to others. Or to be more precise, they will be visible to the fighters, if they are still around. Hopefully they will have moved on. As it turns out that is what they have done. But Edgar, Edith and Edmund aren't to know that, as they make their way away from the settlement. They keep in cover as much as they can, and keep their eyes peeled for any movement that catches their eyes. Initially there is nothing, but then they soon begin to spot evidence of where the wildlife has gone. It doesn't take them long to close in on a couple of birds to hunt. Edgar is skilled at tracking these birds and while the first one gets away, the second one is not so lucky. It isn't long after that that he manages to bag a further three birds. The game on four legs proves to be too elusive for him. Their sense of survival exceeds his power of killing them on this occasion.

The next problem they have to overcome; is how they are going to be able to cook these birds. There is no way they are going to be able to gather any wood that will be dry enough to burn. Everywhere is absolutely soaking, if not under water a few inches. Even if they can find something to start a fire with and cook the birds, they aren't too sure how good an idea it would be, to advertise their presence with a smoking fire.

It is Edmund who comes up with a potential solution. He isn't at all sure that there will be anything there they can use, but if there is, then the place will be ideal for them to have a fire, after it gets dark. Even though the rain has stopped, the sky is still very overcast. There is no sign that it is going to give way to clear skies in the foreseeable future. In terms of making it easier for them, they are hoping things will stay the way they are, the longer the better.

It is tricky making their way across the valley. They have to turn back a couple of times, when they can't get across the streams they come across in their way. None of them are swollen in the way their stream is, but they are still too wide and possibly too deep to cross safely. There is no point in taking any more unnecessary risks that they don't have to.

Eventually they find a place where it is relatively safe to cross. Someone at one time has placed a fallen tree across the stream. Although the water is lapping almost at the top edge of it, it is possible to cross over safely. What puzzles them all is that there isn't that much water at this point of the stream. What water is in it further down must be joining it from some other source. Don't get me wrong; the level is higher than it normally would be, but it isn't anything like as swollen as the other streams they have seen.

As they move over, it becomes apparent also that this side of the stream and the area in this direction has not experienced nearly as much rain as they have done. As they are going to find out in time, the rain had been fairly localised. Places as near as ten miles away had experienced no more than a gentle rain for some of the three days they had been drenched with rain. It would appear that for some meteorological reason, the depression had moved over their settlement area and then stopped for three days. They wouldn't have known that at the time, but that appears to be what happened.

As they near their destination, they come across some sheep. There is just the odd one or two at first, but then they see a big flock of them. They seem to be unharmed by any rain that has come down, though looking at the ground here; it isn't very wet at all. In fact it is quite dry.

Edmund knows where he is and although they are unable to see it yet, he is leading them to the shepherd's hut. The shepherd always keeps a good store of wood, ready for the nights he would have to spend up here, looking after his sheep. They can only hope that the fighters have not come this way. That hope is soon dashed, when they come across the body of the shepherd. He has been killed quite savagely and then left for the elements. It doesn't seem right to leave him out in the open, even though they need to get where they are going, as the light is all but failing them. A crude covering of stones is enough to keep the carrion at bay for now. They have already had a peck or two, notably the eyes have gone.

They are worried that as the shepherd has been found, then maybe his hut will have been too and then destroyed.

Chapter 4 Edmund

They move quickly on, as the last of the light is on the verge of disappearing. They still can't see his hut. Edgar and Edith are depending on Edmund's information that there is somewhere here, well nearby, that they might be able to use as cover. Edmund has already said it is a hut. Their thoughts are; that if that is the case, then there is a good chance that the fighters will have destroyed it. They have already killed the shepherd, so why wouldn't they destroy his hut. Edmund appears to be more hopeful, but he doesn't say why that is.

It is really getting quite hard to see by the time Edmund stops.

'It's still here' is all he says, with lifted spirits.

'How do you know that? Where is it?'

'That's why I was quite sure it would still be here. They couldn't find it, or see it easily.'

'They aren't the only ones' Edith replies 'there is nothing to see.'

'I know the lack of light isn't helping. I'll show you.'

Edmund starts forward. His parents step forward too. In front of them is some thick undergrowth. It isn't a hedge, as it doesn't run very far. But it is quite tall and maybe twenty feet or so wide and more or less the same in depth; no actually a bit deeper. They can't see much of this as Edmund gets to the edge of it and then goes round to the left, following the edge of the undergrowth round. It is clear that he doesn't know exactly what he is trying to find, by the way he keeps trying to push into the undergrowth. Then at one place, he does push in and he gets through. Edgar and Edith push through after him.

After three or four feet they are through and their hands meet a wall of moss. But Edmund hasn't stopped. He turns left and stops after three feet. He fumbles around in the dark and then somehow the door of the hut opens. He steps inside. It is even darker in there, as not one shred of light filters through from the outside, not that there is any still there by now.

It is too much to ask that any fire he would have had going would still be lit. They don't know when he was killed, but it is a fair guess it was days ago now. It is highly unlikely that any part of the fire will still be there. It is Edgar who feels round for where the fire is. He carefully puts his hand on the ashes. It is clear straight away that he isn't risking much. The ashes are warm, but not hot. He carefully moves them around a bit, in the hope their might still be an ember. He is lucky in that there are some very minor red glows, but nothing that will instantly make a fire rekindle into life.

He instructs the other two to explore their shelter for the night, while he takes out his fire lighting kit from his sack. They are to look for what the shepherd uses to light his fire. If that is to hand, then it might be easier than using his equipment.

It is hard to search for things in the pitch black, but they use their hands carefully and skilfully. The shepherd was an organised man. In that business you have to be, so it is no great surprise. Edith comes across what they need and hands it over to Edgar to light the fire.

The sparks created give them a micro second view of the inside of the hut every couple of seconds or so. It isn't instant success in lighting the fire, but Edgar very quickly gets the process going in the right direction. With his encouragement, the sparks take hold and from that point it is only a matter of time for them to have a proper flame to move things forwards.

It is surprising how much light even the smallest flame throws out into a dark room. The shepherd's hut is very compact. That is all it needed to be when he was alive. It is all they need this night, to have cover from the elements. In one corner is his bed, just a comfortable thickness of straw to lie on. There is also a crude chair near to the fire. They knew that was there, as they have already bumped into it in the dark. There are some crude utensils near to the fire, which he would have used when cooking. Over in the corner are some of his things stored. In one place are some spare clothes and then they find what is much more use to them, his supply of food.

It is still hard to see what there is, but Edith takes it over to where the fire is growing by the minute, so that she can see what they have. Edmund ferries bits of wood over to his father from the large pile of it stored in the far corner, the other side of the fire. There are plenty of twigs and smaller, thinner bits of wood that will burn easily. The great thing is the fact that the wood is really dry. It is easy to light and ready to burn. Edgar takes it steadily all the same, as he doesn't want to pile too much wood on too early, a mistake that is common when a fire appears to have got going.

The light from the fire is increasing now by the minute. The fire isn't exactly roaring, but it is well on the way, particularly as Edgar is using more of the thinner bits of wood. He too now takes in his surroundings. They have certainly landed on their feet with finding this bit of shelter, undamaged both by the fighters and the days of rain. He will have a good look at its construction in the morning, when it becomes light. Until then there will be no need to go outside. The sheep have obviously been untended for the past couple of days, but they appeared to be alright when they passed them earlier.

Edmund puts the bar across the door, to in effect lock them in. Edith and Edgar start to get the food on the go. Now they have a fire going and the means to cook the birds they caught earlier, they are all feeling the pangs of hunger they have managed to set aside up to this point.

If the cave they had spent the previous nights in wasn't that cold, then their current place of rest for the night is very much a great improvement on that. Already they can feel the warmth of the fire making a difference to their surroundings.

It takes some time for the birds to cook, but it is worth the wait. They have a bird each and there is little left when they have finished. Edgar stokes up the fire and makes sure that there is sufficient wood on there, to keep the fire going well through the night. They have no need of the coverings the shepherd had used on his bed, as the fire is heating the room admirably. They settle down for the night with full bellies and feeling much more relaxed than they have been on the previous two nights at least.

There is no light to tell them when morning comes. They sleep well beyond when that light comes up outside anyway. They feel safe where they are and make up for the patchy sleep they have experienced, in fear of their lives in the cave, however unlikely it was that the fighters would have found them there.

Making sure that the fire is made up for a good time, they make their way outside, to inspect the shepherd's hut. It is well built to say the least. They find a large extra store of wood round the back of the hut too. Edmund sets about topping up the supply inside the hut. They have already decided that they will take advantage of this place to stay for another night at least, or until they can assess exactly what is open for them to do.

The next thing that they do is to dig a proper grave for the shepherd. It is easier said than done though, as the ground in most of the area is hard. That is because the rock isn't too far below the surface. They manage to find a place in the end and although the grave they dig isn't particularly deep, they make it safe from wildlife by making sure there are plenty of stones on top of him, above the thin soil layer.

The flock of sheep seem to be happy enough. A few have strayed away a bit, but they bring them back together. From what Edmund tells them, the shepherd had been alone and has no family. That is about all he knows about him. He came across him one day and had helped him get a ewe out of a ditch it was stuck in. He had visited him a few times and sat and talked to him. Edmund says that he showed him how to lay traps for small wildlife. He says that the shepherd never seemed to be short of food. He traded with others for the things he needed. The sheep gave him good wool and of course there was the meat itself too.

They walk back down to the stream, to see if the water has receded much. It has gone down by a surprising amount, but it is still well above normal levels. They don't bother to go all of the way down to the settlement to check there. If this stream is still swollen, then theirs is going to be too.

While Edgar and Edmund go off to do some hunting, Edith decides that she will tidy up the inside of the hut. In that she means no offense to the shepherd. But if they are going to stay there even for a short time, then there are things that she wants to do, to make it more acceptable. In other words he may have had it the way he liked it, but she wants it the way a woman wants it.

She is still busy working on this when the others come back. Once again they have been successful in their quest for game. They have also come across another place where wood has been stacked by someone. It may have been the shepherd, but they aren't to know if it was or not. They leave Edith to carry on with what she is doing, while they go back to carry some of this wood back to the hut, to store it there where it will be handy.

All of the time they have been out, they haven't seen a single soul. Of course they haven't gone that far in directions where they know there used to be settlements, but even so they would have expected to see someone, on a normal day like this. But then they don't know just how ruthless the fighters have been in killing everyone who crossed their path.

They make two journeys with wood back to the hut, before calling it a day in that direction. Each time they return to the hut, they are amazed at how camouflaged it is, until you are actually in the undergrowth around it. It is little wonder that the fighters hadn't stumbled onto it. They probably didn't think that the shepherd had anywhere to stay, so close to where his sheep grazed.

The hut is much tidier and neater when they walk in there, after they have finished their tasks. Edith has the dinner cooking on the fire and the fire of course is still going strong.

Chapter 5 Elizabeth

When Elizabeth becomes aware of things around her again, she knows that something different has happened. That is the first thing that comes to her. She has no idea at this stage what that might be, but she is aware that things aren't as before.

She tries to concentrate. She tries to remember what she was doing before this happened. She can't remember anything initially and she can't remember anything that might have made her black out, or whatever it is that has happened.

What she does know is that she is feeling drained. She is feeling extremely drained and very tired on top of that. In fact she can't remember ever being this drained or tired. She looks around her, but as usual there is nothing to see. There is absolutely nothing to see at all. There hasn't been since she came into this state who knows how many years ago. She has no idea how long it has been, but she does know it is since the time when she had heard a whisper and no one would listen to her, or her warnings about the content.

Elizabeth can remember that much about her time before being here, wherever here is, but she can't remember anything else. She can't remember anyone else either. She knows she tried to pass on the warnings to the people around her, but she can't remember who they were, or if they might have been her family. She has tried on occasion to think carefully through everything and see if she can delve further into her own past. But she has been, so far, unable to shed any light on those people she had tried to warn.

All she does know is that she is where she is now and that she has been here for a very long time. As far as she knows she is alone, as she hasn't seen anyone else here with her. She does see people when it is time to go out though. She can see not only people, but she can also see the places they are at. She can see the huts they live in and the land around them. She can see the sun in the daytime and the stars at night, if she is out then.

But, and this has become apparent to her over time, these people cannot see her. On top of that they cannot hear her either. Either that; or they have never taken what she has said seriously. But she knows in her head that realistically they have not heard the words she has whispered to them. There has been no reaction, ever, to her words of warning. She has lost count of the number of times she has gone out and tried to warn people. She knows they have not heeded her warnings, as she has been out there repeatedly, trying to get her warnings through, before disaster strikes. She is always there when disaster strikes and she can see the effect that not taking her warnings have on those she has tried to tell.

Then when she sees them perish, which they inevitably do, she comes back to her place, until the next time. Elizabeth is not in control of this coming or going though. She does not choose when she goes out and when she comes back; she just does it. Something inside her triggers and then suddenly she is out there. She doesn't hear a whisper herself. She just has the information she is trying to part with, in her head. She has no idea of how much time there is in between these visits, if that is what we can call them. They just happen when the need arises. In between time she is just here, doing nothing, looking at nothing, eating nothing, just waiting. But she isn't aware of the passage of time and she isn't bored, or feels anything at all. The fact she does nothing is not something that she thinks about or worries about. She is just there, ready and waiting for the next time.

Edmund. The name pops into her head as she is trying to remember what she was doing before becoming aware of her surroundings again. Edmund is the name of someone she has spoken to, well whispered. She gives herself a bit of time, without trying to force any more than that out of her memory.

While she waits, she thinks that this is the first time that a name has ever come into her head. She knows she has tried to warn people, but now she is thinking about it, she can't remember a single name. But the name Edmund has just come to her. Why would it do that?

She waits for something else to pop into her head. Nothing appears to be forthcoming, but she isn't in any hurry. She knows that she isn't the one who decides these things; well she doesn't think she is. Nothing she does seems to be a conscious thought or action. She is no hurry as far as she knows. It is interesting a name has popped into her head. She is feeling confident that more will come to her, when it is ready to.

As time goes by she feels less tired and not so drained. Part of that is the excitement she has felt at remembering Edmund's name. Most of it is the time that passes before she remembers anything else. She has no perception of how much time that is, but it is not important.

Then she remembers a bit more. By this time she is no longer tired and she is no longer drained. She now knows that she has whispered to Edmund before. The things she said were warnings about things about to happen. Edmund has always been able to hear her. Why has she only remembered this now and why has she only remembered his name now too? But then she has never known his name before, when she has whispered to him. Something is very different this time, but she doesn't know what.

She has tried to warn some others about their lives being in danger from the fighters and the floods that would follow. But as usual there was no response by any of them. She remembers that she kept trying and that she came across this small boy. He didn't tell her his name. She remembers that much. She just knows his name is Edmund.

That makes her stop in her thoughts. She knows his name is Edmund, not that his name was Edmund. Is that significant? She instinctively knows that it is. Edmund is still alive. The she remembers a little bit more of the sequence.

Elizabeth can now recall that she whispered to Edmund. She is not sure if she noticed it at the time, but she is recalling now that Edmund reacted to her whispering to him. Edmund heard her. Not only did Edmund hear her whispers, but he also did something about it. Then she suddenly remembers that Edmund has listened to her warnings before!

More is coming back to her now as her mind follows what happened. She can see in her head that Edmund told others. She thinks they were her parents, but that isn't totally clear. She knows he told these two people close to him and then either he or they told others. She can see that bit now in her thoughts.

She can see that no one was exactly keen to believe what Edmund was telling them, but then he is just a boy and why would they listen to a warning from a boy. She remembers seeing that most didn't, but eventually a small group of people did take heed. Several people left the settlement just in time. It was closer than she would have liked. It was closer than was actually safe, but at least they did leave. Elizabeth knows she was still around then. She can see all this happening again. She is seeing it all as it played out at the time. She can see that they got away in time, but were still not safe. She stayed with them as they climbed onto the escarpment and three of them constructed a shelter. The others did not and were reluctant to be there.

Something inside her told her that even though they had escaped from the settlement in time, they were not safe.

'You are not safe. Go to the cave.'

She knows they were the words she whispered to Edmund. Edmund had reacted to the words as soon as he heard them. Unfortunately the others did not want to listen to her warning through Edmund. She can only remember giving it once. She didn't have to say it again, as Edmund didn't waste any time leaving their shelter. Only three people heeded the warning and made towards the cave.

She remembers the cave, now that the thought is in her head. She also thinks she remembers telling Edmund that the cave should be made as hard to find as possible. Then she also remembers telling Edmund about the space above the passage and making a cover for it, so that it would be very hard to find by anyone who didn't know it was there.

She knows that Edmund did some things there. She didn't see him do them, but she knows that he made some preparations for a time when they would be needed most. That time has now been.

Elizabeth remembers following Edmund and the other two out of where they had made the shelter. She knows the others stayed behind and she doesn't know any more about them, or what may have happened to them. She doesn't know, but she is virtually certain that they will not have survived. These two warnings that she gave to Edmund this time were by far the most serious threats to their lives ever. She knows that. She can't remember specific previous warnings he heard from her, but she just knows they weren't as serious as these were.

She followed them as they made their way towards the cave, but not in a direct route. She worried at first that he might have lost his bearings, but he soon turned in the right direction and made for the cave. She watched as he opened it up and she watched as they went in and closed up the entrance behind them. She watched in the pitch black darkness inside the cave, as they moved into the concealed area above the passage. She thought she was going to stay with them. That would have been what happened in cases when the warnings were this severe. She would watch as the disaster strikes and the lives were lost, because they hadn't heard her warning. She wouldn't be as close as she was this time. She appreciated now the difference in that she was there with them. She would normally have looked on from afar, but not this time. No, she was right there with them.

They had no sooner put the piece in place to cover their way up into this space, when she remembers knowing that these three people were no longer in danger. They had heard her warnings and escaped in time. That is the last things she remembers about what happened, until the moment she resurfaced in her place, both drained and tired.

Is this what happens when she is successful in a life and death warning? She doesn't know, as she can't remember any specifics about previous warnings, other than the ones Edmund had heard before weren't this important.

Elizabeth wants to know for sure that they have survived. She wants to see what has happened where they are. She wants to see that Edmund is indeed alive. She also wants to see if any of the others she tried to warn are alive too. But that can't happen just because she wants to. Or at least she doesn't think it has in the past.

Chapter 6 Edmund & Elizabeth

Edmund, along with Edgar and Edith, feel much safer in the Shepherd's hut the second night. Part of that is that it is much more prepared for the second night and part because they have the knowledge that the surrounding area is void of fighters. Edmund and Edgar haven't seen a single soul in the time they were out this day.

The fire is burning well and the food cooking in a less hurried manner. All in all they feel they have landed on their feet, in finding this place to replace the roof over their heads, at least for now. They could do worse than use this place until they decide what course of action they are going to take. There is little point in returning to where their old hut is. Not only have the buildings been destroyed, but the flooding has taken a great toll on the surrounding area too. If the fighters hadn't been there first, then the flood would have maybe taken them instead. Until now they had not realised how vulnerable the place they had chosen to live was.

Feeling more secure this evening, they feel more in the frame of mind to turn their attention to the future. They make a plan to take them through the immediate future. First of all they will give the waters time to recede. Then they will be able to assess if there is anything to salvage from their old settlement. They think at the moment there won't be anything, but they will know more when they can actually check properly. That will also be the most likely time that any other survivors might return also, to see what is left. They don't know how many may have survived the fighters, if any. Or how many then who might have perished in the ensuing floods.

I think they know in their hearts that the answer will be that they are the only survivors, but they aren't ready to just accept that at this time.

In the meantime, Edith will gather more wood to add to their store during the days, while Edgar and Edmund will scour the surrounding area for more game and possible supplies, to add to their food store. They will also hunt around to see if any of the flock might have strayed further. They will also look out for any other flocks that now appear to be untended. There is little point in leaving them unprotected unnecessarily.

With that all decided, they eat their food and afterwards turn in early for the night. There is still plenty of sleep to make up on after their recent events. If they slept well the first night in the Shepherd's hut, then the second night finds them totally relaxed in their new temporary home.

The next day Edgar and Edmund move in an ever increasing circle away from the shepherd's hut. They keep their eyes well peeled throughout the entire day. On the one hand they want to come across other people; or at the least spy them in the distance. On the other hand they do not want to come across anyone, because they fear it could be some of the fighters returning. The last thing they want to do is to bring unwanted attention onto them. As it turns out, they do not see anyone at all in the entire day. As far as they are aware too, no one sees them either. They come across no evidence that tells them there are any survivors in their area.

The water has receded some more since the day before, but is still far from back to normal levels. They manage to bag some more birds and a rabbit. The rabbit is a lucky shot by Edgar, but that is how it happens sometimes.

They have even more success with rounding up some more livestock. It would appear that the sheep in particular have had much more success in avoiding the fighters, or at least not being part of their target. It is hard to tell if the sheep they come across are part of their shepherd's flock, or belonged to another shepherd or family. There are no markings on them. But there is no one around to contest their taking them home with them either. In the course of the day they return several times with rounded up strays or otherwise. Edith has constructed, reconstructed rather, the crude pen to hold them in. The shepherd had three of these pens to hold the flock close to his hut, in times of bad weather. All three have suffered severe damage in the inclement weather, or by the hands of the fighters. They will never know which.

Edith is skilled with her hands and does an excellent job of re-establishing the pens. Edmund and Edgar bring their finds back and leave them with her each time. She puts them in a pen away from the flock they already have. Then she checks each one out, to assess what state of health they are in. What she is maybe looking for is a weak one which they could kill and butcher for meat supplies.

Sheep aren't the only livestock they come across. They manage to add three cattle and one horse to their stock by the time the pair returns late in the afternoon for the final time that day.

It is about mid-way through the morning of that day that Elizabeth finds that she is somewhere different. One second she is in her place of nowhere and the next second she finds she has been transported back into a place where she can see around her. She can see the sky and she can see the trees and the open grasslands. She can see areas which are covered in water and she can see places where the water has obviously receded. She knows straight away where she is. She also knows that what she is seeing in places is the aftermath of the floods she had predicted and warned about. But as hard as she looks, she does not see a single person from the point where she finds herself standing. Also she is a bit confused as this, she realises, is not her usual viewpoint on the world when she does normally return. She seems to remember that she would normally have an elevated view on things.

She takes her time taking in her surroundings, before moving off in one direction. She doesn't know why she chooses the direction she does, but something inside her tells her; this is the way she should go. The weather gives no clue as to how vile it has been days before this. Not that she has experienced that weather first hand; she knows it has been bad. Now that she is here, the sun is shining and there is even some warmth in it she can feel. That is unusual for her too. She would normally just be there, but this day she is feeling things that she can't remember having done previously.

She moves away from the old settlement that she has arrived near and makes her way up the escarpment. She knows she is following some sort of trail, but is not aware of how she is doing it. She comes across the wrecked shelter on top of the escarpment, but from the feelings that she has within her, she knows Edmund is not here anymore and that he had moved on from here in time to escaper the fighters.

Her journey takes her round to the cave on the side of the escarpment. The route she takes to get there is the exact same one that Edmund had taken days before. When she arrives there she knows she does not have to open the cave up and go in. The way the cave is disguised lets her know this work has been done from the outside by someone who wants to preserve this place for any possible future use. She spends a minute or two taking in the situation here. She needs to know in her mind whether it was Edmund and his family who have been here. The fact she has arrived here makes her think it must have been them, but she wants some kind of confirmation. She doesn't have any idea how she is going to achieve that, but she knows that she needs something. Maybe the cave has not been used as a shelter, but she knows it had. The thought comes to her that she has already been this far with them before. Before she returned to her place, they were here in a safe place, well safer than they had been. She thinks it is odd how she doesn't always remember things in sequence that she has already experienced. It is almost as if someone or something is controlling her and what she can and can't recall at any specific time.

She remembers for sure that Edmund has been here and she finds she is now ready to move on. She lets her feet guide her in the next direction. It takes her up onto the escarpment and then down the other side. She skirts flooded areas and makes her way alongside a stream, before eventually finding a way across. She knows this is the place where Edmund crossed the stream. She doesn't know how she knows it, but she knows it is since the flooding happened.

Then suddenly she spots something moving. She takes cover; not that she has been walking more out in the open than she has to. She sees some sheep moving in the distance. Was this the movement that caught her eye? At first thought she thinks it was, but then a few seconds later, she sees a woman come out from a bank of bushes. The woman walks over to where the sheep are in a pen and goes in with them. Elizabeth stays exactly where she is for the time being. She recognises this woman. It is Edith; Edmund's mother.

She moves further back out of sight and watches for a time, but no one else appears. Ideally she would like to be a bit closer. But she wants to see the others first.

She waits for well over an hour before she sees anyone else. Edith has been busy all of this time. She moves from the pen Elizabeth saw her going into first to another pen, which she repairs, before anyone else comes into view. Elizabeth keeps a good look around her. She guesses that Edmund and Edgar are out and about somewhere. She doesn't want them to stumble across her, without her seeing them first. But eventually she spots them coming back towards Edith. They are driving a small group of sheep, maybe six or seven of them.

They put the sheep in the pen Edith has just repaired, before making off again. Elizabeth guesses what they are doing and follows them discreetly, at a distance. At times she moves further away from them and at times she moves closer. On a couple of occasions she comes across a stray sheep and manages to drive it closer to them, so they can find it, without disclosing her presence to them. She can tell that they are totally unaware of her presence. Thankfully the sheep she comes across does not act in a startled manner either, to give her game away.

Several times they round up livestock and return to where Edith is. It is clear when the time comes, that they are going back for the last time that day. The light is just beginning to go. She watches them put the last of the livestock in the pens and the wood they have been carrying, down on the ground. They then stand together, looking at their animals and then turning their gaze to the countryside around them. It is at this moment that Elizabeth chooses to stand out in the open so they can see her; and they do.

Chapter 7 Elizabeth and Edmund

Seeing someone standing there is quite a shock. They have all got used to seeing nobody when they look around. Thankfully looking around them is still a habit. After all, it isn't very long at all since their lives have been devastated by the fighters who had ransacked their settlement and killed everyone left there. But funnily enough they have just not been expecting to see one person watching them outside their new home. On top of that this isn't an adult that is looking at them; it is a child, probably not much different in age to Edmund.

The first question in their heads; is where has she come from? That is a two part question really. Where has she come from just now, because they have not spotted her approaching and where is she from? Where is her family? I suppose another question would be; are you alone?

There is only the one way to find out, carefully. The girl is standing there quite still. She looks calm and unruffled as she stands there, maybe a hundred paces away from them. She is looking directly at them. She does not appear to be concerned about anything that might be behind her, but that doesn't necessarily mean anything. Edgar and Edith scan the horizons, not only in her direction, but all around them. They do that carefully twice, before coming back with their eyes to her again. All this time she is just standing there. It is as if she is waiting for them to feel safe before she moves again.

In the meantime, Edmund is looking directly at her. He thinks she might look familiar to him, but then he thinks he might be wrong. There is something about her though that has his attention.

For her part, she knows she will have caused them some concern, just appearing from nowhere quite close to them. There was never going to be another way she could do this. Well actually there might have been, but she didn't think that would be such a good idea either. She had thought about whispering to Edmund to announce she was coming and then come into view at a distance a few minutes later. But she didn't want to do that. She doesn't know why not, but maybe it is because it would bring a whole heap of questions on her, which she would be unable to answer, purely because she doesn't know the answers herself. She had decided in the brief time before she made herself seen by them, that it would be better for her to keep the whispering out of things for now, if not forever, if that is possible.

There is a part of her that wants to look around too. Maybe she is not alone. She can't really say so or not. She has no idea honestly about anything. She doesn't look round, but just keeps her eyes in their direction. She tries not to stare, but it is hard not to when Edmund is staring back at her.

It appears to take minutes before anything changes. But eventually Edgar and Edith are looking back at her again. She isn't going to move closer though, until they indicate she can. They don't do that. Instead they start to walk towards her. They do this slowly and are obvious about keeping their eyes peeled as they approach. When they are only a few steps away from her they stop.

'Hello' Edgar was going to be the one who speaks, but it is Edith who does so first.

'Hello' Elizabeth replies with a smile. It is not a broad smile, but it is a smile nevertheless.

'Are you by yourself?' Edith continues.

Now Elizabeth does not know for sure, but then as she has never seen anyone else she reckons that she must be. There is no way she is going to say anything different.

'I am' she says without any delay.

That doesn't stop Edgar and Edith from taking another look beyond where she is standing. There is no one there for them to see.

'I'm Edith and this is Edgar and our son Edmund.'

'I'm Elizabeth'

There is something in the way that she speaks that Edmund finds familiar, just like he had originally thought she looked familiar. But he can't place her at all. But then that is because he is thinking of people he has previously met in real life, and not a whispering voice in his head.

'Where do you live?'

'I don't know.' And before they can question that statement further she continues. 'Something happened and I don't know what. I just can't remember anything from before.'

She isn't telling a lie in that. She is just talking about a different before. Not the one she thinks they might be asking about. There would be little she could expand on that anyway and it would make them suspicious of her. She wants to avoid that if she possibly can.

Of course they can't just accept that. More questions are on the way.

'Have you come far? I don't think I have seen you around before?'

'I haven't seen you here either.'

She is trying to be careful with her answers, without taking time to think them out either. She knows she hasn't answered the have you come far part of Edith's question. She tries to answer it now as best as she can, before Edith asks her again.

'I have walked some distance today. I don't know exactly how far, but I don't think it that far. I don't know how far I came the days before that, because I just can't remember anything.'

'It is nothing to worry about. Do you know if there are any others left where you came from?'

Now this is an awkward question for Elizabeth. The truthful answer is that she hasn't got a clue. She knows what time frame that Edith is talking about. She is referring to the time before the fighters came. She is making the assumption that where Elizabeth is from was also attacked by the fighters. It may well have been, but it is unlikely. Elizabeth hasn't been part of any community, as far as she is aware, for a long time. Although she has no definition of what a long time is, in relation to that. This is the first time Elizabeth has been visible to people, as far as she knows, in her current state. But is her state the same now she is here in front of them? She really doesn't know the answer to that one.

'I don't know. I just can't remember anyone.' And before they can jump on that she keeps going 'Something must have happened to me, because I just found myself walking slowly, not that far away from here. I have no idea what happened before that. My people may have been attacked, or not.'

She hadn't meant to say that about being attacked, but she knew that they would accept her more because of this. The fighters are why they are here now. Well actually they are here now, because she managed to get through to Edmund and he persuaded them that the threat was real, which of course it was.

'I think we should move inside. You need to stay with us. You shouldn't be wandering about by yourself, especially as it is getting dark.'

'I am not afraid of the dark.' She spends so much time in the dark that it really doesn't worry her.

They take another good look around them and particularly beyond where Elizabeth is standing, before they turn and walk back towards the shepherd's hut. As they start to walk away, she walks behind them. Edmund has stayed back and he walks with her. She knows he has noticed something about her, but she isn't going to tell him yet, if she ever does. No, that is wrong. She knows that she will have to tell him sometime.

Edith leads the way round to where they go through the bushes. Edgar stands to one side and waits for them all to pass him. He takes another good look around. The light is fading fast and he can't see that far now particularly well. But there is nothing there for him to see, in the way of people that is. He doesn't feel there is a threat, but you can never know. It is just odd that a child this young should be out there on her own and with no memory of what has happened. He isn't concerned that she might be not telling them the complete truth. He thinks that maybe she has seen something terrible and that has caused her to forget what happened where she lived. He'd had a good look at her while she was talking to Edith. Her clothes are undamaged. In fact they are in good condition. They don't have the look of having been slept in either, so that raises the question of how far she has come today and where was she last night, in that she didn't get her clothes crumpled.

There is little doubt in his head that she doesn't now have anyone to look after her. He believes the fighters must have destroyed her settlement too. Maybe they will wander further in the morning and see if they can come across anyone else. But which direction did she come from. She hasn't said much so far. Edgar doubts that she will know. It would appear that she has just wandered and then suddenly come across them. But then, how could she have got that close without them seeing her? He thinks about it and he doesn't know the answer. It is more likely, he decides in the end, that she spotted them from quite a distance. Then she must have decided to move closer, while staying in cover. She must have been trying to see what sort of people they are, before revealing her presence to them. He supposes that if he were in her shoes, he would probably have done the same thing.

He realises that he has been standing there thinking about all this. The others have gone in a minute or two ago now. He quickly follows them in and secures the door as he enters the hut. Edith has turned her attention to the fire and the meal she has been preparing on it. Elizabeth and Edmund are sitting by the fire, staring at the flames. They appear to be at ease with each other.

Edith serves up the food in bowls. Elizabeth is unsure about it at first and carefully tastes it. Edith tries not to look at her as she does this. She expected the child to be starving hungry. If she has been wandering around for a day, two or three, then she should be hungry. Maybe she is not sure about the type of food in the bowl, but it is fairly ordinary fare for folk to eat.

Elizabeth is unsure, because she can't remember eating like the others are doing. It is not something she has done, or at least she does not remember doing. She is just where she is. She does nothing. But now she is here. She tastes a bit of the food she has been given. It tastes good and she feels the need to eat it come over her quite suddenly. Then quickly, she feels that she really needs it. She tucks in heartily and ignores everything else, until she has finished everything in her bowl. When she has finished she looks up and sees that the others are looking at her, with smiles on their faces. That is good, because she knows she has done what is expected of her.

Chapter 8 Elizabeth & Edmund

The next morning they tend the animals. All appear to be in good shape. They do need to be let out to pasture though. There is plenty of grass for them to feed on near to the shepherd's hut. The rain has encouraged good growth already and the landscape is looking lush and green.

The debate they have; is do they separate? On the one hand it would be good, almost advisable to have someone on hand, to keep an eye on the livestock. The last thing they would want is for someone to come along and assume that the livestock is without ownership. In normal circumstances that would not be a problem. It is something that would never happen. But these aren't normal circumstances. The fighters coming through and devastating these small settlements will possibly, maybe even inevitably, have left survivors. By that I mean not only human survivors, but livestock too. Livestock like the shepherd's flock and the others Edgar and Edmund found wandering. Others may hunt around to see if there is any wandering livestock that they can gather into their own flocks and herds.

But on the other hand, they want to try to see if Elizabeth belongs somewhere where there are more survivors. It is quite possible that she has family, or at least people who know her, who might be trying to find out what happened to her. They can't just let her go on her way and they can't ignore the fact that she is someone else's child. They might be searching for her.

They decide that they need to protect what they have here, but also make a determined effort to track down where she came from, within limitations. They decide that they will try today and go as far as they can in one direction, taking in as much as they can see in either direction side wise as they go. They think that quite possibly three, maybe four days of this will be enough to complete a reasonable search in all directions. They could go further but surely, if there is anyone left alive where she comes from, they will be making the effort to search for her.

Edith stays behind to look after the livestock. She is comfortable with that. She knows what to do if anyone comes on the scene, both friend and foe. Edgar takes Edmund and Elizabeth with him. They start off in the direction she appeared from. There is no particular reason for doing this. But they have to start somewhere and Elizabeth is unable to assist with any helpful information as to where she might have come from. She can hardly tell them that there is no point in what they are doing. She doesn't know for a fact that they won't come across someone who might recognize her, but she is 99.999% sure that she isn't even from this time.

For the first hour they walk at a steady pace, with all of them watching around them as they go. The only things that move in that time other than them; are the birds they see flying in the sky. They don't see any livestock and certainly not any people. To be honest though, they hadn't expected to. They have already been this far out previously.

For the next two hours the pace slows a fraction. Partly this is because the land is harder to cross and partly because it is more difficult to see if there is anyone who might live here still. There is only the one time when they feel it worth the detour to check on something, but it turns out to be nothing more than a couple of huts that must have been destroyed by the fighters. There is no trace of anyone who might have lived there and there is no livestock.

They stop by a stream to have a drink and something to eat. The water looks as if it is still above normal levels, but it isn't that far above; as far as they can tell by the signs on the banks. Refreshed and fed, they continue on their way for another couple of hours. Edgar is getting to the point when he feels that they can go no further before they will have to turn round, so they can make it back in daylight. They climb to the top of a small hill. Edgar says that they will be able to look around the area ahead of them and all around them before they turn back.

Strangely enough it is Elizabeth who spots the smoke from a fire in the distance, to the left of where they are standing on the hill. They can't exactly see what is there, but their best guess is that the smoke is coming from some kind of building.

Edgar is in two minds what to do. He knows he has left a bit of leeway in his timings, but not overly much. But to come this far and then not investigate the smoke would have been a defeatist attitude on the entire task they have taken on.

It only takes them seconds to start on their way towards the smoke. That is only after they have scoured the horizons in the other directions, to see if there is anything else they need to investigate as well. That would have presented a different set of issues to overcome. Edgar has discussed the possibility of exactly what has happened and the chance that they might run out of time and not be able to make it back in daylight. In that circumstance they will seek some kind of shelter from the elements and return as soon as they can the next day. Of course there is no way that he will be able to let Edith know if this happens.

It takes them the best part of half an hour to even get close to where the smoke is coming from. As they approach they can see that there is a small group of huts close together. The smoke is coming from the largest hut. If there is any livestock, then they haven't spotted it as yet. Nor have they seen anyone, but obviously there must be someone around, because of the fire.

They are within a hundred paces before they see anyone. It is immediately apparent that they have been spotted much earlier than they have spotted the inhabitants. When they do step out in front of them and appear from the side, the greeting is a guarded one. That is despite the only thing that Edgar is carrying, is his staff and the bag with water and food in, on his back.

Edgar has never seen these people before, but then he has never travelled this far before. He has had no need to up to now. If it hadn't been for the fighters, then it is doubtful he would have left his settlement.

Edgar remains relaxed. He can see that they are not so much looking at him as a threat because that is how they greet people passing through, but this reaction is because of the fighters.

'We found this girl wandering. Or to be more precise she came to us. We are just trying to find out if her family have survived. She has no idea where she is from. We believe the fighters may have attacked her settlement and killed her people and destroyed the buildings, but we don't know. We think she must have seen some of this and she has forgotten who she is, other than her name.'

'I don't recognize her. She isn't from around here and she hasn't been past here either. We keep a good eye on who comes towards us, or past us in the distance. We saw the fighters when they came through. For some reason they did not come our way. We thought they must have seen our fire, like you have done. Maybe it was because there was little smoke from it that day. There is another settlement that way.'

He points in the direction away from where they have come from and continues:

'There is nothing left there. They destroyed everything and they killed everyone and what livestock they caught. It is the same for the next settlement and the two either side of that one. We have only just returned earlier this afternoon with what livestock we could round up.'

Edgar looks around, as he hasn't seen any livestock on the way here. The man sees his confusion.

'We keep them in a dip over there'

He is pointing over their huts to somewhere beyond. Edgar finds it surprising that he has offered this piece of information. He must have made up his mind that they do not offer a threat to them.

Edgar has also been looking over at Elizabeth. She has shown no signs of recognition, either of the people standing around them, or the place where they are at.

'I take it you survived the fighters then?'

'Only a few of us from our settlement managed to escape. In fact only my wife, my son and I did. Everyone else left at the settlement was killed. Some did come with us initially, but they didn't move on from where we stopped and they tracked them down too. We hid in a cave.'

There is a kind of puzzled tone when one of the other men speaks to Edgar next.

'It seems to me that the way you tell it, that you knew something bad was coming, but not because, like us, you saw them coming?'

Edgar isn't sure what he is getting at. His tone is quite odd. It is not accusing, but it certainly seems to be questioning how and why he left his settlement. The words are out of his mouth before he knows he is speaking them.

'My son here told us to leave. He said that we were in danger. He has done it before and he has been right on those occasions too.'

They all turn their attention onto Edmund. The atmosphere has changed since this conversation began. Edgar is starting to feel a bit unsettled by the way things have just turned. He wishes he could say something to Edmund without these people hearing him tell it, but he knows that is not possible. He just knows they are going to ask Edmund something and they are not going to like it if he tells them that he heard a whisper.

'Edmund, do not tell them about the whispers.' Edmund hears this in his head. It is the same whisperer as before. He looks quickly across at his father and then at Elizabeth. His father is looking a bit concerned, but Elizabeth has a little smile on her face. It is at this second he knows the words in his head have come from her

'So what made you tell your family to leave?'

Edmund knows by the way the question is being asked, that the voice in his head is correct. He must not possibly tell them that he has heard a whisper in his head. He almost smiles as he realizes that it is the whisperer again who is warning him of this situation. He knows that he shouldn't take too long before responding to the man's question. He doesn't look like the kind of man who has to wait to be replied to.

'I was out of the settlement on the hill. The wind was blowing into my face. I heard these sounds from the distance. I couldn't see anyone, but I heard their voices. They were shouting and roaring. I didn't know what they were saying or roaring, because they were so far away, but it made me afraid, so I ran back and told my father. He listened because I have never told him something that is not the truth. I do not lie.'

Chapter 9 Edmund and Elizabeth

The men listen to Edmund and then give each other a look. It is impossible to tell what that look means. Edgar is feeling rather uneasy about the situation. He doesn't know why these people are acting this way, but he doesn't like it. Anyway they have achieved what they came here for, even if that is only to find out Elizabeth is not from here. He doesn't really want to get into a long discussion about how they managed to avoid the fighters. He knows that some people do not like things that they don't understand. In fact he doesn't really either, but he can't deny that Edmund's warnings do carry weight with them. Edmund for some reason has not told them about his whispers. These people obviously do not like to hear about these things. Edgar thinks they were expecting to hear something different from Edmund.

Edmund is trying to look serious, as nothing is said for well over a minute. Edgar isn't keen on letting this silence turn into something more awkward than it already is. He isn't quite in time.

'We did hear some time ago about some people who know when something bad is about to happen. Is that why you were away from your settlement on the hill?'

'I often go there, after I have done my duties in the settlement. I like to look around at the countryside around us.' He wants to say that he often wonders about the world beyond what he can see, but he doesn't think that is wise at the moment.

'It's time we were moving on' Edgar interrupts the line of questioning and answers. 'We need to keep looking for her family.'

There isn't any response from the men. There isn't any move to stop them either, which is good too. Edgar hopes that Elizabeth and Edmund will not say that they need to go, so they can get back before dark. Thankfully they remain silent and in fact start to turn ready to leave.

Edmund and Elizabeth have both turned to go back in the direction they arrived from. Edgar has noticed this and wonders if they will be questioned about it. He decides he needs to say something before he is asked about it.

'We need to get back to the line we were following before we saw your smoke.'

'Well there is nothing that way' one of the men says, pointing in the direction they say they have just returned from.

'That helps knowing that' is all that Edgar says.

He turns away and starts to leave the settlement. Edmund and Elizabeth are at his side. They don't rush away, even though that is what they really want to do. The sooner they get away from these people the better they will feel.

The temptation is to look over their shoulders as they move away, but none of them do it. They don't want to provoke any further reaction, if they can possibly help it. They don't talk as they walk either. It isn't as if Edgar has told them not to. It is something they all feel instead. They are on edge. Something isn't quite right about the people they have just left.

They have been walking for maybe five minutes before they say anything. They have not even nearly reached the point where they saw the smoke yet. Edgar has been trying to work out if they have enough time to make it back to the shepherd's hut before they lose the light of the day. He knows they will have to pick up the pace if they have any chance of making it back. He is concerned though, about the people he has just left. He doesn't know where the thought has come from in his head as he walks, but the thought is that these people may follow them, to see where they come from. That thought makes him want to turn round even more. He is just thinking he must when Elizabeth speaks.

'Someone is following us.'

'Have you looked?'

'No, but I saw the looks as we were leaving. They signalled to a man who was standing out of the settlement. I noticed him while we were there. He was trying to keep out of sight, but he didn't manage that. I saw him move just as we left.'

'We are short of time as it is. I am finding this very worrying.' Edgar replies just loud enough for Edmund and Elizabeth to hear. 'I don't want to lead them back to where we live.'

'So which way are we going to go?'

'I don't know as yet. We need to try to establish if we are definitely being followed.'

'We should stop then' Edmund says 'and get a drink or something as our reason to stop. But we must do it suddenly and then try to look round us, without letting him know we think we are being followed.'

'Or I could just trip and fall' Elizabeth says, as she does just that.

It takes everyone by surprise, including the man who has been tracking them behind them and to one side. As Elizabeth tumbles, she manages to roll round, so she gets a view of every direction behind her. She sees the man quickly falling to the ground, trying to get out of their sight. She continues to roll and ends up facing ahead of her again, all in one continuous movement. Edgar and Edmund have stopped. They bend down and help Elizabeth get up. She brushes her clothes down and is smiling when she speaks to them.

'He is behind us, maybe fifty paces away. He dropped to ground as I fell and rolled. I don't think he will believe I saw him. He will think I just tripped and fell over and then rolled.'

'That was very clever of you. We should start walking again now. We will have to make a decision what to do next.'

'We mustn't go towards our hut.' Edmund has a hint of concern in his voice.

'I agree. I don't know why he is following us, but I don't like it. When we get to the point we saw the fire we will stop. What we need to decide is what direction we go in. The question is which direction do we choose? It will also mean that we have to make camp and not go back until tomorrow.'

Edgar is racking his brains trying to work out which is the best direction to go in when they reach that point.

'I think we should carry straight on.'

Edmund has suggested this and Elizabeth is already nodding gently at this. He doesn't give Edgar time to give a comment back.

'It is hard to know which way to go. Obviously we can't turn and go back towards them. They know we haven't come from that way. We don't want to lead them towards where we live, so we can't go that way. So we have the choice of carrying on in the direction we were heading; or going straight on from where we are. The first one will lead us away from home. At some point we will have to try to lose him, unless he only follows us so far. If we do that, then he will guess we have not been going in the right direction. Because of that we could make towards our home, but that is too risky. So we should go straight ahead.

That way at least we aren't going overly far out of our way when we turn, after we lose him.'

'That makes sense.' Elizabeth says.

'It does' Edgar agrees with them both. 'How long will he follow us though and if he doesn't give up, then how long before we try to give him the slip. And how do we intend to do that?'

'We will have to wait until dark probably before he gives up. Maybe when we stop, he will have had enough and turn back towards home. It is a shame it doesn't get dark earlier.' It is Elizabeth who says all this.

'Why?'

'Because when it is dark he won't see us go and …' Elizabeth doesn't voice the next words.

The other two look across at her with questions in their eyes. She knows she will have to say something.

'I have a plan' she starts with, but knows that will not be enough to satisfy them. 'I just know things. I am not sure if I have just remembered this, or whether I knew it all the time. But I now know you will not find my family. I don't want to say more about what I know at this moment. I will tell you later, because for now the priority is to stop this man and any other of those people back there from following us home.'

Edgar doesn't know what to make of this. But what she is saying does not surprise him for some reason. There is something about her, something different. But if she has a plan, then that is more than he has, so he will listen to it and follow it if it sounds good.

'So what are you planning to do.?'

'We are going to make for the nearest trees, but if we can, still roughly in this direction. As we approach, I am going to trip up again and this time I will stay on the ground, pretending I have hurt my leg. I am sure he will come in closer if he can. You and Edgar will talk louder to me, asking me if I am alright. I will say I need to rest, as I have fallen because I am so tired. You will say that we will make camp for the night. Both of you will then go and start to gather materials to make a makeshift shelter from woods.'

'What will happen then?'

'Do you think he will approach us?'

'No, I don't expect he will. Nor do I think he will return to his settlement, so I will just have to do something.'

'What will you do?'

Edgar doesn't know what she can do against a grown man, but something in her voice tells him that she can do something.

'He will do what the whispers tell him to.'

Edgar almost stops when he hears those words. He looks at Edmund, but he is just listening to what she has been saying. He looks at Elizabeth and she is just smiling a sweet smile.

There is a small bit of woodland just over to their right. Maybe it is half a mile away. Before Edgar can ask her his question she says to him.

'We should make for those trees now. It won't look a sharp turn as they are pretty close to being on our path now.'

Without breaking stride they angle towards the trees, as if that is the direction they had been heading for all along.

'He will probably come closer now anyway.' Edgar says as they get closer to the trees. 'He may want to keep closer, so he doesn't lose us.'

'That is a good point. I won't trip over yet. Let's actually go into the trees before I trip and fall down. It will make it easier for us all that way.'

Edgar really wants to give her a good look, but he doesn't dare. He also wants to see if the man has moved closer, but he can't do that either. He will just have to trust in Elizabeth and whatever it is that she has planned. What can a young girl do to stop this man following them?

They enter the trees and go in about twenty feet, when Elizabeth falls to the ground again. This time she just falls down on to the ground. She squeals as she does so.

Chapter 10 Elizabeth & Edmund

Elizabeth knows she needs to be careful. She needs to concentrate and not let any thoughts go outside of her own head. It is important that she doesn't whisper to anyone. She doesn't need to whisper to Edmund, but she must make sure that she doesn't to this man. It will only bring more attention on them from these people.

Edgar and Edmund bend down to her on the ground.

'I'm fine' she says to them quietly. 'Now you stay here for a minute and then get up and look around you into the woods, not outside where he is. Then I want you to wander off and start gathering pieces of wood to make a shelter. We will not need this shelter, so don't bring much back the first time. I may have done something by then. It will depend on how he reacts to us potentially stopping for the night.'

Edgar doesn't know what to say or ask, so he doesn't. He plays along with her suggestion. They don't have another plan, so this is better than they have alternatively.

They stand up and look into the woods as agreed. Then they walk off together into the woods. They don't look back, as Elizabeth says they shouldn't in case the man sees them.

She lies on the ground and listens. At first she doesn't hear anything, but then after a few seconds she hears something. Her ears are hunting for a certain sound and they have found it. It is the sound of someone creeping closer. She knows which direction the sound is coming from and she knows how far away he is. In her mind a picture appears and she can now see him, creeping closer to try to see what is happening.

Elizabeth rolls over and slithers over the ground. She won't look back to see where she was, where she is maybe. She is not going towards him, but is moving away, slithering along the ground almost in the manner of a snake. She is moving fast now, very fast. She is now out to his side. She would not be in his line of sight, if she was visible. She is visible, but not here where she is now. She gathers more pace and then turns towards him. She approaches him at speed, raised slightly higher off the ground. Even if he could see her coming he wouldn't, as his concentration is on the people ahead of him in the woods.

Then she is upon him. She is still bent over as she gets to him. Suddenly he stops. He has heard something. He has probably heard her, the noise in the undergrowth she is racing through. She is right there when he stops. She doesn't stop. She throws herself at his lower legs. The force of her hitting him is much more severe than her size would suggest is possible. It takes him off his feet and he lands hard on the ground. She hasn't stopped just at taking him down. She grabs the large boulder beside her. It looks as if it should be too heavy for her to lift, let alone thrust down on his ankles, which is what she does all in one movement. So within a few seconds of hitting him, she has also smashed the boulder down on him.

For his part, one second he hears something in the undergrowth and then he stops. He has no sooner stopped than something hits his legs. He has never been hit into like this before. It has hit his leg just above the ankle. He falls to the ground and looks down at his leg to see the boulder there that he thinks he has just fallen onto, but it is the other way round. The pain is immense and he is confused by the pain he is experiencing and what he can see with his eyes. He can't quite understand how he could have tripped over this boulder and yet fallen so close and be in such pain. But there is nothing else there. There feels as if there should be, but he can see nothing. He feels down there carefully with his hand. He is afraid that he might have done some serious damage by the way he has fallen. He can feel his leg throbbing badly. It now doesn't feel as if it is his. It is numb on the one hand, but painful on the other. He must have trodden on something else, whatever it was and fallen onto the boulder.

Suddenly he hears movement in the undergrowth, maybe three or four feet away from him. He must have trodden on something living. Did he do that and something bit him? He stays still, hoping that whatever it was will move away if he does so; it does; she does. She has completed her task. He looks down again at his leg. He is shocked as it has started to swell. A panic comes over him. Something is wrong. Whatever it is that has happened, he is now badly injured. The pain is excruciating as he tries to move his leg, but he has to keep that to himself. He wants to scream out loud, but he can't do that. They would hear him and he would then have to explain why he was following them. They may not take that lightly. If he was uninjured that would not be a problem, but with his leg as it is, he would be severely disadvantaged. He doesn't think they are physical people, well the man isn't, but you can never tell.

He has no choice but to try to retreat, but that too will now be a problem. He has no desire whatsoever to stay on the ground. There may be others of these things in the undergrowth, if indeed it was something that tripped him. But he does not want them to see him. He decides that staying safe from whatever it is on the ground overrides being seen. He tries to stand up, but the initial pain from his leg stops him from doing that. He sees on his aborted attempt at getting up, that the man and the boy are returning to where the girl fell. She must have been tripped up too by something, like he was.

He knows for sure that he will not be able to follow them any further. Even if they stop here for the night, it is doubtful his leg will be better by morning to allow him to continue his pursuit. He stays where he is for a minute or two and then tries to get to his feet again. Again he fails, but he does see the man and the boy going away into the trees again. He waits for a few seconds for the pain from his efforts to subside again, before he attempts to retreat on hands and knees, or whatever way he can. Suddenly he feels a sharp pain on the back of his head and that is all he remembers as he falls to the ground. Elizabeth puts the rock she has used, on the ground by his head. She is hoping he will think he has fallen to the ground with pain from his leg and banged his head on the rock when he fell. That is in fact what he did report to the others, when he eventually made his return to them.

When Edgar and Edmund return with some materials a few minutes later, Elizabeth is standing waiting for them.

'I think we should move on now.'

'What about the man who is following us?'

'He won't be bothering us for some time.'

'Why is that?'

'That is because he has fallen too and hit his head on a rock! He has hurt his leg in the fall too.'

'How do you know this?'

'I was there when he fell. Come with me and I will show you. Then I believe we should leave.'

They walk over quickly to where the man is lying on the ground. Edgar bends down and checks the man is still alive. He then stands up again quickly.

'He has knocked himself out, but I don't know how long he will be out for. We should hurry.'

He is about to say more, but Elizabeth taps his arm and makes the sign for him to not say any more. They don't want to say too much while standing by him. He may be unconscious, but there is always the chance that he could still hear them and maybe remember what they said when he wakes.

They move swiftly away. They have spent a fair amount of time detouring to where they saw the smoke and also back to this point, although they have not gone any further than where they started their detour from. They were tight for time anyway, to be able to make it back to their hut this day, but now they are even shorter of time.

When they are a good distance away from the man, they make their way round so that they are heading in the direction of home. They are stepping out, not because they have discussed it, but because they want to get as far away as soon as they can, from the man.

Something has given them good energy and they are making good time. The only direction they look, other than the way they are going, is behind them. But they need not worry on that score. He is still in exactly the same position as when they left him.

Edgar has based his timings on how long it took them to reach where they saw the smoke, but he hasn't taken into account that on their outward journey they were slower in their progress. They had scoured the horizons in all directions, to see if they could see anyone or any settlements. They were also in a way, conserving their energy so they would last the day out. Now he can see that they are making good time. It will be tight he thinks, because he is uncertain just how far they still have to go. But if they can manage to keep up their current pace, then he thinks there is a chance that they will just about make it back to the hut in daylight, or as it is fading.

He judges whether he should tell the young ones that, or keep it for a time if and when they start to flag. Surely they won't be able to keep up this pace forever. They reach a stream, where they stop for a drink and the last of the food they have brought with them. That is another reason to make it back to the hut. Edith will have prepared something nice for them to eat on their return. He is sure that although she will understand if they don't return today, that will not stop her worrying about where they are and their safety out in the open.

Edgar remembers the stream from their way by here in the morning. He knows it took them about two hours to reach this point then. It should take them less time to make it back from here. He decides now is the time to tell Elizabeth and Edmund how close they are to making it back today, in the hope it will help them keep going. He needn't have been concerned. They too are in the mood for making it back and they say they should keep going now, even if they lose the light. By the time that happens, they reckon they will know roughly where they are and be able to finish their journey even without the assistance of daylight.

As it turns out the light is just fading when they reach the hut. Edith is outside looking for them as they come into view. Even at a distance they can tell she is relieved to see them.

Chapter 11 Elizabeth and Edmund

Over a welcome hot meal by the fire, they tell Edith of their visit to the settlement and how suspicious of them they were. They make light of the man who followed them and make even less of how they managed to evade him. They also assure Edith that he has no idea which direction they have come in.

Elizabeth says that there is no need for them to go out again in the coming days, to try to find her family. As she has said to Edgar and Edmund earlier, she does not think they are to be found, near here or now. No one questions her wording, because she asks them not to. She says that if they will have her, she would be happy to stay with them and do her share of work to pay for her keep. It doesn't take much agreeing to. So Edgar and Edith now have a daughter too.

Over the next few weeks the waters slowly get back down to normal levels. All four of them go back to the old settlement, but there is nothing there that they want to salvage. Anything of any use has been washed away. There is no one left there from before, as they have all perished. If it hadn't been by the hands of the fighters, it could well have been from the sudden flooding that had occurred. So there is literally nothing left there for them. They could rebuild a shelter, but they feel that they are safer from everything where the shepherd used to live, than here.

None of the settlements that are within a reasonable distance are still standing. They don't come across a single soul left living near them. They are reluctant to travel too far from home.

In time a few folks move through and then another settlement springs up near to where theirs had been. They keep away most of the time, but do trade a bit with them, when the need arises.

Elizabeth and Edmund appear to get on really well. In fact they become very close. They work well together and they seem to understand each other. They enjoy each other's company too and very rarely spend time apart from each other.

It is maybe three or four years later that things change and not for the better. More people have joined the new settlement and they are surviving well. Edgar takes some sheep there one day, with a view to barter for some things that the settlers have, in exchange. The thought had never entered his head that someone would ever try to find them. Why would they after all? But apparently they have, or that is the way he chooses to interpret what he has been told.

Two travellers had come through the settlement a day or so before. They'd stopped for a rest and had asked while they were there, if anyone knew of a certain boy. The description fits, in Edgar's head anyway, Edmund. What makes it fit is also the description of Elizabeth and him. He can also tell that the woman, who tells him this, is also fairly certain that they are describing Edgar, Edmund & Elizabeth. They say they have not told the man that they recognised the descriptions, but she thinks that someone else may have reacted differently. That person had told them that Edgar mostly, but sometime Edith, would come into the settlement about once a week. They had been unable to tell them where Edgar and his family live.

Edgar isn't exactly in a panic, but it is close to that. Why would they have come here after all this time, to look for them? What on this earth could they want with them? It was Edmund they had questioned at the time, but in reality it probably should have been Elizabeth. There is something about her that they know nothing about. He can't put it into words, but she is different and there is just something about her that he does not understand. She is with them and she does her chores and everything else that Edmund does. He has always felt this about her, but until this day, faced with the knowledge that some people appear to have come a long way to seek them out, he has never worried about her. Now he is worried, not just about her, but also what she may have brought upon the entire family. Maybe that is a bit unfair of him, but that is how he is thinking about it.

He completes his business in the settlement and starts off on his journey homewards with his goods. The woman didn't say what had become of these travellers. She didn't know and from what she said to him, they are no longer in the settlement. But that doesn't mean they have moved away. If they believe they are close, they might be out there looking in the surrounding area, or maybe they have waited for a day like today, when he has visited the settlement.

It turns out to be the latter of those. He is about half the way back home, when he knows he is no longer alone on his journey. They haven't joined him, but he suddenly notices that he is being followed at a distance by two men. They are not really trying to keep out of his view, when he turns. But they do stop when he stops and they are there at the same distance every time he turns to check on them.

He is unsure what to do. Ideally he does not want to lead them back to the hut, but realistically there is little other choice open to him. It is virtually certain that they will not allow him to give them the slip a second time, although hopefully they are not aware that he is responsible for their man not being able to follow them before. If he does stop and confront them, they might overpower him easily. He has nothing with him to defend himself, other than his staff. He is not a fighting man either and so he is not going to willingly enter something like this situation. He is assuming that they have more than just come to resume their questions.

They do not seem to want a stand-off here either. They will not get the result they want by confronting Edgar here. They want to find out where Edmund and Elizabeth are before they get close to Edgar. They continue to follow him and they stop when he stops and resume their trailing when he starts moving again.

For his part Edgar wishes he had some way of forewarning the family back at the hut, before he actually arrives. (Today we would use a mobile phone, but back then, well there was nothing, except of course, Elizabeth.)

Elizabeth is surprised that it only came to her after Edgar had left. Was there some reason for the timings to be like this? Maybe, as she decided as she shared her vision with Edmund; it was because Edgar as such is not in any danger, as isn't Edith. It is only Elizabeth and Edmund who are in danger. That she knows in her head.

Her first reaction is for them to gather some things and make their escape before Edgar can lead them back here. But when she thinks that, another scenario comes to her. If they do that, then Edgar and Edith will be in severe danger. They might be killed for not having Elizabeth and Edmund with them. They both decide they cannot allow that to happen.

Edmund listens to what Elizabeth tells him. She has been speaking to him quite a lot recently, about how at some time they will have to move away from here. She doesn't know where this information has come from, but then she never does. As time has gone by, with them being together, Edmund has become very much like her. They even have managed to have conversations, very basic ones that is, between them, without actually speaking out loud.

They approach Edith who is busy with the sheep, checking them over to make sure they are all healthy. As soon as they approach her, with looks on their faces she has never seen before, she knows something is wrong. She listens carefully as they say what they fear is coming. She is surprised by how well she receives their words. It is almost as if she has known this would happen one day and she has been prepared for the time she hears the words.

Elizabeth assures her that they will be alright, her and Edmund that is. They will not be going away, but they won't be here for her to see.

'Sometimes I have to go away. This time Edmund will be with me. We will be together now for a long time, beyond the time you will know.'

Edith just nods at this. She somehow knows there is worse to come. Elizabeth then tells her what she thinks might happen. She also says that although she knows Edgar and she will be scared, that they can do nothing to change things and they must believe that she and Edmund will be safe. They will know this when they cannot be found afterwards. Elizabeth does not say what the afterwards bit is about. That would not be helpful to anyone at this stage and would only result in Edgar and Edith putting their lives in danger.

The three of them move back to the shepherd's hut. They stand in front of it, looking out for Edgar's return. They don't have long to wait. They also see very soon after he comes into view, that he is not alone.

'You must go forward to Edgar. We will stay here. We love you both.'

'We love you both too. You are always in our hearts and our minds.' Edith replies.

'Go now, you must move forward' Edmund says these words 'We love you both.'

Edith steps forward. As she does, she turns to look at them. They are smiling and encouraging her to move further forward to meet Edgar. She does so when they are about thirty paces away from them. Edgar stops and she talks to him. He looks at his children. They smile back at him and they both say.

'We love you.'

They then turn, as the two men now make their way right up to them.

'You already know' one of them says, as they stop in front of them.

'What are you going to do?'

They don't answer, but one grabs hold of Edgar and the other gets hold of Edith. They were not expecting this so suddenly. Within seconds they have been tethered and are helpless. The men have only been concentrating on

Edgar and Edith for a matter of seconds, but by the time they return their attention onto Elizabeth and Edmund, they have moved. They have moved towards the entrance of the hut and are standing by the entrance through the bushes. As the men make a move towards them, they go in, and are out of their sight. The men run forward and follow them in. They then stop when they realise there is a path round the shepherd's hut. One of them stays on guard, so they can't get out past them, while the other one checks out the path, before going into the hut when that search proves fruitless.

He is soon back outside. There is no sign of them. They ask Edgar and Edith if there is another way out of the hut. No there is not. The only way in and out of there is where they are standing. The other one goes in and searches, but he doesn't find them either. They check the outside of the hut area, but it is quickly apparent that the geography of the land does not allow for there to be any other way out. They must be in there somewhere.

They start to bring the wood outside from the wood store. They make a pile against the hut and the vegetation around it and then set fire to it, using the fire from inside the hut. Once it is all alight, they step back and watch it burn. The fire is ferocious and it burns extremely quickly. Soon there is nothing left to burn. The bushes have all gone and there is nothing left of their hut and their possessions. More importantly there is nothing left of Elizabeth or Edmund. There are no human remains, or any other for that matter, in the ashes. But it is also clear for all to see that they could not have gone anywhere. There is absolutely nowhere they could have gone. The two men smile at them as they loosen their tethers and walk away. They know they have burned them to death. Edgar and Edith have no such concern, despite the evidence in front of their eyes.

They sit where they are, staying awake throughout the night for as long as they can. They want to shed a tear, but they aren't able to. Eventually, just before dawn, they fall asleep. They wake a few hours later, when the rays from the sun hit their faces. They open their eyes, only to find that nothing has changed, well nothing from before that is. The bushes are there and when they investigate, they find their hut is there too, fully restored. The only things that are not there are Elizabeth and Edmund. They have gone and they never see them again.

Part 2
Chapter 12 In Between

That event changes things for Edmund and Elizabeth. It is not a conscious change for them, but something has changed nevertheless. In fact they are not aware of any change, as everywhere they are in the future; they are just Edmund and Elizabeth. They could not tell you of their past. Edmund has no memory of his parents and that time in his life. Elizabeth was already in that position when she met Edmund.

In between 'visits' they are nowhere. They are only aware of the actual times they appear and not any of the years in between.

It is many years later that they make their first return. They emerge from the shepherd's hut into the bright sunshine. There is no one around. If they could have remembered it, the hut is in the same condition as when they were last inside it.

The settlement, when they reach it, is much more established than it had been when they last saw it. Not that they are aware of that of course.

Like she has done so many times before, Elizabeth tries to whisper her warnings to those it will affect. Unlike before, she is now visible to those who she tries to warn of impending doom. Edmund is with her every step of the way.

The King is not a popular man. Time and again he makes calls on the landowners to raise money for the war against the Scots, originally in the 1630's, and now in the 1640's, the time they are now visiting. His quest for more money has pitted him against Parliament, about how he has sent soldiers to arrest some men in Parliament. Now he has started a war against Parliament too.

The Royalists and The Roundheads are involved in many battles for towns and castles in the area, from 1642, for the next 3 or 4 years. Families are at odds with each other, with some members being split about who they support.

Elizabeth and Edmund gather from those that they speak to, that the majority of the landowners and their tenants are Royalists. But there are supporters of Parliament too. Elizabeth and Edmund try, whenever they can, to give advance warnings of when their area is going to be subject to soldiers passing through, or even trying to enforce calls for more money to be raised for the King, or to support the local landowners' own armies with food and money. There is no money to pay for these local garrisons, so the local towns, farms and villages are expected to provide food and money to pay for this support. If people do not provide this support, they will get a visit from the soldiers, who will confiscate everything they can carry away. Often they will burn down the buildings as punishment too. Naturally this causes resentment and in time, turns many against the King, as his soldiers are often the worst offenders.

Elizabeth has little success in her whispers. People can see her, whereas before they could not. Even though what she is saying always proves to be right, the people she has warned are not around afterwards to verify her warnings were correct. Three times over the period of time they visit in that period, she is not just accused of being a witch and a traitor, but they are also followed home and the shepherd's hut is burnt down, supposedly with them inside. Each time they reappear a short time later and continue to warn the people of the settlements round and about, of impending visits by soldiers to punish people for not paying enough money and providing enough food.

The people of one settlement in particular are more resistant to her warnings. It is one of the larger ones in the district. It is also one where the people who live there are more critical of each other, particularly of people who move in. This is the case even by relative newbies. They will talk about people and spread malicious gossip, which on occasion leads them to be raided and have their things taken and houses burned. There is something about this particular settlement that brings the worst out in some people.

Then one day Edmund and Elizabeth go to this settlement, to warn certain individuals. There has always been an element of people who have kept together and done their worst. They were not born here, but have taken the settlement as their own. It is almost as if they have set Elizabeth up. Well, if they have, she has not gone there this day because of anything she has heard. No one tells her about things around and about anyway.

She doesn't even get as far as to speak to the two people she has gone to warn of impending events. A group of people are waiting for her as she enters the settlement.

They knew she was coming, or so it appears to be. As she turns the corner close to the hut she is aiming for, they jump out in front of her. Others close in behind her, cutting off her route of retreat. Edmund is not with her at this stage. He has gone off to do some hunting, to replenish their food supply.

The ring tightens round Elizabeth, until her attackers are close enough that there is no possible way she can escape.

'You think that you know about impending doom? You didn't see this coming. That is the problem with witches. They only see what they want to see. There is no room for people like you here. Did I say people? You are not a person, you're a witch. You know what they do to witches? They get burned at the stake; that's what happens around here. You will regret coming here, trying to spread your malicious gossip about the people here.'

Elizabeth remains calm. It is not the first time she has been accused of being a witch. It is not the first time she has encountered most of these people who are surrounding her now. She has not encountered them all together as they are at this moment, but she has seen them virtually every time she has been here. One or two of them talking and watching her. Sometimes it has been the same ones, but often others. They have not done anything up to now, other than the odd call of 'witch' to her from a distance. They have seen her with Edmund almost every time. She is thinking that this is probably the first time in she can't remember how long, that Edmund has not come with her to this settlement. In fact he has warned her about walking here alone. But then she hadn't any intention of coming here today, until after he'd left to go hunting. Then she'd felt the message come to her. She knew that she couldn't wait until Edmund returned, to come and try to deliver the warning. Now it would appear that she is in trouble. She knows it is not the first time.

Elizabeth remains calm, despite the fact that several of them are now prodding her with their wooden staffs. She knows they have not brought her here, but it remains an open question as to how they knew she would be coming round this particular corner today. She has not been to see these particular people before. It is rare that she does come to see the same people, if they do not heed her words. Often they are not still around to be warned. No, it isn't possible that they could have arranged this, whatever they are saying. She also doubts the situation would be any different if Edmund was with her. Then the thought strikes her that they were not expecting Edmund to be there. Now that is very strange. Some power must be at work here, or the coincidence is a very odd one.

She feels a rope being put round her wrists and then around her legs. She is then lifted by some of the menfolk. They carry her high and start shouting to everyone who can hear them, about the witch they have caught and are going to deal with. The question will be whether it will be the Sherriff they take her to, or if they are going to mete out their own punishment. She suspects it will be the latter.

As they turn into the main area of the settlement, she sees that it is definitely going to be the latter. They have built a tent of wood in the middle of the square. There are one or two others coming now, to see what the uproar is about.

Just as they reach the pile of wood, she sees Edmund come into view. She wants to shout out, to warn him to keep away, or they will catch and burn him too. As hard as she tries, she cannot open her mouth to shout her warning to him. But she knows that he has seen her and what is happening. She knows he can see the danger, but he is looking remarkably calm.

Then she hears his voice. She is not sure that he is talking from where he is, or if his voice is just in her head.

'I am here now. They cannot see me. I have been told this, so I have to presume it is true.'

She looks at him as he approaches. Surely he can be seen by her captors. Some of them are facing in his direction. But they are not reacting to his presence. Edmund is now almost at her side. He doesn't come straight to her, but goes over to the wood pile. In a second there are flames starting from the point where he is. The fire whooshes up as it takes control. It is far fiercer than the fire should be in such a short time. It takes her captors by surprise. None of them has lit this fire and yet here it is burning strongly. It is burning too strongly for them to tie the witch to the wood, before burning her.

A jet of flame leaps out of the fire and scorches the people who have hold of her. They have no choice, but to let her go. The jet has also burnt the ties that hold her. A jet of flame jumps to her side. The people shrink back from her, in fear of this. The flames are hot, too hot for them to be close to. But Elizabeth does not feel this heat. Nor does she see it as flames, because all she can see is Edmund.

'They will pay for this' is all he says, as he takes her hand and walks through the group of people. They open a path for them to walk through.

They watch as Elizabeth walks away. Only when she turns the corner and disappears from their view, do they make a move to follow her, to follow them.

Chapter 13 In Between

They see the fire start up and they are bemused by this. They see the jet of flame leap from the fire. Some of them do not see it in time to jump back away from the scorching heat and burning it brings with it. Everyone backs away enough in the end to be clear of it. That of course has meant that they have let her go. She does not appear to be affected by the flames. In fact what they see in front of their eyes; is that she appears to be in control of the flames. Maybe she, as a witch, has brought the fire to life like this. Maybe she, as a witch, has brought the jet of fire out to make them let her go. Maybe she, as a witch, has made the jet of flame burn her ties and release her. But they have not seen Edmund. They can't see Edmund. So they do not know that it is Edmund who has done all this and not Elizabeth. But of course it does not matter, for if they had known this, he too would be looked on as a sorcerer or such likes.

They just stand and watch as she slowly walks away from the fire, walks away from them. Only as she turns the corner and is lost from sight of them do they move again. The thoughts they have been having in their heads are now being voiced to those around them. The noise is loud and confused, as everyone is speaking at once. They are all talking and not listening to what the others are saying. It matters not, as they are all saying the same thing. They are not saying it word for word, but there isn't a huge diversity in their words.

Edmund's actions have succeeded in releasing Elizabeth from her captors, but he knows he has probably only increased their suspicions and fear of them even more. They will not let this go now, but then they weren't going to anyway. He is sure that when they had burnt Elizabeth on the fire; he is quite sure this was their proposed course of action. Then they would have come for him too. If not today, it would have been sometime soon.

They can hear the babble of talk as they turn the corner and keep walking away from the crowd. They hear it turn into a shout, as everyone tries to get their words heard by the rest of the crowd. Inevitably the noise brings others into the arena, as they wonder what is going on.

When the crowd had been leading Elizabeth towards the fire, they had been determined. I wouldn't have said they were angry at that time, but now they are angry. An angry crowd is a dangerous crowd in any situation.

Edmund realises there is no point in running. He doesn't want to and he doesn't need to either. They aren't going to catch him as such. It is like when he walked towards Elizabeth, standing by the fire. He had been told that the crowd would not see him, but he didn't know that for sure when he came into their view. It soon became obvious that what he had been told was correct. He does know that Elizabeth can see him and he also knows that Elizabeth can be seen by the crowd. But he has been told that now she is with him, now that she is holding his hand as contact, then they will not be able to harm them. They will not be able to capture them. They will not be able to stop them. He knows this, but until the time comes he does not know how any of this will work. He doesn't know if it will work, but he has been told, so he is fine with that. As long as he has hold of Elizabeth, then she will be safe too.

They have walked maybe a hundred yards beyond the corner, when the first of the crowd turn it. They had expected that Elizabeth would have made a run for it, but she hasn't. She is still walking at the same pace away from them. She isn't turning round to see if they are following. Surely the noise that they are making should be enough for anyone to turn round to see what is coming towards them. But, as a witch, which is the way they are thinking of her, she is not bothered by them. There is no way they can do anything right now in the eyes of the crowd, but this lack of reaction from her only raises their level of anger and hate against her.

Some of those who are arriving have weapons with them too. When they see that Elizabeth is still in sight, some of them run forward. Still she does not turn towards them. Only when they get closer, do they realise that Elizabeth has some of the fire still with her. The jet of fire that had leapt out of the fire appears to be with her. It is almost as if she is holding it. There is definitely part of it and her that appear to be connected.

It slows them a little, but not totally. Some of their number runs on ahead, in an attempt to cut off their route of retreat. Elizabeth does not break her stride. She continues towards them. As the gap closes, the fire, while staying with her, also sets out a jet of fire towards them. That causes them to back off and a channel opens up for them to walk through. An attempt to close in from the sides is dealt with promptly in the same manner. The fire is strong. The fire is hot. The jet burns severely to the touch. While all of this occurs, Elizabeth does nothing other than carrying on walking, as she has been told to do by Edmund.

Edmund has his eyes everywhere. He feels he has to do so, even though at times he thinks the fire jets are deciding when they will strike out at anyone who dares to come too close. There are a few episodes with members of the crowd daring to grab them, but each and every one is repelled with ease by a jet of fire. By the time they are at the edge of the settlement there are no people trying to head them off. There are some away to each side, but most of the crowd are behind them. The numbers are swelling all of the time. It would appear that virtually everyone from the settlement is now out in the crowd, possibly even more if that is possible. Some are wishing that soldiers would come along at this moment. That would change things they are sure, but that just isn't going to happen. They do not know that.

They continue walking beyond the settlement. Some of the followers decide they have come far enough, but the vast majority keep following. They don't understand why they can't get close, but they believe they are correct about Elizabeth being a witch. Surely the fire jet verifies that. Elizabeth is keeping quiet. She knows that Edmund needs to concentrate. She is not afraid of these people, but she does not understand why they are behaving like this, when all she has tried to do is to warn some of them about impending doom.

In the meantime back in the settlement virtually the only ones who have not come out to see what is happening, are the people Elizabeth was on the way to warn. They are now about to get a visit from the four soldiers who have just entered the settlement. But before they can get to the hut in question, they are approached by some of the ones who had turned back. They tell the soldiers about Elizabeth and the fire jets that are protecting her. The soldiers know they can come back to address this issue at the hut, so they turn their horses and ride off in the direction the crowd has gone. As they depart, the occupants of the hut come out. They quickly gather their possessions and load up their cart. In less than five minutes they are on their way out of the settlement, in the opposite direction. They have survived the day despite Elizabeth not reaching them, not that they would probably have heeded her warning. That is what is so confusing. It is not the information that is brought, but by whom it has been brought that appears to matter whether people take heed of it or not.

The soldiers soon catch up with the crowd. They make their way to the front and surround Elizabeth as best they can. Edmund is more careful with the fire jets. It is not the fault of the horses that they have been put in this position.

But on the other hand they are trying to stop Elizabeth and Edmund getting to their destination. A brief jet is enough to unsettle the horses enough for their riders to back them off. It is clear that Elizabeth isn't going to be stopped from getting to where she is going. In their minds they can wait a while. It will only be so long before the fire burns out. Then what will she do?

That thought is fine if the fire is real, but it is not. Nor can they yet see Edmund. All they can see is Elizabeth and the fire she has beside her, connected to her in one place.

It doesn't take long for them to be at the stream and go across it. Ahead of them are the bushes that shield the shepherd's hut. Surprisingly not one of the followers has been here before. As far as they are aware, there isn't anything here. None of them realise this is where Elizabeth and Edmund have been living.

About twenty feet short of the bushes, Elizabeth suddenly turns around. Edmund turns with her and sends out a jet of flame in an arc, which stops anyone from coming closer. The four soldiers are at the front of the crowd now.

'All I have ever done is come to some of you and whisper to you something that I know will happen. I have done that to give you an opportunity to escape from the impending danger. You have chosen not to do that. But now you are accusing me of being a witch. I am not a witch.'

'Put out that fire then, if you are not a witch.' Someone shouts from the crowd.

'It is not a fire. You are wrong. It is a person I have beside me.'

At that the fire all but disappears and Edmund is visible to them all. A gasp comes from every mouth when they see him.

'You will pay for what you have tried to do. You will pay and the people who come after you will pay.'

At which they both turn and walk round to the side of the bushes and walk in. before anyone can think of following, there is a huge whooosh, as the bushes burst in flame. The heat is intense. The flames are intense. The fire is intense. It only lasts for just over a minute and then it has gone. So have the bushes. So has the shepherd's hut and more importantly, so have Elizabeth and Edmund. All that is left is a large scorched area on the ground where they were.

Part 3
Chapter 14 Where Now?

Mick has been busy in Broseley. It wasn't always that way, but recently he has hit a relatively rich vein of business there. Of course he puts that down to him. He is an easy going guy, compared to some of the others out there who ply the same trade. He is also more accessible than most of his competitors. He makes it easy for his customers to get what they want, and most of the time, when they want it too. Well, more or less. It has to be worth his while to come over here, but most of the time it is. He has a merry band of regulars to keep supplied. Another reason he does so well, is that he is competitive. He doesn't take advantage. He tries to keep his prices right. He doesn't want his customers to get in too deep. When they do that, then it is not good for business in the long run. If they get in too deep, then they stop buying, well they stop buying from you, because they avoid you. If they get in too deep, they owe you and they can't afford to buy and you don't want to extend their credit.

Ideally he would not have to give credit, but in his case, he found it works for him. It has certainly got him more customers. Yes it has occasionally meant he has had to work a bit harder to recoup potential losses. But thankfully the type of customer he has; soon gets to be in the pay for it now class. They work off the initial credit he has extended when they start buying from him and then it becomes a cash business after that.

Mick is cash rich. He doesn't take cards and he doesn't take cheques. He doesn't take anything but cash. He has been known to take gold and watches, but he isn't that knowledgeable on valuing them, so if he does, then the balance is heavily weighted in his favour.

The car door slams shut and his last customer of the day in Broseley walks away from him. The hoodie is pulled well down over his face as he slinks away. His hand is in his pocket, grasping hold of his purchase from Mick. Mick waits until his customer disappears round the corner before he starts the engine of his red Ford Fiesta. The car is his means of getting round his customers. He doesn't want anything too flash when he is delivering and collecting. It wouldn't do for them to see how well he is doing. At home in Telford, he keeps another car parked in his garage. That is for when he goes out with the family. At the moment that car is parked where he keeps the Fiesta. He drives there from home and swops vehicles to do his work and then at the end of the day, he parks up the Fiesta and drives home in his other car.

Mick pulls away from the curb. A couple of minutes later he is on his way out of Broseley. He goes down the dip and up the other side, going through Benthall and onwards towards Much Wenlock, his last delivery of the day. He wouldn't normally be going there on a Tuesday, but Nigel had sent him a text saying he had not only the money he owed, but quite a bit more he wanted to spend with Mick. The offer to collect the money owing, plus the added incentive of a good cash sale, was enough to make him detour there on his way home.

As he drives steadily along the winding road towards Wenlock, he sees the night sky coming in ahead of him. But every mile brings darker skies too and it is not just the time of day making the skies so dark ahead of him. It doesn't really matter to him what the weather is doing out there. He has no intention of getting out of his Red Ford Fiesta, until he swops cars on the way home. That only takes ten seconds or thereabouts, so the weather is neither here nor there. He doubts it will affect Nigel either. To be honest the weather very rarely affects his customers meeting up with him. They want what he has to sell, more than they don't like coming out in bad weather. Not everyone who sells goods has that sort of customers.

It takes him less than ten minutes to reach Much Wenlock. By the time he gets to the 30 sign and turns the bend into Barrow Street, the daylight he'd had when he left Broseley has disappeared. The first spots of rain hit the windscreen by the time he drives past The Raven. By the time he passes the end of High Street, the spots have become a steady rainfall. By the time he reaches the junction at the end of Sheinton Street the rain is hammering down. He turns right onto the main road and then immediately right on to Station Road. There are a couple of cars parked on the right as he enters Station Road. He drives up about fifty yards and stops just before the coach bays. It wouldn't have bothered him if he parked in the coach bay. He isn't bothered where he parks, as long as his customers can find him.

The wipers are worker hard, sweeping the rain away. They aren't winning the battle. As fast as they sweep one way, the rain falls again on the windscreen and makes seeing ahead almost impossible. It doesn't matter for the moment, as he is where he needs to be. This is where Nigel meets him.

Mick looks at his watch. He is a few minutes early. Nigel will be bang on time. He always is; whatever the weather. He turns off the engine and the wipers stop where they are, mid sweep. Almost as if the engine has been making it rain harder, as soon as he turns the engine off, the rain eases back tremendously to a drizzle.

Mick reaches into the back for his notebook. He will need to mark off the debt when Nigel pays him. He doesn't need to look at the book to know how much that is, as he already knows exactly what Nigel has got to pay him, to square things from last time. He has what Nigel ordered too, ready on the back seat next to his notebook.

As he reaches into the back, the wind suddenly springs up. Well he thinks it is the wind that is making the sudden noise. It sounds like wind when it starts, but it now sounds different, very different. Mick's hand is poised over the notebook as he hears the sound change. It doesn't sound like wind anymore he decides. It sounds like whispering. But it isn't as simple as someone whispering would be. It is not like that. It has the force of the wind blowing behind it. It has the sound of wind rustling through the trees. It has the sound of the wind trying to talk. Yes that is what it is like. The wind is talking, but not talking very loud. Yes, it sounds like the wind is whispering. But that doesn't seem to make sense. The wind should roar when it blows this strong, but it isn't. It is almost as if it is holding itself back. It wants to roar, but it is afraid it will lose control, so it is whispering instead. That is all well and good, but the wind isn't just whispering to keep control and hold back from forcing its way through the obstacles.

Mick is concentrating on the sound. He has never heard the wind sound like this before. Then it changes from just a whispering sound to words, words that he can hear and understand.

'Mick . . . . Mick Devlin . . . . Mick . . . . Mick Devlin'

Mick shivers and a jolt of panic courses through him. His hand snatches back to the front again, as he sits up and pays attention. Strangely he feels fear, something that he hasn't felt for many a year. The sound has gone back to a general whispering. It has not gone back to the sound of the wind blowing, but back to a whispering. Long slow whispers of words that he just can't quite make out.

Then in an instant, the wind roars up again, overpowering the whispers. The car shakes with the force of the wind pushing into the side. There is no warning to what happens next, but it has a definite effect on Mick. A branch breaks off from one of the trees he is parked under. It isn't a big heavy branch, but it is big enough. It breaks off from the tree and drops down onto the windscreen and bonnet of his car, just as the wind stops completely. The whispering can be heard clearly once more, with a long slow whisper of the one word:

'M…………i……….c………..k'

Mick has never been so afraid. He isn't sure which has scared him more; the branch hitting the car, or the sound of his name being drawn out by the whisper. The branch landing on the car made him jump, but he decides it is the whisper he is scared of. He is jumpy. He looks out of the car ahead and behind him. There isn't anyone there. He thinks there must be. Someone is playing a prank on him. It is not the sort of thing Nigel would do. Nigel just isn't that kind of a guy. Nigel is serious. Nigel is depressed most of the time. Nigel hasn't got it in him to do anything to anyone. That is why Nigel is buying gear in the first place. So it won't be Nigel, but who else could it be? Who else could know that he was going to come here this evening? The answer is no one except for him and Nigel. He is stopped from pursuing this line of thought by the whisper coming again.

'Mick Devlin, yes it is you I am whispering to. I know who you are and I know what you do. I know your family from now and before. I will make an example of you.'

That does it for Mick. He is scared out of his wits. He doesn't know where the sound of whispering is coming from. It is definitely not coming from inside the car. There is no one outside it could be coming from either. But then it isn't the sound of someone whispering from the outside. It is the sound of someone whispering on the wind, but the wind isn't there anymore. It isn't like anything he has experienced before. It isn't something he thought he ever would, not that he would have thought about it.

As if all that isn't enough for him to try and cope with. He isn't expecting what happens next. Suddenly something taps his driver's window, then the passenger side. Then it taps the back window and then the windscreen. And when it taps the windscreen, there is a face in the air over the bonnet, as the branch is swept aside. It is the face of a girl, maybe a young woman. Mick doesn't see any more, as he loosens his bowels the same moment as he passes out from shock.

Chapter 15 Nigel

Nigel sits there looking at his phone. He has sent a message to Mick, but Mick hasn't replied yet. Nigel finds that more than slightly annoying. After all he has said in his message that not only is he going to pay off his debt, not that it comes to that much in real terms, and on top of that he has indicated that he wants plenty more stuff.

'You'd think he'd sprint a reply back to me' Nigel says out loud. There isn't anyone else in the room to hear those words. Nor is there anyone else in the house. Nigel lives alone, well he does these days.

He has another glance at the screen, but is to be disappointed still. He lets his mind wander, to try to make the time pass quicker.

Nigel Melvin-Coots; that is his name.

'Twats' he says out loud as he thinks of this. The people who gave him that name think that it is the be all and end all of the world, having a double barrelled named.

'Twats' he says a bit louder at that.

Yes, they really think it makes them special. They're special alright, but not in the way they think they are. They think that having a double barrelled name makes them superior.

'Twats, they couldn't even spell superior' is his outburst this time, followed by a glance at the screen. There is still no reply from Mick. He lets his thoughts continue with their theme.

The double barrel comes with his step-dad. It certainly didn't come from the aristocracy. He inherited the name from a previous generation who had decided to join their surnames, in an effort to raise their profile in the area they lived in. It didn't work. You either have it or you don't.

'Twat' he says again.

Nigel has no time for his step-dad. He thinks he is better than everyone around him, but he isn't. He thinks that he is clever and knows about stuff, but he doesn't. Nigel has experienced how shallow the man is and how shallow his knowledge of things really are, when you actually challenge what he does or says. Of course his step-dad does not like Nigel.

Nigel gives out a huff as he looks at his phone again. He turns his thoughts briefly to his mother. She is almost as bad as he is. She seems to have adopted the double-barrelleditis. Sometimes he thinks that is why she got together with him, after Nigel's dad had left them, in a permanent kind of way. She had nothing when she was left alone. Their world fell apart for a time, until his mother picked herself up and got on with life. It is all way back in the past now. The problem, as far as he is concerned, with her picking herself up again, is that she met his step-dad. His mum made it work as best she could, but she was also concerned with getting her life on track. And whatever Nigel may think of him or her, they did that. In relation to where she had been, she landed on her feet. They certainly had a better life than when his mother was alone, after his dad left them. But of course in his eyes, this all came at a price.

Nigel could never have been said to be a good scholar. It isn't that he is thick or anything, because that is not the case. One of the problems is that when his dad was alive, they moved from place to place quite a lot. That meant that Nigel got popped into the local school when they got there. One of the problems with that; is that different schools teach different things at different times. They are all supposed to be covering the same program, but it never works out like that in practice. It would have helped if Nigel had been a bit more confident, but Nigel wasn't a child with great confidence.

As a result he failed to pick up more than the basics. Because he wasn't maybe at the stage a class was, he muddled along as if he understood everything. He had the teachers fooled most of the time. The exceptional time to this was when they got to do exams and tests. If he could, he managed to avoid a lot of them by being conveniently sick on those days. But when that didn't come off, there was a realisation that Nigel wasn't up to speed with the rest of the class. But then they'd move on again and it became someone else's problem, or not, as the case was most of the time.

The only thing that changed when his mother and step-dad got together; was that they didn't move around nearly as much. But by this time Nigel was so far behind everyone else, that the void was too big to bridge. He truanted, feigned sickness and invented family tragedies, all as excuses not to attend school. It is no surprise to learn that as soon as he could leave school, he did. Of course that didn't solve the problems at home. In fact it probably made them worse. As he reached the later years of his teens, he became more distant from both of them, trying to defend the fact he was doing nothing with his life. Inevitably it was only a matter of time before the relationship at home broke completely and it did.

Nigel has another look down at his phone. He sees that Mick has responded. He has also given him a time to meet him at their usual rendezvous.

He still has time for his thoughts. That wasn't a good time in his life. He had fallen out with both of them and his step-dad had more or less told him to sling his hook. If Nigel thought he was going to be supported throughout his life by them, then he had another think coming. Of course that is more or less what Nigel had been doing and he hadn't given it much thought as to what he would do with the rest of his life.

He spent a few nights here and there, staying with friends. But that soon enough came to an end, when they realised in turn that Nigel was more or less moving in and wanted to stay there indefinitely.

Nigel stands up and moves into the kitchen. He wants a cup of tea before he goes off to see Mick. There is plenty of time to review what happened next in his life when he left home. Needless to say that the path has not been a smooth one and has varied from downs, to deep downs, to rock bottom downs, before the occasional lift up from somewhere that miraculously saved him from the absolute pit of no return. Sometimes he manages it by himself, but more often or not it is because someone takes pity on him, or likes him enough to try to help him. Occasionally a good bit of luck comes his way and he finds he is in the right place at the right time.

It is a mixture of all of these that brings him to Wenlock. He has, for him, been on one of his better runs and then hit a blip, when somehow he re-established contact with his Mum and Mr double-barrelled twat. Of course it was they who made the contact. Initially it wasn't of the face to face kind, but more of the Facebook kind. He had always been quite careful just how much information about himself he puts on his profile page. You never know who might decide to drop in and read it. So he doesn't incriminate himself, if he can help it. He only paints a general picture of his life. God forbid he dare put on how he feels when he gets depressed. That would scare anyone who might want to contact him, off. Anyway as I said, he had been on one of his better runs before the blip.

Before the blip everything had been going so well. Life is never smooth as such, but at that time he was alright. He had a roof over his head, he had a woman in tow, or was he in tow with her; probably that actually. Not only that, but he was also employed. It was nothing of great shakes, but it was a regular job and he was paid through the books. That in itself was a bit of a novelty. They had a little problem finding him on the system; it is that unusual for him to have a job where he pays tax and NI.

The relationship he was in was quite a volatile one. The woman was quite headstrong and occasionally she could be violent too. But on the positive side, as far as he was concerned, she appeared to like him. She actually appeared to like him a lot. She told him that he was good for her and that he had changed her life for the better. She was never that explicit as to what her experiences of relationships have been like in the past, but Nigel thinks he could have a good guess at it, and often did when she went off on one. But overall his life was better with her. He wore better clothes, never mind they came from the charity shop. They were good clothes wherever he bought them; he just got them cheap as someone had given them in to the charity shop, to support it. She introduced him to that style of shopping. It had never crossed his mind to buy his clothes from a charity shop. But he did remember his mother doing so. More when they were alone and before the Twat came along, but she never gave up the habit even afterwards. His mother was always one for a bargain; a bargain for her of course. She doesn't believe in giving other people bargains though. That just isn't in her nature.

Anyway the introduction to buying clothes from charity shops wasn't the only thing she introduced him to. She wised him up on the entire benefit system. She knows how to get money out of the system if the situation arises. It did quite often, as she lost her job frequently, due to her volatile nature. It was always someone else's fault and she soon got her income stream reconnected on benefits. She even tried to get Nigel to get his own place. Not because she wanted him to go, but to get him housing benefit to pay for it and then sub-let it out. Nigel wouldn't go along with it. I think he knew he needed to bank some things for the future, when he might need them more.

She also introduced him to modern technology. He acquired a smart phone from one of her acquaintances who had got themselves something better. She spent a good amount of time getting Nigel to learn how to use it. Once he managed to get his head round the workings, he took to it like a duck to water. In time he wondered how he had managed to live without this kind of technology for so long.

And then there are the two other things that she introduced Nigel to. Both are things that he hadn't encountered before or had done, surprisingly enough. The first is she taught him how to drink and my; she knew how to drink. She could so easily drink him under the table. At first he tried to keep up, but that was before he found out he never could. The other thing she introduced him to is drugs.

Chapter 16 Nigel

You can say whatever you like about his Mum and the Twat step-dad, but of all things they are, from his point of view, boringly straight. He doesn't know if they were always like that, or maybe had experimented with things in their youth and then grown out of it, or whatever. They had never commented to him while he was growing up about drugs.

At first all his lady friend introduced him to, was a bit of weed. He is a smoker anyway and although he had heard of people smoking a spliff, he had never indulged in one before this. And that only came about as he was out of fags one night and she offered him one of her rollies instead. Naively he thought it was one of the hand rolling tobacco cigarettes that she smoked all the time that she was offering him. Only when he started to feel the effects of what he was smoking, did he think about the smile that had been on her face when she gave it to him.

Nigel remembers that he quite liked it at the time and the many times he has indulged since. What he particularly liked was that one benefit of this was that she appeared to like Nigel even more. Now that he was smoking weed with her, she felt better and for a time was less volatile than normal. In fact she was totally calm for months after the first time. But then as with everything in her life, somebody got the wrong side of her, or did something that she didn't like, and the balance was tilted out of kilter once more.

It was soon after this that Nigel noticed that she has started taking other drugs. Her highs and lows were extremely pronounced. She lost her job again and although as usual she picked up benefits easily enough, there wasn't enough money for her needs this time. Things disappeared from their home and her attitude to him changed for the worse. Things were getting so bad between them that he really thought that he couldn't take much more of her strange ways and the way she was distancing from him. He was also struggling with the fact that it was also some of his things that were disappearing.

Then one evening when he got home from work, she was all over him. She wanted him, she needed him, she loved him emotionally and on that evening, physically in a way that raised things to a new high. And when they just had to stop for a rest; that was when she persuaded him that this was the time to take what she had taken that day. This, she insisted, was why they have had such a good evening. After the months of a declining relationship, he found it hard to argue that this evening had been anything but a more than pleasant experience.

The result of that was ok for a short time, but then he stopped going into work. He just didn't feel like it when it came to the time to leave in the mornings. It didn't take that long for his employer to lose patience with him. So, it wasn't that long before he lost his job. And from that moment what they had between them, more or less disappeared overnight. She would disappear for hours on end and come back with a strange smile on her face. Even though it was obvious to Nigel that she was on something, she shunned him. She shut herself in the bedroom and locked the door. When he tried to bridge the gap between them, she became violent towards him. She would not only hit him with her fists, but also with anything she could grab hold of. Never once did he hit her back. He just retreated to a safe place and tried to keep out of her way.

This only lasted a week or so, before she demanded that he leave. He had nowhere to go, and no money to rent anywhere either. Any money he got was going on his new drug habit. He didn't even have enough money for that. He sold whatever he had that was worth anything, except for his phone.

She had been particularly nasty this day. He'd said he would go out and try to find somewhere he could go. He had no idea where that might be, but he did go out to look for something. When he got back home an hour later, not really having tried as he had got something from their dealer who he'd bumped into. Not that he had the cash, but they were willing to advance him a bit, at a cost. But when he got home he finds what was left of his stuff was piled up on the doorstep. She hasn't even packed it in his bags.

He banged on the door but she wouldn't open it and told him in no uncertain way to 'f*** off'. He did, after stuffing what he could into the bags she'd put out with his stuff.

That night he slept rough before he found someone who'd let him stay for a couple of nights. He tried to go back round a couple of times over the next few days, but he didn't get a reply when he knocked at the door. It was maybe a week later when he went round that the door was opened by a man. He was wearing a pair of jeans, but had nothing on his top half. She appeared a second or two later and stood about three feet behind him.

'You must be Nigel. As you can probably guess, she is with me now. I won't tell you this more than once. You must not come here again. If you do I will sort you out. I will sort you out so you can't come round again. Do I make myself clear?'

Nigel just nods. To be honest he had never thought that this would happen with him and her. He had no idea that she would just jump from one man, him, to another.

'And if you see her out in the street or somewhere, or me for that matter, the same applies. You don't come near either of us and you don't speak to us. We won't speak to you, so don't you worry. If you don't do as I say, then I will sort you out; sort you out so you can't. Do I make myself clear?'

Nigel just nods again. But he doesn't make to move away. It is almost as if he is transfixed to the spot. The truth is that he is in shock. He never thought that she would just throw him away and get another man just like that. He is interrupted in his daydream by this man.

'Do you want me to give you a taste of my fists? The way you are just standing there is as if that is what you want. I thought I had made myself clear. I'll give you five seconds to turn round and walk away or you won't be able to.'

Nigel thought about saying something, but by the time he has, the five seconds are up. The man steps forward and swings his fist at Nigel. On reflection Nigel reckons that the man aimed to miss, but at the time it had the desired effect. He stepped back quickly and then turned away. He wasted no time starting to run along the street to get away from him; to get away from her. All he could hear as he ran was the sound of the man laughing at him, and then she started too. Nigel is a broken man.

Over the next few weeks, maybe a couple of months, his existence was one of hand to mouth. He crashed on whoever's floor he could. He borrowed money to buy drugs. All he wanted to do was retreat from the reality that had spoilt his new life.

Then as happens when you borrow money and don't pay it back, the day comes when they try to get it back from you. If it had been ordinary people then they might have pursued that through the courts, but these aren't that kind of people. They wanted their money back. They wanted it with interest too; high interest and more importantly they wanted it now. A visit late at night with a taster of what he would get if they didn't start getting their money soon, was funnily enough the start of things changing for the better for him.

He has been in contact with his Mum on Facebook a few times. He hadn't intentionally sent her the message she received that night. He wasn't thinking straight. In fact he was in a blind panic, so he wasn't really thinking at all. He was just trying to get anyone he knew, to lend him something to get him out of immediate trouble. But he sent the message to his Mum too.

The next thing he is getting a reply, asking where he is staying and then the next day, they turn up; her and the Twat. But the Twat has brought some money with him. As it turns out it wasn't nearly enough to clear his debt, but it is enough for them to allow a bit more time for the debt to be repaid. When I say a bit more time, I mean a couple of days for her and the Twat to go back for the rest.

Nigel knows that he doesn't really deserve their help to this degree, but he doesn't admit that to himself. Of course the money comes with certain terms and conditions. They take him to a guest house. They aren't going to splash out on a hotel for the three of them. There, over a drink in their room, they lay out their terms for helping him out. The first surprise is that they aren't going to ask for the money back. That is a real surprise to him. In fact there are only two, maybe three terms that they are insisting on, in exchange for getting him out of this mess. Firstly that he gives up the drugs that he is clearly on, secondly that he comes back to Wenlock with them, until they get him a place of his own, and thirdly that he does some work for them, for which they will pay him. But they don't specify what the work is and how much they will pay him.

It is a no brainer. He is in s*** street here. As things stand it is only a matter of time before he gets injured badly by those he owes money to. Also he has nowhere to live and no prospects of work either. Also it has been hard going around the town, always on edge in case he sees her, or the man she is now with. He has no wish to let them think he has crossed the line with what the man has warned him about. He can't go on forever worrying every time he goes out, or goes in a pub or shop, that they might be there.

What his Mum and his step-dad (he decides to drop the other reference for now) are offering, will give him the opportunity to start over again in a new place. He doesn't hesitate in agreeing that he will agree to their terms. He thinks that he will try to give up the drugs if he can; they are after all just a habit he has picked up from her. But he also knows that saying he will give them up and actually doing it, may be quite different things.

Chapter 17 Whispers

A day is all it takes to get everything wrapped up where he is living. The debts are cleared and what little personal goods he now has are bundled into the back of their 4 x 4. The 2 hour or so journey back to Wenlock is taken more or less in silence. Nigel thinks that his Mum and step-dad are surprised, at how ordinary the people are that he had owed money to. He thinks they thought they would look like down and outs, not realising the level of income their dealing allows them.

Eventually they pull up in front of their house, near the centre of Wenlock. Nigel's step-dad turns off the engine and then gets out. But before Nigel can do the same, he opens the back door to have a word with him.

'Nothing goes on in my house, you understand! You will only be here a few days, the fewer the better as far as I am concerned. I'll make no secret of the fact that I would rather you didn't stay here at all, but until things are ready, you will have to. So don't let your mother down.'

Nigel just nods. To be honest he has been expecting this. He has always known that it was his Mum who arranged all this. He doesn't know as yet why all this has happened. It is so out of character for her, or him, for that matter, to spend money in the way they have just done. Nigel is sure that even though they have said they don't want it paid back, that there is some ulterior motive in their helping him out of his predicament.

It is 3 days before they move him out of the house and into his new home. There is very little that transpires during his stay. He stays in his room unless they go out, which they do thankfully. They haven't enlightened him as yet what they go out for. They say they want that to be a surprise.

He is pleasantly surprised when they announce they are ready to show him his new home. They walk along Victoria Road and across into High Street. Nigel has already taken note of the Gaskell pub on the corner and the Fox Inn, as they walk past them. As they walk into the narrower section of the High Street, where it becomes a one way street, he notices the Talbot and just as they stop, he thinks he sees another, The George and Dragon, further down. Things are looking up, he thinks. Where there is a pub there is always the opportunity. He leaves his thoughts at that, because they are stopped in front of an empty building.

'We've bought this' his Mum announces. 'We are going to run our business from in here. We've been doing some things from home up to now, but we are so good at it, that we need more room. So we have bought this.'

She stands back, with a silly look on her face. It is one that Nigel remembers well. She always thinks she is so clever, but never mind! She can have her moment as far as he is concerned. All he is really interested in is where he will be living and what they will be expecting him to do for them.

The long and the short of it is that they have bought the entire building, all four floors of it. The ground floor is accessed from High Street and the other floors are accessed from the back of the building. The previous owner lived in the upper floors. The downstairs part has been empty for a while, as she was too ill to do anything about getting a new tenant, after the last one quit, due to lack of trade. When she died, her family went for a quick sale and put the building on at a reasonable price. Nigel's Mum and stepdad made a cheeky offer and nearly got their hands bitten off by the family, impatient to get their hands on their inheritance.

Nigel walks with the others round to the back of the building. They show him the living space above. He knows straight away he isn't going to be given all of it. It isn't long before they show him their plans, literally. The way the stairs run on the upper floors, makes it quite easy to separate two of the floors from the other one. He is given the choice of having the 1st floor apartment, or the bigger one on the 2nd and 3rd floors. He immediately goes for the 1st floor one. It will be plenty big enough for him

There is some furniture left in the apartments and they keep that for Nigel to use. Once the apartments have been split, which is done a few days after he moves in there; his job is to decorate the new 2 floor apartment and get it ready for renting out as soon as possible. Then they require him to do some alterations and decorating to the premises they are using for their business on the ground floor. Once he has finished that, they then get him to help with the donkey work in their business. In time he gets things to settle down a bit. The only part of refurbishment that is not yet completed is his apartment. By the time he has done all the other places, he is inclined to leave it for a time. His Mum doesn't mind. They never come upstairs. Nigel is charged with doing the monthly inspection on the rented apartment. His Mum and step-dad never bother him in his apartment and Nigel is never invited up to their house either. The arrangement suits all of them.

To be fair to Nigel, he does manage to stay off the drugs initially. But that is while he is busy. When things start to settle down, he has more time on his hands. He still doesn't feel like starting on refurbing his apartment, so he starts going out. He tries all of the pubs in turn, finding his step-dad in one of them when he walks in there. Surprisingly he is nice to Nigel. He even buys him a drink. But as Nigel is to find out later, he has then proceeded to run him down to everyone he speaks to. But back to the here and now!

Nigel puts down his mug of tea. Even while he has been drinking he has noticed the weather has turned for the worse outside. He can't remember hearing there was going to be a change like this, but sometimes you get that here. Wenlock can often have its own climatic conditions. It is something to do with the escarpment; he thinks he has heard that said in the pub.

The windows in his apartment aren't too bad. The old girl who used to own this place had them replaced sometime in the not too distant past. But at this second you wouldn't realise it. The wind appears to be whistling through them, as if they aren't shut properly. He gets up to check, even though he knows he keeps this one at the front closed. It helps keep out the sound of the street.

The window is shut and as he checks it, he hears the sound that has made him do this. Sitting in his chair, he thinks it sounds like the wind whistling through the window, but now he is standing there, he realises that is not the case. He can still hear the sound, but now he knows it is not the wind. It isn't coming from the windows and it isn't coming from outside. The sound is actually floating in his front room. As he stands and listens, he also notes that it is not just in the one place. He turns slowly round in a circle, trying to establish exactly where the sound is coming from. The best he can up with; is that it is in two places; one to the left of the window and one to the right.

Also as he has turned, he now thinks of the sound not as a whistling sound at all. It is more like a whispering sound that he can now hear. He steps back over to where he was sitting. It still sounds like whispers. He sits down in his chair. Now the sound is still like whispers. It definitely isn't a whistling sound like it was at the beginning. He can't get his head round it, so he goes back to the window and looks out. He can see it is raining, raining quite hard at that. He can also see that the wind has sprung up, as the string of lights that goes across the street are swaying in the wind. But the sound he can hear is definitely in the room. And if he is not mistaken, the whisper sound is moving; well at least one of them is. He turns slowly to get a handle on it. Yes the sound from the left of the window is now coming from further in the room. Then the other one moves too, but this one comes towards him. He can hear the noise getting perceptively closer and louder, well to a degree. Then a cold draft sweeps past him and as it does so, he hears a whisper in his ear.

'It is time.'

That is what he thinks it said. He hadn't been expecting anything like that. The draft keeps going. It is almost as if someone has just walked past him, close to him. The draft has gone now, but the sound hasn't. It isn't in his ear though; it is back to what he heard before. Then the other sound comes towards him and another cold draft washes over him briefly and as it passes he hears the same words again in a whisper.

'It is time.'

He feels a shudder course through his body. Part of that is because this draft is even colder than the first one, but there is another difference. Both times they have been a whisper, but the second time he thinks the voice is different, maybe slightly higher. But it isn't that that really gets to him, it is the tone of the whisper. The second whisper has much more meaning, much more definition, and much more threat. Is that the right word he has found for it? Maybe not threat as such, but certainly with more intention.

The second sound has kept going towards the window. It now turns and sweeps past him, but not right by him this time. A little pit of fear drops into his stomach as the two sounds come together, not too far away from the door. Nigel thinks it is almost as if they are getting ready for something. He doesn't know what makes him think that, but he does think it.

The only time so far the whisper sound has had something that he can understand, is when they pass very close to him and whisper in his ear. The rest of the time it is just an undefined whisper sound that he can hear. It is much clearer now that it is whispering and not the wind whistling. It is much clearer this is for him to hear. He is guessing that if he wasn't alone, then everyone there would be able to hear this whispering too. Then the whispering becomes much faster. It gets faster and faster, almost as if they are saying the same thing again and again, but quicker each time. Then he hears it quite clearly. It is the same three words again that are being spoken.

'It is time.'

Then in an instant the sounds rush towards him. The icy blast chills him and he hears the words as they stop by him. Then the whispers stop.

Chapter 18 Whispers

Nigel stands still and shivers. The icy chill is still with him, but the whispering is not. He is starting to feel afraid. Something is about to happen; he is sure of that. All thoughts of anything else have gone out of his head. At this moment all he is concerned with is what has been happening over the last few minutes and seconds. His eyes are all around him, but there is nothing for him to see that isn't normally there. Everything is as it should be, except that he is icily cold and there is a feeling around him, a feeling of something touching him but not quite, if you know what I mean.

He stands there for what seems like absolutely ages, but in reality it is only a few seconds. He is just waiting for whatever it is to happen. He is so cold. He doesn't think about moving. He isn't sure he could if he wanted to. He isn't sure he wants to either.

Then the whispering starts again. At first it is very faint, so faint that he thinks he is imagining it. Then it gets slightly louder, but still not to the level it was when he first heard it. He can't define the words that are being whispered, but he guesses it is the same as before. His mind tries to make those words fit to the whispers.

He almost jumps out of his skin when something actually touches him. Well, that is what his brain is telling him has happened. Something has touched his face. It feels like a hand, but it could be anything in reality. The touch feeling stays with him and then he hears a single word whispered in first his left ear and then his right ear.

'Edmund'

'I'm not Edmund, I'm Nigel' he replies straight away.

The touch is removed from his face, but it is then replaced almost immediately by another on the other cheek. Then another word is whispered to him, again in the left ear first followed by the right.

'Elizabeth.'

This time Nigel says nothing at all. The whispers were definitely different. The touch is removed before he hears a very faint whisper in both ears, one from each of them, but both saying the same words.

'It is time.'

Then as suddenly as the icy chill had come, it goes. The whispers have stopped too. His eyes are darting all around the room. He can't see anything and he can't hear anything, well nothing that isn't normally there to be seen and heard. He waits for a few seconds, but nothing changes. His head is asking him where they have gone, but he isn't getting any answers. He is finding it quite unsettling. He is just getting his nerves stretched to the nth degree in fear, when he hears the whispering start again, except it is now not whispering he hears. What he hears is now more like the whistling that he heard when all this started. But instead of being from the window, it is by the door, yes it is definitely by the door. It isn't moving from there and it appears to be one sound, much like it had started. Strangely, he finds that it is drawing him in. He takes a step towards the whistling sound, but as he does so, it comes towards him. When it gets to him, it separates and goes round both sides of him. There is no whisper this time, nor is there the cold or icy chill. It just goes round him and keeps going. Nigel spins around and watches, although there is nothing to watch. The sound reaches the window and stops, stops moving that is. This is the sound he heard at first and this is the place he heard it coming from. Once again it sounds just like the wind whistling through the window. He hears it like that for maybe thirty seconds and then as suddenly as it came, it is gone.

Nigel walks over to the window, but there is nothing there. There is no cold or icy chill and there is no sound.

There is no whistling and there is no whispering. He knows it has gone now and it, they, are no longer in his room.

He shudders and gives himself a shake. It wouldn't surprise him to wake up and find he is in his chair and had a dream. But that isn't the case. He stands where he is for another minute, waiting to see if they will return, but that isn't going to happen.

Then he glances down at his watch.

'Damn' he says out loud, as he sees what the time is. He is going to be late meeting up with Mick. He is never late meeting up with Mick, but he is going to be today. He can only hope that Mick will hang on for him. He has a look out of the window. It is still raining hard and the wind is still buffeting the string of lights. Hopefully Mick will think he has waited a few minutes for the rain to let off. He will find out when he gets there.

Nigel puts on his waterproof jacket and opens the door of his apartment. He goes down the stairs and lets himself out into the back courtyard. It is gloomy out here, as the rain clouds have darkened the sky much more than the time would normally suggest. The rain hits him as soon as he is out in the open. The wind doesn't hit him until he makes it out onto the road at the back, by the car park. He has another look at his watch when he gets there. Even though he is late already, he is not going to go the obvious way to get to Station Road. The obvious way and the most direct way, the quickest way too, would be to go left out of his gateway and cut through The George Shutt onto High Street. Then take a right and a left at the bottom into Wilmore Street. From there walk down past the Guildhall and the Church, along Sheinton Street to the junction and then take a right into Station Road, past the pillars and then up to where Mick should be waiting in his Red Ford Fiesta.

But Nigel isn't going this way. Nigel has always gone another way to get there. He has done that because he has given Mick the impression that he lives somewhere else in the town. Not that Mick has ever asked where he lives. Mick would always be able to find him if the need arose, he guesses.

Anyway, although he has never told Mick where he lives, he has given him the impression that he lives in the Southfield Road direction. He comes to meet Mick from that direction and he walks away in that direction. He has watched Mick watch him go. Mick never drives off until he is out of sight.

So Nigel walks through the car park and takes a right into Falcons Court, well towards Falcons Court. He walks through the open car park and out of the walkway at the bottom onto High Street, by the plot where the new house was ordered to be taken down again. He turns left and walks along past the Fox Inn. The rain is lashing down and even with his waterproof jacket on, he is getting soaked. The wind is buffeting him from side to side on the pavement. It is slowing him down a fraction, but he will get there when he does. If Mick is still there then good and if not, so be it.

He gets to the Gaskell corner and turns right into Smithfield Road. If anything the wind is blowing even stronger at this point. He is heading right into it. It makes walking even harder, but he keeps going. So far he hasn't passed a single soul on his journey, but then why would anyone be out when the weather has turned so bad, the way it has.

He walks past the old police station and at the fire station crosses the road and walks up Bridge Street. Over the bridge and then turns right. There are lights on in the houses, but still no one is out. He reaches the bottom and walks through the walkway and out onto the pavement on the bend. Station Road is straight ahead of him. The wind drops a fraction, as does the rain, as he walks across the road and into Station Road. He can just make out the red car parked about half way up on the right hand side. At this stage he can't see anything other than the car ahead of him. As he gets closer, he can see a branch has dropped onto the bonnet. That is strange, as you would think Mick would get out and move it off the bonnet. Maybe he has gone somewhere and just parked the car up.

Nigel reaches the car. By this stage he would normally be able to see Mick sitting in the driving seat. This isn't the first time he has met him when it isn't exactly daylight. But normally he would be sitting in there, with the inside light on. That isn't the case today. Nigel reaches the car. He is sensing that everything is not as it should be. He can just about make out something in there; hopefully it is someone, in there. He steps into the road, as he normally does, and makes for the passenger door. Before he tries the handle, he bends down and looks through the window. He can see clearly now that someone is in there, slumped over the wheel. He is just about sure it is Mick. The question now is; what he should do? Is this a case of Mick taking a nap because he is late, although to be honest it doesn't look like he is resting? He looks more untidy than that. But the other thing that is going through Nigel's mind is; maybe Mick has been attacked. And if he has been attacked, it is more than likely by one of his customers. That could make things awkward for Nigel, if he were to open the passenger door and get in. He decides not to do that.

He stands up straight and goes round the back of the car and goes to the driver's door. He taps on the window and waits a second. Mick doesn't respond. Nigel taps again, but much harder this time. Once again he gets no response from within. He pulls his hand up into his sleeve and gets hold of the door handle to open it. Half of him thinks that it might be locked, but he is wrong about that. The door opens as he pulls the handle. The first thing that hits him is the smell. Basically the car is stinking of s***. The smell is quite overpowering, but thankfully the wind is still blowing a gale and it soon disperses a lot of the smell. But it is still there. He shakes Mick's shoulder, but still there is no response from him. He feels for a pulse and he finds there is one. It is faint, but it is still there. He gives him another shake, but that doesn't wake him. Something isn't right here.

Nigel takes his phone out and he stands back from the open door. It lights up, but he can see straight away there is no signal. He walks away a few paces to try to get signal, but even when he reaches the bottom of the road, he hasn't got any. He looks up the road and is surprised to see that the driver's door is no longer opened. He is about to walk back up to the car, when a massive clap of thunder comes out of nowhere. It lasts for the best part of a minute and is followed by a huge gust of wind. It catches Nigel off guard and he is blown to the ground. On the way there he bumps into one of the pillars at the bottom of station road. By the time he hits the ground he has lost consciousness.

Chapter 19 Whispers

'It is time' Edmund says to Elizabeth.

They have followed Nigel out of his apartment. It is clear that Nigel has no idea that they hadn't gone, as he thought they had. They have no idea how they came to be in the room with him. It was Elizabeth who suggested they do what they did. But she knew this wasn't like before, when she whispered to people to warn them about some impending doom. That isn't what they are here for. The words had just come to her so she told Edmund and they worked on it together. They weren't trying to scare Nigel and to be honest he hadn't looked too scared. He'd looked a bit confused, but not exactly scared. But then they had been quite tame in their actions.

As soon as he went to the door to leave the apartment, they knew where he was going. They had already been to Station Road just a short time before. They knew about Mick sitting slumped in his car. They now knew that Nigel was going there.

At first they are a little confused by the direction he takes to get there. Although they haven't actually travelled from Station Road to High Street, they just know the route he is taking isn't the most direct.

They follow, but only just behind him, as he makes his way there. Even though Nigel is struggling against the force of the wind and the rain, it has no effect on them. They can see both are present, but they can't feel anything. In their world they do not experience these things.

As soon as Nigel opens the car door, they can smell briefly what he can. It is no surprise to them that he doesn't shut the door and walk away from there. As soon as they see he is going to summon help, they block the signal. Ideally they don't want him going further away. If he does there will be more likelihood that other people might be about. They don't want that.

Elizabeth closes her eyes and thinks. A huge thunderclap sounds from above. There has been no sign of one up to this point. It roars and rumbles for nearly a minute. Edmund closes his eyes and thinks. A great gust of wind blows just as the thunderclap ceases. It catches Nigel off guard. He is blown to the ground and on the way down; he bumps his head against the pillar he is standing by. He is unconscious by the time he hits the ground. As far as Elizabeth and Edmund are concerned, that is ideal.

'Which one shall we take first?'

'Probably this one, as he is out in the open. Have you shut the car door?'

'Yes I did it as he walked away.'

'How do we move him?'

'As we would move anyone I think. If we go beside him and try to lift him, we will see.'

They do that and bend down to pick him up. They are surprised by how little effort it takes to put a hand under his armpit and bring him upright. He is as light as a feather to them. They lead Nigel with them as they turn into Shineton Street, as it is named coming in at this point. The wind and the rain are still raging on around them, but they don't feel that. It takes them just a few minutes to reach their destination; the Guildhall.

You may or may not have noticed if you have ever stood outside the Guildhall that there are some black chains and cuffs hanging from the bars. They are not that obvious if you don't stand there for a minute. They blend in with the bars on the street side of the Guildhall. I have no idea what they are there for and I have no idea when they were put there, but they are there. Edmund and Elizabeth know they are there too and it is at this point they stop.

While Edmund takes sole hold of Nigel, Elizabeth takes hold of one of the cuffs. On first look it is just a circle of metal, but as she takes it in her hands, she pulls the cuff open. Edmund moves closer and Elizabeth takes one of Nigel's arms and slips his wrist into the cuff. She then closes the cuff and rubs her hand round it. When she takes her hand away, the cuff is closed and there is no visual sign of where one can prize it open.

The two cuffs are close together on the bars, but this is not ideal for Elizabeth. She intends to use them both, but she doesn't want the two men to be close enough to be able to touch each other. She touches the end of the chain and it comes away from the bars. She steps three paces to her left and fixes the cuff and chain onto the bars at a point there. She judges it will be far enough away so that the two men will not be able to reach each other.

With that done, they return quickly to the car in Station Road. With a wave of the hand the situation about the smell is resolved. Edmund pulls Mick out of the car and between them they lead him away. The key is out of the ignition and is now in Mick's pocket. Within minutes they have Mick secured in his cuff. Edmund takes a string tie from his pocket and ties each spare hand to the cuffed one. Although neither man is actually conscious at this stage, they are both standing cuffed to the bars. What Elizabeth has done to them will ensure that they remain this way, even though they aren't conscious. They will not be able to move their feet. They will not be able to slump down, but even if they could, the cuffs will not allow them to sit on the ground.

'They will be safe here until the morning. No one will be able to see them, or feel them, or even hear them. They will not regain consciousness, until we decide it is time.'

'Shall we wait and make sure?'

'There is no need. I know this will be.'

'Where shall we go? I only ask because I can feel that we are different. I know we have to be somewhere, rather than this being an in between time.'

'There will be somewhere we can go, let me think please.'

'Do you think it is still here?'

'Do you mean the shepherd's hut?'

'I do.'

'I am not sure. Even if it is, I suspect we are not meant to go there, otherwise we would know. Also I think we would have come from there and we did not. We came from the sky.'

'Do you know why we are here?'

'I don't know exactly. I think the world and time we have come to are more settled than the times we have been here before. I would use the word civilised, but I am not sure that the meaning is relevant. There are still people who behave in a way that is not good. No doubt we will be guided in what we have to do.'

The wind starts to die down as they talk, as does the rain. They stand over the road and look at the two men cuffed to the bars. As they stand there, a man walking a dog turns the corner from High Street. He walks straight past them without realising they are standing there. His dog is no wiser either and doesn't pick up their presence. It is obvious the man can't see them, or the two men cuffed to the bars.

'I know where we will go' Elizabeth suddenly announces. 'There is a place that a girl called Anne went when she returned. It is only just down there.'

She points back in the direction of Sheinton Street. They start to walk down there. Less than a minute later, she stops outside a door. She tries the handle and the door opens. Even though there is a pile of letters and flyers lying in the doorway, the door opens over them and they step inside. Elizabeth closes the door and leads Edmund upstairs. She goes into the front bedroom. Edmund is surprised to see a bed in there. Elizabeth walks over to it and lies down on it. Edmund goes and lies down beside her. They cover themselves with a blanket and close their eyes.

It is daylight when they open their eyes in the morning. There is the occasional sound of footsteps, as people walk by. At first it is not a sound they recognise, but a quick look out of the window tells them that that is what they are hearing.

It is still early, so they sit and wait. It is not yet the time when they need to go and show off their two captives. More than another hour passes before Elizabeth announces that it is time they went.

'How do you know?' Edmund asks her.

'I can feel that the one we need to be there will be there soon.'

'Have we seen this person before?'

'No and I don't know his name. I just can feel that the time will be when he arrives at the Guildhall. Until then, there is nothing to be seen or heard by anyone in the town.'

'This is most odd.'

'I agree, but it is as it must be.'

They move quickly and silently down the stairs. Elizabeth leads the way and she opens the front door onto the street. There is no one in view and no one is looking out of their windows to be able to see them. But of course, even if there had been anyone who might have sight of the doorway, they would not have seen them leave the house.

They walk the hundred yards back up to the Guildhall. The two men are still standing there, cuffed to the bars. Inside the Guildhall Marketplace, there are tables with fruit and vegetables laid out. To the left is a stall with jars of jams and other delights. Just the other side of the bars, on the inside and opposite the fruit and vegetable tables, are some tables with eggs and flowers for sale. There are people in there serving and there are customers in there buying. It is apparent that not one of them is aware that there are two men cuffed to the bars on the street side of the Guildhall.

There are people walking along the pavements almost bumping into the two men, but not seeing them.

'We are nearly at the moment. Come with me and stand over there. We can watch as they are revealed to the world.'

'Is he here then?'

'He is close. He will be the one that changes this situation. It is not up to us apparently.'

They cross over the road, nearly getting hit by a car that comes round the bend from Barrow Street too quickly.

'We need to be careful of those' she warns, as they just get out of the way in time.

'I don't think they can hurt us.'

'I think that very shortly we may find that things will have changed for us too. I think that maybe as soon as these two men are visible, then we might find we will be too.'

Chapter 20 Whispers

They stand where they are for a couple more minutes before anything changes. There are quite a few people walking down the High Street and also in the square too. There are several people already in Viv & Rod's fruit and veg market under the Guildhall. All of them are oblivious to the fact there are two men chained up outside on the pavement.

From where Edmund and Elizabeth are standing, they have a good all round view. They are standing by the bench, behind the wall between them, the road and the Guildhall.

'Look' Elizabeth nudges Edmund.

His eyes turn to hers and then follow the direction of her look. Along the direction of Barrow Street towards the Raven, there is a man walking towards them, well in their direction. He is tall, maybe six feet tall. He is walking in an unhurried fashion, not in a rush to get to wherever he is going. He is dressed in black. His shirt is black, his coat is black, his trousers and shoes are black as well. He is wearing a brimmed hat which is also black. It is pulled slightly forward, shielding his eyes a little from the light. His head is slightly bowed forward too, which makes is hard to get a good look at his face. He may or may not be looking at them, they can't tell as yet.

The man is walking on the same side of the street that they are on. It is as if he is going to somewhere in the square, or maybe in High Street.

'Are you sure it is him, that he is the one we are waiting for.?'

'I am fairly certain it is, but no matter if it is not. It will be soon.'

The man walks into the section where the square is. He starts to cut across the square, when his eyes turn to his right. First of all his eyes land on Edmund and Elizabeth and then they keep moving on in the same direction and he looks across at the front of the Guildhall. He stops. His eyes are on the two men chained to the bars of the Guildhall. He doesn't move, but turns his eyes back towards Edmund and Elizabeth. He sees that they are looking directly at him. He points towards the two men. They turn and note what he is pointing at. They then turn back towards him and Elizabeth nods.

'He can see us.'

'I said that would happen.'

At that moment someone brushes past Edmund and sits down on the bench.

Edmund leans into closer to Elizabeth and whispers in her ear.

'Apparently others can't yet though.'

'They won't be able to hear us either' she replies.

The person who has sat on the bench is unaware she is sitting so close to them. The man in black is still looking at them. He is watching not only them, but also the people walking up Wilmore Street and straight past the two men, taking absolutely no notice of them. It hasn't quite clicked with him yet that they are not ignoring them, but in fact can't see them. He stands there for a good two minutes before he does anything else. Then he starts to walk over to them. That is over towards Elizabeth and Edmund, not the two men. He doesn't say anything until he is standing maybe five feet away from them.

'Are they there for a reason?'

'I beg your pardon.' The person on the bench answers him.

'The two men attached to the railings over there. Are they there for a reason?'

'What two men?'

The man in black looks over at the two men and points. He looks back, but the person on the bench is looking blankly at him.

'She can't hear us, but she can hear you. She can't see them either, but you can. Go over and touch them. That may change things.'

The man in black says nothing more, but turns away and crosses the road. He doesn't go up to the two men attached to the railings, but instead he goes into the market. A minute later he is out, with Rod.

'Tell me that you can see them.'

'See who?' Rod replies.

'These two' the man in black says, as he steps forward and touches the first of the men.

'Where did he just come from' Rod exclaims.

The man in black quickly touches the second man too.

'There are two of them now. Where have they just appeared from?'

On the other side of the road where Elizabeth and Edmund are standing, the person on the bench who had been watching the man in black, suddenly stands up and points at the two men who have just appeared.

'They weren't there a second ago.' She isn't saying it to anyone in particular, just making a statement. She still cannot see Elizabeth and Edmund.

The two men are now not as the man in black had seen them just a minute ago. Then they had been dressed in casual clothes. Now as they have appeared to others, so their dress has change. They now appear to be dressed in rags. They have also started to stir. Rod and the man in black take a step back, to give them a bit of room. No one knows why they are there and what they might do or say, now they are waking up.

Almost at the same moment, they both come alive to the present moment. They also very quickly realise that their movement is restricted, very restricted. Then they open their eyes and see the world around them. The first thing each of them sees is the cuffs that are holding them where they are.

Even while they are struggling to move, they ask the first question.

'What's happening?' they both ask in unison.

Hearing someone else ask the same question makes the two men look at each other.

'Mick, what's going on here?'

'Nigel, I have no idea.'

They both try to free themselves from the cuffs that are restricting their movement, but to no avail.

'What are you two doing?' Rod breaks their attention from each other.

'I don't know.' Mick replies 'What time is it?'

'It is about ten o'clock.' Rod replies.

'What day?'

'It is Friday today.'

'Friday morning. How can it be Friday morning?'

'Why do you say that?' The man in black asks.

'Well it was Thursday afternoon when I came to Wenlock.'

'It must have been a good night then?'

'What do you mean it must have been a good night?'

'Well on the beer, you must have had a good night on the beer and someone tied you to the railings. Was it a stag night?'

'No it wasn't. I haven't been out on the beer. I'm driving, so I don't drink. Anyway I only came to Wenlock to …….' He stops as he realises he can't admit the next thing he was going to say.

'The last thing I remember is' Nigel is going to say something next, but he too stops short of saying it all.

'So what is the last thing both of you remember? I take it you can't remember who chained you up like this?'

'I have no idea who might have done this. Can't you get these undone?'

Rod and the man in black step forward and have a close look at the cuffs that are holding the two men. They touch them and look closely, but there is no obvious way to get them undone. They appear to be all in one piece, with no breaks and no place for a key to go in. Nigel and Mick can see this too, as they stand and watch.

'I can't see how they are done up.' the man in black states. Something is bothering him and then he remembers the two people standing on the other side of the road. He turns his head to look at them, but they aren't standing there anymore. They haven't disappeared from the scene completely, but they have moved over to where he had stood in the square. They are standing by the clock.

'I've called the police' a well-meaning individual comes up to them and says. He doesn't stop at that. 'We shouldn't be allowing this sort of behaviour in the town. It is disgusting. This sort of behaviour doesn't belong here.'

'You might have a point' Rod says 'but first let's get the situation sorted and find out what has happened here, before we start pointing fingers and spouting off.'

The man in black nods his head a fraction as Rod says this. He then asks the next question.

'So what is the last thing you each remember?'

There is a small silence. A few more people have come to gather around and see what is going on. It is not an ideal situation and it is probably not that helpful for them to get a reasonable and truthful answer from the two men. But neither Rod nor the man in black feel inclined to take over the role of policing this, unless they really have to. Anyway, this man has just informed them that the police have been summoned. The man in black thinks it might be more helpful to call the fire brigade to try to release them, but he isn't going to make that call, yet.

'Give them a bit of space' Rod's voice comes clear and loud to the ever growing crowd around them.

'I had just stopped my car in Station Road' Mick is voicing his last recollections 'I switched off the engine. The rain was streaming down and the wind got up.' he stops for a few seconds, as if running the scene through his mind before continuing. 'Then I think it was a branch that either blew into the windscreen, or broke off onto it. Then I don't know. I think something else happened, but I can't remember what. Next thing I know I am here chained to these railings and' he looks down at his attire 'and dressed like this. Someone's having a laugh on me and I don't think it is funny.'

Nigel has been listening intently to what Mick has been saying. He knows exactly why Mick was there in Station road. Mick has been able to tell his story without letting on the true nature of why he was there and the fact he was going to meet up with Nigel, to sell him drugs. Nigel gives a few seconds for people to absorb Mick's story, before he starts on his own. He has wondered about telling them of the incident in his apartment before he left, but has dropped down on the side that it is not a good idea. They will think he was on something and quite possibly the one who was responsible for how they have ended up. The story he tells is quite truthful, just not the full story of events of the previous evening.

'I walked down Station Road. I think there was a car or two there, but I had got to the bottom by where the pillars are, when there was a huge clap of thunder. It lasted for maybe a minute. I didn't time it, but it was probably the longest thunder clap I have ever heard. Then I remember there was a huge gust of wind and I got blown off my feet. I think I hit my head on the pillar, but I don't remember, because the next thing I am here.'

Rod looks at the man in black and he looks back at Rod. They have both jumped to the same conclusion. That is; whatever the stories these two have told, they were either together at one point, or were going to meet up with each other. They don't get the chance to expand on this, as a police car pulls up right beside them.

Chapter 21 Nigel and Mick

Rod gets called away and goes back in to the Guildhall market. The man in black takes a step or two back from where he was standing; to allow room for the policeman. The policeman addresses Mick and Nigel. Rather than ask anyone what stage has been reached, he begins at the beginning. When the man in black hears this, he steps further away, before turning and crossing the road towards High Street. He notices that Edmund and Elizabeth are no longer standing by the clock. He knows they have something to do with all this, but then he also knows that whatever that is, isn't going to have a simple explanation. He has no need to get involved at this stage. His only concern on that score is that he is pretty certain that he is the only one who has seen them. He also has the feeling that releasing them from their cuffs is not going to be as straightforward as most people would think. He doesn't believe that his being here will make a difference; at least he hopes it won't. And then he remembers his arrival on the scene. At that he thinks it best that he get on with what he came down town for, before he gets caught up in this more than he has already done so far.

He wheels off up High Street and picks up the bits and pieces he has come to town for. When he has finished, he debates if he should go back down and see what stage things have reached, on his way home. But instead, he makes a detour cutting up through the car park by Falcon's Court and coming out the other end onto St Mary's Lane. He takes a left and then a right at the bottom by the Raven and then proceeds along Barrow Street to his home. He glances left when he reaches the Raven corner, but from that point he is unable to see what, if anything; is going on.

Meanwhile it has taken the policeman this long to reach the point they were up to just as he arrived. The difference now is that Mick and Nigel have become a bit more agitated as the time passes and they are still chained up to the railings. On top of that it would appear that the policeman and a few others have also come to the same conclusion. That is that Nigel and Mick were going to be meeting in Station Road. They keep to their stories though, but don't deny they know each other. The policeman has called for back-up and also for the fire brigade to come to cut the men loose.

That not unexpectedly, is a job that is more easily said than done. Try as they might with all the cutting tools in their armoury, they are unable to cut the men loose. More than that, they aren't even making an impression on any of what is holding them to the bars of the Guildhall. Mick and Nigel of course cannot remember the cuffs being put on, so they have no idea how they come undone.

In the end they have to cut the bars themselves, just above and below where the cuffs and the chain fix to them. There is no other way to release them, even if that is only partially. As can be expected these days, there are people there filming everything on their mobile phones. A couple of men come huffing and puffing down the road when they hear about the bars being cut. One is a councillor of the town and in the case of the other one, the father of one of the victims. He only realises that his stepson is involved when he pushes his way to the front of the small crowd looking on. A minute later he is joined by Nigel's mother. She wastes no time in berating her son, about bringing shame on the family and how could he do this to them. She lets off at him for a good couple of minutes, more reminiscent of an olden day's fish wife, but then maybe that is her roots coming through. She always thinks she is better than she actually is.

When she is finally quietened down by the policeman, the councillor learns that despite his protestation, there is no choice but to cut the bars to release them. So at least they are free of the bars, if not the cuffs. Back up for the policeman arrives and then as soon as the two men are released, they are taken away in one of the police cars. It is not at this stage because they have been accused of doing anything, but more because there is nowhere locally they have to take them while they work out what is the next course of action. Only after the cutting of the bars and the two men leaving, do the police turn their attention to the people standing around. They are asked what has occurred, so of course they are directed to Rod. In his turn the name of the man in black comes up. He knows his first name, but that is it. Where he actually lives is not part of his knowledge. The policeman doesn't view it as a matter of importance, so doesn't pursue getting that information.

Later in the day, the cuffs are still very much on Nigel and Mick. They have tried all sorts to try to remove them. But nothing has any effect on the metal. Questions have been asked back in Wenlock, as to where the cuffs have come from. No one knows specifically their source, but it is thought that they have been there for years. No one can say anything about the mechanism that must make them open and close, or about what material they are made of. Due to the way their hands are tied, they can't do anything about the clothes on their top halves. They are given new trousers to put on.

It is in the process of doing this, that they discover three things on Mick's person. Firstly they find his car keys. Secondly they find a small roll of money and thirdly they find some small bags in a bigger bag. These bags have illegal substances in them.

That discovery leads to Mick's car being towed in. They don't even try to search it until they have it recovered back to the station. When they do search it, they come across a good deal more cash and a varied stock of drugs. While that changes the complexion of his stay at the police station, it does not give any answers as to how they came to be chained up, or how they can be released. They found quite a sum of cash on Nigel too. Putting two and two together, it is clear that Nigel was on his way to meet Nigel when he got caught out by the thunder clap and the gust of wind. None of this comes close to explain how they came to be chained up at the Guildhall.

The why is briefly guessed at, as a probable case of some locals taking the law into their own hands? But there are several flaws in that argument. How did they get the cuffs on them, if there is no mechanism? Why was it that even though it is likely they were chained to the railings possibly overnight, that no one saw them until morning, and not first thing at that? Rod says there was no one there when he set up. He can't say for definite, but he thinks they weren't there when he eventually finished the last of his unpacking, round about 9 o'clock.

Eventually the conclusion is reached that the one person who might know more than anyone else about the situation, is the man dressed in black.

The man dressed in black is way ahead of them though. He'd reached that conclusion fairly early in the day. Once he heard from the jungle drums that the fire brigade had failed to remove the cuffs from their wrists, he knew he would receive another visit at some point in the day. The fact is that he has no more information about the whys and wherefores than they have. But he does have a lead which might prove fruitful. There is the fact that he has seen Edmund and Elizabeth. He is 99.9% sure that he is the only one who saw them. The person on the bench hadn't been able to. The people passing by them by the clock hadn't noticed them either. That was obvious, because not one of them had turned to look at them as they passed them and they would have done, because of the clothes they were wearing. Neither of them was dressed in anything like current day clothing, let alone fashion. It is hard to place their clothing, but it can't be described as anything like modern. It isn't that the clothes are dirty or torn or anything, because they aren't. It is just the way they are dressed is not of this time, or a recent time for that matter.

The man in black knows that it will be easier for him if he can try to get some answers before the police come to ask him about it. Surely enough they will come sometime, when they can't get the cuffs off the two men. Something inside him tells him, he just knows they won't get the cuffs off them, otherwise what would the point be? A statement is possibly being made here he believes, or they are out to prove something, or do something. It never occurs to him for one second that there might be a sinister side to what has happened. He doesn't give it a thought at all that he might be stepping into something involved with dark powers.

To be honest when he spoke to them briefly, they hadn't appeared to be evil. But then in today's society you can never tell. What does any person look like? What does a terrorist look like? There is no one look for a good person and or a bad person. It is generally their actions and not their looks that describe who and what they are.

With a brief word that he is going out to try to find someone, the man in black makes his way back into the town. As he reaches the square, he looks in all directions, but there is no sign of them. He didn't really expect there to be. He pops into the fruit and veg market and has a quick look around there, in case they are hanging around. He has a quick look at the cut bars, but you can't see much as they have police tape wrapped round the cut ends. He wanders up High Street and round about the rest of the town, but he fails to get even a sighting of them. He stops off in one of the coffee shops, Tea on the Square, to have a coffee and also because it gives him a good view of the comings and goings at the junction of High Street, Barrow Street, Wilmore Street and the Square. There are plenty of people about as he drinks his coffee, but not the ones he is after. He makes it last a bit longer than it should have taken to drink, just to give them time to appear. After all, in his thinking on reflection, he thinks they were waiting for him to appear earlier this morning. So maybe they would know he was coming down town again and would come to meet him. By the time he is leaving the tea shop, they have still not made an appearance. He does another quick circuit of the town centre before calling it a day. He is just coming back down High Street passing the Corn Exchange, when he gets the urge to sit on one of the benches under there.

Chapter 22 Andy

The man in black sits down on the bench. He closes his eyes for a few seconds, to try to locate the reason he has felt the urge to sit down here. There must be a reason; everything has a reason, in his eyes. He hopes that no one will see him there and come to see if he is alright. He hasn't always been in the best of health and although it is nice to have people looking out for you, there are times, in the nicest possible way, when you need to be left alone. This is one of those times.

It doesn't work out that way. He has been spotted wandering around town and now the same person has spotted him sitting down under the Corn Exchange.

'Was it something to do you with you?'

He hears the voice a few feet away from him. He knows it is aimed at him too. There is no point delaying the inevitable. He has recognized the voice anyway. He opens his eyes and turns in the direction he knows the voice is coming from.

'Hi Andy; I thought I recognized that voice. What brings you to town, as if I didn't know?'

'I'm sure you do and I mean that in multiple meanings, as I expect you to understand.'

'I was there, when they were discovered. Up to that point I was blissfully oblivious to anything being out of the ordinary this morning.'

'Would you oblige me by telling me everything from your point of view, literally, from the moment you got involved? They still have those cuffs on you know. I don't know what they are made of, but nothing and I mean nothing, is touching them to be able to release them.'

'I have no idea what they are made of either. To be honest, when I first saw them attached there like that, I thought they must have been brought there in them and then attached to the railings. But then I thought about it later and I remembered seeing them, or something like them, on the railings well before this. How long they have been there is anyone's guess. What they are made of is anyone's guess too. But I suspect that what they were made of when they were put on there; is completely different to their state now and why they can't be cut to release those two men.'

'Is there anything in particular that is making you make that statement?'

'I guess it will become clear if I start from the beginning of my involvement. You will then understand why I say that and what I am doing here now, although I have failed in that part, as you have turned up early.' He smiles at Andy as he says this.

'Be my guest.'

'I had to come down town to do some chores. You know where I live. I walked along Barrow Street. It was when I got over the road at the corner of St Mary's, by the Raven, that I felt the first inkling of something being different today. At that stage I didn't have a clue as to what the feeling meant, or was going to lead to. At first I couldn't see anything that might have made me feel that way, but as I drew closer to the square, I took note of a couple of people standing by the wall, in the corner by the museum. Do you know where I mean?'

'I'm not sure, but you can show me in a few minutes when you're done telling me what you have to.'

'Ok, I'll continue. The reason I took note of them was twofold. Firstly it was because they were so definitely looking at me, not in my direction, but straight at me. The second reason was because of how they were dressed. It is not as if they were dressed badly, because they weren't. It was because they were dressed in clothes that were not of this time. Before you even ask, I can't place the time. I just know they aren't of this time. Then as I approached, someone walked past them without even seeing them, as far as I could see. They just walked past them as if they weren't there and sat on the bench. That notched my feelings up a little more. I don't think the obvious had quite got to me at that point, but it probably should have done. Anyway, they watched me walk across the square and across the road towards them. When I reached that side, I stopped a few feet away from them and asked them a question.'

'What did you ask them?'

'Let me think for a minute and I'll try to remember the exact words.'

He thinks for a minute or two and then he is ready.

'The whole scene goes something like this. It may not be word for word. I started it off.'

"Are they there for a reason?"

"I beg your pardon." The person on the bench answered me.

'I then said':

"The two men attached to the railings over there. Are they there for a reason?"

"What two men?" The person on the bench said.

I looked over at the two men and pointed. I then looked back, but the person on the bench was looking blankly at me.

'Then one of the two people I had come over to see spoke to me.'

"She can't hear us, but she can hear you. She can't see them either, but you can. Go over and touch them. That may change things."

'Then I knew that this was something just for me, if you know what I mean. I said nothing more, but turned away from them and crossed the road. I didn't go up to the two men attached to the railings, but instead I went into the market. A minute later I was out again with Rod. Rod owns the fruit and veg stalls in the market. I said to him.'

"Tell me that you can see them."

"See who?" Rod replied.

"These two" I said as I stepped forward and touched the first of the men.

"Where did he just come from" Rod exclaimed.

I quickly touched the second man too.

"There are two of them now. Where have they just appeared from?"

'On the other side of the road where the man and the woman were standing, the person on the bench who had been watching me go over there, suddenly stood up and pointed at the two men who had just appeared.

"They weren't there a second ago." She wasn't saying it to anyone in particular, just making a statement. It was obvious she still couldn't see the man and the woman beside her.

'The two men by the railings were now not as I had seen them just a minute ago. Then they had been dressed in casual clothes. Now as they have appeared to everyone, so their dress has changed. They now appear to be dressed in rags. They have also started to stir. Rod and I took a step back to give them a bit of room. No one knew why they were there and what they might have done or what they might say; now they were waking up.

Almost at the same moment they came alive to the present moment. They also very quickly realised that their movement was restricted, very restricted. Then they opened their eyes and saw the world around them. The first thing each of them saw was the cuffs that were holding them where they are.

Even while they were struggling to move they asked their first question.

'What's happening?' they both asked in unison.

Hearing someone else ask the same question made the two men look at each other.

"Mick, what's going on here?"

"Nigel, I have no idea."

They both tried to free themselves from the cuffs that were restricting their movement but to no avail.

"What are you two doing?" Rod broke their attention from each other.

"I don't know." Mick replied "What time is it?"

'It is about ten o'clock." Rod replied.

"What day?"

"It is Friday today."

"Friday morning. How can it be Friday morning?"

"Why do you say that?" I asked.

"Well it was Thursday afternoon when I came to Wenlock."

"It must have been a good night then?" Rod put in.

"What do you mean it must have been a good night?"

"Well on the beer, you must have had a good night on the beer and someone tied you to the railings. Was it a stag night?"

"No it wasn't. I haven't been out on the beer. I'm driving so I don't drink. Anyway I only came to Wenlock to ...." He stopped as he realised he couldn't admit the next thing he was going to say. Rod and I knew they had been up to something, or about to be.

"The last thing I remember is" Nigel was going to say something next, but he too stopped short of saying it all.

"So what is the last thing both of you remember? I take it you can't remember who chained you up like this?"

"I have no idea who might have done this. Can't you get these undone?"

'Rod and I stepped forward and had a close look at the cuffs that were holding the two men. We touched them and looked at them closely, but there was no obvious way to get them undone. They appeared to be all in one piece with no breaks and no place for a key to go in. Nigel and Mick could see this too as they stood and watched.'

"I can't see how they are done up." I stated.

'Something was bothering me and then I remembered the two standing on the other side of the road. I turned my head to look at them, but they weren't standing there anymore. They hadn't disappeared from the scene completely, but they had moved over to where I had stood in the square. They were standing by the clock.'

"I've called the police' a well-meaning individual came up to Rod and me at that moment and said. He didn't stop at that. 'We shouldn't be allowing this sort of behaviour in the town. It is disgusting. This sort of behaviour doesn't belong here."

"You might have a point" Rod said "but first let's get the situation sorted and find out what has happened before we start pointing fingers and spouting off."

'I nodded my head a fraction as Rod said this. I then asked the next question.'

"So what is the last thing you each remember?"

'There was a small silence. A few more people had come to gather around and see what was going on. It was not an ideal situation and it was probably not that helpful for them to get a reasonable and truthful answer from the two men. But neither Rod nor I felt inclined to take over the role of policing this unless they really have to. Anyway, this man had just informed them that the police have been summoned. I thought at the time it might be more helpful to call the fire brigade to try to release them, but I wasn't going to make that call, yet.

"Give them a bit of space" Rod's voice came clear and loud to the ever growing crowd around them.

'Then the two of them started to give their stories about where they were that they could last remember. I can't remember too much about what they said because as soon as they started I knew they weren't telling the whole truth. Rod looked at me and I looked back at Rod. We had both jumped to the conclusion that whatever the stories these two have told, they were either together at one point, or were going to meet up with each other. We didn't get the chance to expand on that as a police car pulled up right beside and he took over things. Rod went back to his work and I went to do my shopping.'

Chapter 23 Andy and the man in black

'So what happened next?' Andy asks the man in black, when he has finished.

'I did my shopping and then took a detour to get home, so I didn't have to get more involved there and then.'

'But you are back here now, why is that?'

'I guessed that it would only be a matter of time before the enquiries would move on from the two of them and back to who was the one around when they were discovered. In the light of that, I wanted to try to be able to have some sort of answer for when I inevitably got questioned. So I had to come down and try to find out what was really going on.'

'And so what is really going on?'

'I honestly don't know. I haven't got anywhere. I was hoping that I might come across the man and the woman that I saw first. I am sure they know what this is about and how things have turned out the way they have.'

'What do you mean by that?'

'Well, there are many bits I don't understand. Starting at the beginning of my involvement, I saw them straight away, but no one else did then. I don't think they did after the two men appeared, attached to the railings, when they moved over to stand by the town clock. Then there is the way the two men appeared to everyone else when I touched them. The other two told me to touch them. I have no idea how me touching them made them appear, but it happened as they said it would. As soon as I did, then everyone could see them. I don't understand why their clothes changed when I saw them dressed differently and when everyone could see them.'

'They were up to something those two. The car in Station Road had more drugs and money in there. He has been arrested for possession and supply. The other one, we believe was on his way to buy drugs, so he says and I think I believe him. He has a history of it. His mother wasn't too pleased at his involvement, so I understand. She had a proper rant at him in the street when she came down and saw him chained up there. So carry on then.'

'Well there isn't that much more to tell. As I said, I was hoping that I might bump into them round town somewhere. Taking that I am somehow involved, I was kind of assuming that they would appear if I came down town again. I am thinking that my involvement can't be over just with touching the two men and letting everyone see them.'

'Not that I know anything about these things. I'm tending to be in agreement with you. So what were you going to do next and why are you just sitting here?'

'I'd looked all around the centre of town for the man and the woman. I guess they might have gone off with the other two, when your lot took them away, but I think that is an outside chance somehow. My belief is that this is something to do with Wenlock. And while those two were found here in Wenlock, they are only part of this, not the why this is happening. So the man and the woman wouldn't have gone off after them. So although I don't have anything to back up why, I think they will be here in the central part of town, this is where I think they are to be found. I just haven't found them as yet. Anyway if they aren't here, then I would have no idea where to look for them. I have no idea who they are, what time they are from, or anything at all about them. Then I was about to give up. I have been around town as much as I can and have had no luck. But, as I was passing here, I got the urge to sit down. I don't know why, but as I had the urge, I listened to it. I'd just sat down and closed my eyes when you came along and here we are.'

'So has anything come to you?'

'Other than you, no, but I haven't really given it a good chance.'

'Very funny! What do you want me to do?'

'I'm not sure. Let me just sit here in silence for a few minutes and see if there is something that is going to come to me.'

The man in black closes his eyes again. He doesn't wait for Andy to reply and he really doesn't want him to. He knows he has to close his eyes now. Something has indicated to him that he needs to. He sits there, trying to block out the sounds of the world going on around him. He manages to do that quite easily. He shuffles over on the bench about a foot, still with his eyes closed. It happens to be in the direction away from Andy, but he doesn't think about that too much. He doesn't do it to move away from Andy. He does it to move closer to something he needs to be closer to. He knows he is now in the right place. He lifts his arm up and reaches over the back of his head. His fingers feel along the wall. He doesn't know initially what he is trying to find, but as soon as his fingers feel it, he knows exactly what it is. This is definitely a sign. His fingers have found the letter A carved in the wall. This is the letter A carved by Anne. He doesn't try to make sense of it. There is no point. From experience it is not about a conscious thought. This is just him being guided and not necessarily by Anne. How does he know that? Well the answer is that he doesn't, but he knows instinctively that the man and the woman that he saw earlier, and Anne, are not from the same period. He also knows that they do not know each other. So this is not a message from Anne to him, trying to tell him something. He knows this is a message from the man and the woman, trying to get him to get on their wavelength.

Unfortunately he doesn't have a clue what this clue means at this moment. Maybe it is just that, a clue. Why would the letter A that Anne carved in the wall lead him to them? He keeps his finger tracing out the figure of the letter A, while he tries to let his mind go clear. This is no time for conscious thought. In fact conscious thought is only likely to lead him on a wild goose chase. It is only likely to hinder his chances of finding them sooner rather than later.

His finger goes round the letter again and again. As hard as he tries not to, he can't stop the image of Anne coming into his mind. It is inevitable really that it would when he is sitting here and running his finger round the letter she had carved in the wall. It takes him a minute or two of trying not to think of this, before he realises it is exactly this that he needs to be thinking of. Having got this far, he then lets his mind follow its natural course. As soon as he does that, then he has what is being told to him come into his mind. He now knows why he has been guided to stop and sit here.

The man in black opens his eyes and stands up. It takes Andy a bit by surprise. He has been watching the man in black. His face has been expressionless as he sits there, moving his finger around something on the wall.

'Let's take a walk down the street. I'll show you where they were standing. Then we'll have another look at where those two were chained up. Then we'll go to somewhere else we've been to before. That is why I had to stop here; to be told where I need to go.'

'I'm surprised they didn't whisper it to you?'

The man in black laughs.

'I know this place is full of whispers, but most of them are by folk who haven't got enough to do with their lives, or by the ones who just can't help themselves by making up stories about people. I have been the subject of some of those, probably more than my fair share at that.'

'I'll bet you have.'

'Don't say any more.'

The man in black smiles as he is saying this to Andy.

They step out from the Corn Exchange. They both look around to see who is around. There isn't anyone paying them any attention in particular. No one is watching them, other than being in their line of site. They walk down past number 63, the old HSBC bank and Spar and then across the front of the museum. The man in black walks over to where the bench is and stops.

'This is where they were standing when I first saw them. Then at some stage they went over to stand by the clock over there. The men were by the railings over there.'

He is pointing at the place under the Guildhall where he had seen the two men. But that wasn't like it was the last time he'd seen it.

'What's wrong?' Andy asks as he sees his reaction.

'That's what is wrong. Look carefully.'

They both look over the road at the Guildhall. The police tapes have gone. The gap in the railings where the cuffs were cut out has gone. There are no gaps any more. The railing has been repaired, but it isn't quite as simple as that. That isn't all. The two of them move round the wall and cross the road to get a closer look.

'It's like nothing ever happened.' The man in black says to Andy.

'Is this how it looked last week then?'

'I would say so.'

The railings look as if they have never been touched. The cuffs are hanging from the bars on their chain. They aren't new and they definitely haven't been replaced by new ones. These are the original ones.

'If these ones are here, then what is on the two men?'

'That's a good question.'

Andy takes out his phone.

'I haven't got any signal.'

'Move down past the church. You'll start to get signal about there, just before you get to the Bull Ring. We're going that way in a minute anyway.'

Andy wanders off to make his phone call. The man in black stays back at the Guildhall, to have a look at the cuffs. He is about to touch them, when he thinks better of it. He takes a clean tissue out of the packet in his pocket and holds the cuffs in that. There is no doubt in his head. These are the cuffs that have always been attached to the railings here. He doesn't really want to think about what is really going on here. There is little doubt he will find out more in good time. Wenlock Whispers are the words that come into his head, as he stands there watching Andy walk past the church to make his phone call.

Chapter 24 Andy and the man in black

He turns his attention back to the bars on the front of the Guildhall market place. He has a closer look, without actually touching them again. They show absolutely no sign of having been cut away, let alone any signs of having been mended again. The paint matches perfectly on these and the other bars around them. In no place could you describe the paint as being new. If he was asked for his opinion, he would answer that these bars had never been cut. He also inspects the cuffs and chains. They too are as if they haven't been touched or cut, which to be honest is the situation anyway. There are no signs of where the firemen and others have tried to cut them; not a mark and not a scratch.

He is just about to turn away, when he hears something. At first it sounds just like the sound of wind whistling gently through the bars. It is enough to make him stand still and hold his breath. He feels his heart rate go up markedly and then the sound changes from a whistling sound to a whispering sound.

At first he struggles to make out what the whisper is saying, but it becomes clearer to his ears by the second. Soon it is extremely clear and there can be no doubt as to the words being whispered.

'It is time, it is time……'

The same three words are whispered time after time. Not fast, but in a steady whispering tone. He is expecting the words to change after a while, but they don't and maybe after two or three minutes the sound changes back slowly to the wind whistling sound again, before it disappears totally. All the while he has been listening to it, he keeps his eyes peeled. He is half expecting the man and the woman to appear somewhere close to him, but that doesn't happen, or if it does he doesn't see them.

When he knows for sure that the sound has gone completely, he turns away and looks to see where Andy is standing. He must have been engrossed for a bit longer than he thought, because he is a bit shocked to find Andy is standing only a few feet away from him. He is looking at him with a question on his lips. The question is soon to be voiced.

'Was there something happening there? You looked rooted to the spot. I could see something was happening from way down opposite the church, so I wandered quietly back up here, but I didn't interrupt.'

'I appreciate that thanks. Yes, there was something. There was a whistling sound, but it changed into a whisper. It just whispered the same three words again and again, until it stopped. "It is time" is all it said and before you ask; I haven't got a clue as to what it is time for.'

'Ok, so where was it you were going to take me next?'

'Just down there, at the beginning of Sheinton Street.'

'Ok, but before we go, you need to know what I've found out. Let's go and sit on the wall by the church for a minute.'

They walk maybe twenty metres down Wilmore Street and then stop to sit on the wall. Andy then continues.

'I got them to check on the two men who'd got the cuffs on. We'd sent for some metal expert and they were waiting in an interview room for him to arrive. The door was locked and although they were alone in the room, there was someone keeping an eye on the door every second. When they went to the interview room and opened the door, the two men were fast asleep on the floor. The cuffs had gone and they were dressed in their own clothes again. And as well as that, their hands were tied together with a piece of cord or thick string. They tried to cut it and it cut like a knife through butter. They were asked if they knew what happened, but they had no recollection at all of how they came to be lying on the floor and how the cuffs were removed. The camera in the room just shows snow apparently. One of them is now being held and charged, and the other one has been released for now. He hasn't actually done anything, so there was no reason to hold him. The first one will get out on bail no doubt, once he has been up in front of the judge tomorrow.'

'I have to say that none of that surprises me. I mean the bit about how they were found and the cuffs. It is not that I know anything about it all, it just fits the rest of what has happened so far.'

'I sort of understand what you are saying, but it is hard to explain to everyone else who is involved. I'm kind of getting used to being around you.'

'There is no answer I can give you for that.' He smiles as he says this. 'Let's carry on and see what we find down here.'

They get up and walk down to the Bull Ring. They cross over to the diagonal corner and keep going past the first door in Sheinton Street, but stop at the second door. The door is a wood and glass door. The door is a panelled one with the handle on the left. It is hard not to take note of the pile of letters and other notifications lying on the floor on the inside of the door.

The man in black pulls his sleeve over his hand and takes hold of the door handle. In normal circumstance both men would have expected the door to be locked and therefore the handle wouldn't move. The man in black is half expecting that to be the result of his action. But the other half of his expectation is that the door will open. To his surprise and more to Andy's, the door is indeed unlocked. But actually that statement is not true. The door does open when the man in black tries the door. Oddly enough though, both men can see as the door swings open, that the lock is still across. Yet it has allowed the door to come open.

Carefully both men step inside. They step over the pile of letters. It looks as if none of them are recent.

'I'd be happier if we left this door open. I seem to remember we had to break it open a couple of time before.'

'I'd say push it to, but I don't think you can do that. I'm assuming it will just shut again and that is what you want to avoid.'

'Correct.'

'Let's leave it wide open then. Unfortunately I don't think there is anything we can use to keep it open against the wall.'

They push the door open as far as it will go and walk on into the hallway of the house. The man in black is leading the way. He has a look in the downstairs room, but doesn't go in. That is for more than one reason. Firstly he can see that the room is empty, but it is more because he hears a noise from upstairs. He tenses up a bit. Andy notices this.

'What is it?'

'I can hear something upstairs.'

'Do you think there is someone up there?'

'It's not that sort of noise.'

'What sort of noise is it?'

'Can't you hear it?

'I can't hear anything other than my own heart beating. You don't think that someone lives here do you?'

'I've never seen anyone and if there is, surely they would have moved that mail by the front door. Anyway the sound I can hear is like a wind blowing. It is coming from upstairs.'

'Maybe I should shout out and see if we get a reply.'

'I'm guessing you might as well. I don't think it will make a difference, but it is probably better for you to check.'

'Hello, police, is there anyone in here.'

They both wait for a reply. None is forthcoming and to be honest neither is surprised by that.

'Try again' the man in black says in a quiet voice.

'Why, what's happened?'

'When you shouted out, the wind sound stopped for a couple of seconds. It has restarted again. It is almost as if it heard you, stopped and then decided to start again.'

'Hello, this is the police. Is there anyone here in the house?'

He repeats that a couple more times. Each time he does it, the man in black says the same thing happens. The wind sound stops for a couple of seconds.

'I think that is enough.'

He starts up the stairs, with Andy close behind him. When they get to the top of the stairs, they stand on the landing while the man in black listens intently.

'It is coming from the front room.' He says quietly to Andy 'but there is another quieter sound coming from the back room too.'

'What sort of sounds are they, because all I can hear is how quiet it is in here.'

'The sound from the front room is the wind sound and the sound from the back room is like a very distant whisper.'

'Which room should we look at first? There's little point me taking one and you the other. You are the only one who can see or hear anything.'

'Let's do the front room first.'

They step forward, quickly and quietly. The door isn't shut completely, so they just push it open gently and step into the room. As soon as they open the door and step into the room, the noise has stopped. There is just a bed in the middle of the room. There is some net curtain across the windows. The man in black can't remember what was here before, but he doesn't think there was either a bed or net curtains. But other than those the room is empty. It is empty of noise too. He tells Andy this, as they quickly look round the room. They turn and Andy leads the way across the landing. He pushes the next door open. The man in black has pointed to the room where the other noise has been coming from.

This room is completely empty and from the moment they enter, it is also devoid of the sound that has been coming to the man in black's ears. He tells Andy this. They retreat to the landing and from there back into the front room once more.

'I think they have been here.'

'What makes you say that?'

'I know this is going to sound strange. But when we came in here a minute ago, I felt nothing at all. But now we have come back in again, it feels as if there is something different. I can't explain what I mean adequately to you, but there is something different to the feel of the room now.'

He goes over and looks at the bed.

'There is an indent on here that wasn't visible before. But I didn't see anything before. But it isn't that indent that makes me feel they have been here. It is like their presence has left a mark on the room. I think we should hang around for a bit, just in case they come back. I find it odd the noises stop as soon as we walk into the rooms. Hang on. The noise has started again from the other room. And this one is doing it too now. It is like there is a wind blowing gently round the room.'

He looks at the window and then back at the bed, but they aren't standing there. They are standing in the doorway of the room.

Chapter 25 Edmund and Elizabeth

It certainly gives him a start, even though he was maybe expecting them to be here in the first place. The wind noise has stopped the very second he sets his eyes on them. They are standing there, looking very relaxed. They have their eyes set on him. Andy notices that something has changed in the room, but he has no idea what or why. He guesses the most likely reason for that.

'Can you see something' he risks voices his question.

'I can' the man in black replies.

'Would be it be best if I left you to it? After all there hasn't been a crime as such involving anything other than Mick and his drug dealing.'

'That might be a good idea, except they are standing in the doorway. I'm not sure if it would be a good thing to try to get past them. I have no idea why they are here. Give it a minute and let's see what's going to happen next.'

While he has been answering Andy; Elizabeth and Edmund move out of the room. They walk slowly backwards towards the other room, where there is still a whispering sound floating across to them. They step through the doorway into the other room and then wait there.

'I think they heard what you said. They have moved back into the other room. I'll walk with you downstairs and let you go out and then come back up and see what they have come for.'

'I'll go and try to get a cup of coffee somewhere. If you're too long, I might have to get back to the station, so I'll give you a ring later.'

They walk down the stairs and find the front door is now closed. It isn't the way they left it. Andy reaches for the handle and the door pulls open quite easily, without him even having to turn the handle.

'I'll see you in a bit then.'

'Ok.'

'Do you think you will be alright?'

'I'm sure I'll be fine.'

Andy walks off and the man in black closes the front door again. He walks up the stairs, but the two of them aren't in the back room anymore. He goes into the other room and he finds them in there, sitting on the bed. There is a chair facing them, about three feet in front of them. He has no idea where that has come from. He takes it that he is meant to sit on it, so he walks across to it and sits down.

'Have I met you before?'

'Other than earlier today, no you have not.'

'Is there a particular reason why I can see you and hear things that no one else appears to be able to?'

'That is more about you than them. We all have the capability to see, hear and think things, but not everyone manages to access that capability.'

The man in black thinks that is quite a nice explanation. It doesn't make him feel too different.

'Sometimes people get frightened about what some others can do. Frightened people can get aggressive and do things that really aren't necessary. We have certainly experienced that many times over the ages.'

The temptation is to ask about what ages and when was the first time, but the man in black decides that is not a question he should ask as yet. There is a brief silence between them, which is a good thing. It shows there is a level of trust that has developed between them already.

'This is good.' The woman is the one who speaks this time. 'My name is Elizabeth.'

'I am Edmund. We know who you are. You have a name, but we also know you as the man in black. We have been waiting for the right one to come here. Now we know why we have appeared at this time.'

The man in black has several questions in his head that he might consider asking, but he decides to resist them, just for the time being. If he is right, there will be plenty of time to ask his questions.

'Is there somewhere we can go where this man you were with does not know where we are? I am not saying that he will tell anyone, but experience has told us that when it comes to us, then people talk and they don't behave in a way that is safe for us.'

'But you always come back.'

'We have done so thus far, but now it is time. This will be our last place and we won't come back anymore.'

Then something strikes the man in black. It has been niggling at him for a few seconds, maybe even a minute or so, but now he has a grasp on it.

'I am fairly certain that I was the only person able to see you when you were standing in the corner by the bench and by the clock. But from what you have been saying, there have been times when everyone can see you. Why can't they see you now?'

'I will answer that in the best way that I can.' Elizabeth says. 'In the beginning I was alone. I was not seen by many. In fact I was seen only by few. Then when I met Edmund things changed. People were able to see me all of the time. When we first appeared here a day or so ago, we thought that we had only been back maybe once or twice, but since this morning, we have realised that we must have been back many times. We do not have a clear recollection of these times, but safe to say that we were not received well on any of these occasions. Otherwise we would still be there. It is only now that we know that the time was not right. People were not ready for us and we were not ready to end this for all time, as far as we are concerned. We don't know why only you can see us, but it is obviously meant to be that way. From the very beginning I came to warn of impending disasters. All I could do was to whisper to people and hope they would listen. Some took heed, but most did not. There was nothing I could do about that. Edmund was the first one who really took note of the warnings. I stayed with him for many times, even though he did not know it. Then for some reason we were joined. Maybe they thought that we would be better together. It really did not change anything. In fact it has not changed a thing. Over the decades and the centuries people's attitudes have changed. The world has changed and progressed in some ways, but not in others. The need for warnings is not as vital as it may have been in the early days.'

The man in black wants to ask another question, but he feels he should maybe wait. But Elizabeth is way ahead of him. Maybe she can read his thoughts.

'You would like to know why it was me that was chosen. I have asked myself that question many a time. To be honest I have never had any memory of anything, other than appearing in some manner to give my warnings of impending events. But since we have arrived here this time, I have been permitted to have these thoughts. That is the way I look at it, as being permitted. Something is allowing us to do these things. Then while I was lying here after we had attached those two men to the railings, I had a vision and it was a vision with me in. I was walking on the hills as I often used to do; I know this because that is what my thoughts told me. I sat down in my special place at the top and looked around me. I was very small. I remember that the day was a warm one. I would not have been allowed to wander away if it wasn't good weather. We had not been in this place very long, but already it had been a good place for us. There was plenty of good hunting, the water was good and the ground by our camp was good for farming our crops. It was more than a good place for us to be. But I had taken to going out of the camp and walking up the hill. I had taken a rock up with me each time I went and had made a small pile at the place where I would sit and watch the world. From where I sat I could see our camp, only just, but I could see it. I think from the first time I saw it from there, I realised that it was in a place that might not be as good as my family thought it was. From where I sat, I could see gullies that led to a point where we lived. They were all dry gullies. The stream we got our water from ran across the bottom of the land we tended. These gullies were not so apparent when you were down there, but from where I sat they were obvious. And the point where they all met was the point where we stayed, where we slept at night. I can't say I was uncomfortable about it, until this one day and then I got a feeling inside me, that the gullies were not going to be our friends. I had no idea at that moment what was going to happen. A slight breeze sprang up and it made me look up at the skies. They had been all blue the last time I looked, but now they were starting to change. In the direction the breeze was coming from, there were now clouds on the horizon. It wasn't just a fluffy cloud here and there; no it was like a wall of cloud. Even as I sat there they were moving over the sky and filling it. I knew then that they were menacing. I also knew that they were going to threaten our existence. I got up from my place and started to run down the hill. I got home and started to shout and scream at my family that we needed to move away to higher ground. They would not listen to me. But I would not give up. By this time the sky was dark over half of it, pushing away the clear skies with the heaviness of what was to come. Eventually, because I would not stop and because I showed them what I thought were the gullies, my father came with me up the hill. I showed him the gullies. They were so much clearer from up there. He saw in an instant what I was saying. The dry gullies were exactly that. They were gullies which were now dry. But every now and then when there was an exceptional weather storm, they were going to fill and be the release for the water to flow away. Even in the time we had taken to come up the hill, the sky had completely clouded over. It was as if it were trying to beat me getting my warning across. We ran back down the hill. My father was shouting from the moment he thought he could be heard. My brothers and sisters and my mother saw and heard him. My uncle and his family came out too. But by the time we reached them the skies had opened and the rain was coming down in a manner I have never known. Everyone wanted to get under cover. Even my father said we should wait. But then I went outside and over to the nearest of the gullies. Already there was a stream starting to run down it.'

Chapter 26 Elizabeth

'The rain was really coming down very hard. I don't think I have ever seen and been in rain that was so heavy. By the second, the stream was growing. I had this terrible feeling inside of me that said something really bad was going to happen. I had never felt anything like that before. I ran back to where they were sheltering. Even as I got in there I could see that the rain was making its way through the roof of our shelter. My father and my uncle were looking up at the roof. The sound of the rain in there was terrifying in itself. It was really hammering down. I tugged on my father's sleeve and eventually managed to get his attention away from looking up at the roof. He was still more intent on staying in there and trying to stop the water coming through the roof. I gave him a few more seconds before I went over to my mother. I didn't say anything, but just pulled her by the arm. I think she knew what I was trying to show her was important, because I remember her not resisting my pull too much. We went outside and although it was clear she did not want to be there, I pulled her over to where the first of the gullies was filling. I said filling, because that is exactly what it was doing. The very small stream that was there when I left to go back inside, had multiplied in size many times in the time I'd been away. I pulled her over to the next one. That one had been still dry when I'd gone in, but now there was water in there too.'

'I've never seen water in those.' Was what she said in my ear?

'I pulled her to the next one and that one had more water in than the other two put together. It was also getting visibly bigger every second. Mind you it was no wonder as the rain was falling even harder now, if that was possible. We had been soaked through and dripping before we had taken more than a few steps. I had been soaked already. Our clothes were flat to our skins. The water was running off us, almost as much as it was running along the ground. It was getting to the stage where it was getting hard to see in front of us, the rain was coming down so hard. We went back to the first gully. That had filled alarmingly so even in those short minutes. I could see the panic on my mother's face. She was the one who now took hold of me. We went as fast as we could back to the shelter. Inside when we got there, they were fighting a losing battle with the roof, but they weren't going to give up.

My mother, as best she could, told them what was happening outside in the gullies. My father got angry and said we were fine, but we had to try to stop the water coming through. My mother was not having that. She started to gather a few things with my uncle's wife. She tried to talk to my father and uncle again. She begged that they come out and see what was happening in the gullies, but they would not.

I did not think it was possible for the rain to fall any harder, but it did. Then there was the sound of thunder. At least we thought at the time it was thunder. For the first time it was enough to stop my father and my uncle from what they were doing.'

'It really is time we left. I don't know where we can go, but those gullies are filling by the second. Elizabeth has a feeling of doom and I have seen them filling for myself. I am taking the children with me. I beg you to come with us.'

'We will be fine here. We are safe in here. We have nowhere to go and it is so wet out there. Where would you have us go in rain like this?'

'Anywhere but here will be safer than this. You really need to have a look at the gullies.'

'I couldn't believe that my father, who had seen what I showed him from the hilltop, could now have changed his mind and was willing to stay, just because the rain was falling so hard. How could he be so blind to the danger that he had seen for himself when he was with me. But then I have experienced the same, time over time since. There seems to something inside of people that makes them not react to warnings. I don't understand that, but anyway I will continue.

My mother gathered up what she could carry and gave us things to carry too. My father even tried to stop us leaving, but she wasn't having it. He returned to trying to keep the water out from the inside of the shelter. Even I could see that what he was trying to do was a lost cause. He would have to work from the outside to stop the rain coming through.

We left the shelter and as soon as we had gone only a few steps, we could see how the gullies had filled up even more, just in the time we were in the shelter trying to get everyone to come with us. We ran away and the only place I could think that would be safer than where we were, was up on the hilltop. Yes, there were other places we could go, but looking at the direction the water was flowing in, those places were going to be just as dangerous as staying where we were. My mother let me guide us all. Although she did go out from the shelter, I don't think she knew the surrounding area like I did. None of the other children did, as I was the only one who wandered far away from the shelters.

It wasn't easy walking, and sometimes trying to run, through the pouring rain and up the gentle slope, whilst carrying our possessions with us. The thunder was deafening at times and the rain beat down on us in torrents. Every now and then the sky, which was so dark now with the heaviness of the clouds, would light up as great forks of lightning flashed across everywhere. We could hear the sparking of the lightning as it exploded visually into the darkened sky. In between times it was so dark, we had great difficulty in seeing where we were going. I knew though that we were on an upward course, as the ground beneath my feet was still rising.

The feeling of doom was still there, like a deep pit in my stomach. I wasn't sure in my mind that we would be safe where we were heading, but I did know that if we stayed where we were; then we were definitely in mortal danger. On top of not knowing where we could go, I also was feeling a deep sense of having abandoned my father and my uncle in the shelter. I felt with every step that I took, that I had let them down. I had not managed to be forceful enough to make then understand and agree that they needed to abandon our place of living. They should have come with us, to a place where at least there was more chance of safety.

It took us far longer than it normally took me to get to the top of the hill. When we reached that place I turned to look back down towards our encampment. At first I couldn't see anything as it was so dark, but then a flash of lightning exploded across the sky. It was only brief, but the scene I saw was one that was almost unrecognizable. Where there had been dry gullies, there were now streams running, easily visible from where we were. Then the light went and I couldn't see again. There was more that I had intended to look at, but I hadn't the time to take it all in in that flash. I waited another minute or so, hoping for more lightning to light up the sky. The feeling of doom in my stomach had just deepened.

The others had huddled together and my mother and my aunt were holding the skins over the group's heads, to try to ward off at least the worst of the rain. It wasn't ideal and with the wind that was now blowing, it certainly wasn't that effective either, but it did at least deflect some of the rain from falling directly upon them.

Then the next flash came. Thankfully it was a much longer flash. I took in the sight of the gullies and then let my eyes look in the direction the clouds had started coming in from in the beginning. My heart sank and the pit in my stomach dropped into a canyon. If I had thought the skies were dark here over our heads, then what I saw in that direction was the blackest of black that I have ever seen. It was a solid wall of black, right down to the ground. It was lit up with little sparks of lightning, but even those could not penetrate the depth of the darkness over there. There was a deep rumbling sound coming from over there too. Already the rain was falling harder over our heads. But the scariest of all things was that this wall was moving at a pace towards us. I knew we had to find something more than we had, to save us. Then I remembered that just over the top of the hill, on the other side, was a large rock overhang. There would be enough room for us to huddle under there and the direction it was facing would mean we would be protected from the directness of the wind and the rain too. I went to talk in my mother's ear and told her where I wanted us to go. We did not hesitate and started to move straight away. It took us maybe five minutes to get there and as soon as we arrived, I knew we would be safe there.

But I also knew that my father and uncle were not safe. I went back out on my own to the top of the hill. When another sheet of lightning lit up the sky, I could see that the black wall of cloud was almost on us. I also saw, which struck more terror to my heart, that the streams had now become rivers. I could see them growing by the second. My father was in immediate danger.

I know now that I should not have done it, but my head told me to try. I ran down the hill and when I reached the bottom I had to wade through the water to reach the shelter. As I was about to go in, my father came out. There was no sign of my uncle.

'You were right Elizabeth. The water is coming through the walls now. He took hold of my hand and we started to run away from the shelter towards my hill. But the water in the gullies had risen even in those few seconds. We started to wade through the first one and we were about half way across, when a wall of water rushed towards us. We had no time to do anything before it was upon us. It thrust us apart and I was taken off my feet. I felt that I was being swept away. I tried to shout out, but there was nothing anyone could have done to save me. Another wall of water came over me and that was the last I remember.

The next thing I knew was that I came to warn others.'

The man in black has listened to her in silence. He now knows why she is doing what she does. He does not understand what force is allowing her to do this, but then not everything has to have an explanation.

Chapter 27 Elizabeth & Edmund

Of course what he does not know, and he thinks it unlikely that she does either, is what she is doing here now. He has no idea why Edmund is with her and now she has finished telling him about some of her history, it is very quickly apparent to him that Edmund does not have any intention of telling a similar tale. That is quite possibly because this isn't about Edmund; it is all about Elizabeth.

They are just standing there now in front of him. He didn't notice them get up from the bed. He isn't ready for them to leave yet, which is what he thinks their standing up might signify. He decides to ask a question, to try to keep them there for a while. He knows it is probably not up to him whether they answer and whether they decide to stay or go.

'Why were those two men chosen to make an example of?'

'I am not sure either. I think they were chosen for us.'

It is Edmund who has answered the question.

'Are they connected to why you have returned?'

'I have thought about it over the last few hours' Elizabeth replies 'I think that there is no direct connection, but their actions are a connection. They are people who do not wholly benefit the society they live in. We have returned at this time, but before we can complete what we need to for ourselves, I have the feeling inside me that we have to expose some people to others in the town. That is what we think we have to do. I believe that these two men just happened to come into our sights and were a natural place for us to start. I am not sure if that is the right reason, but it is what happened. We shall see what occurs now they are free of their shackles.'

'You know they have been freed and the shackles are back on the Guildhall bars, as if they have never been removed.'

'We are aware of that. We arranged for that to happen. There will be others too who will receive the same treatment. There will be others who receive slightly different treatment. How they respond and how the people of the town respond will maybe make a difference to what happens to us; we don't really know too much about that.'

'But I have a place to fill in all this.'

'It would appear that you do. I suspect it is because you can see us and hear us. All I can say is that you will come to no harm, but we do need you.'

'I'm fine with that. So what happens now?'

'We have no exact plans. We just know when things are going to happen, right at that moment. It is not a conscious plan and action time, it just comes to us.'

Elizabeth stops talking and goes quiet. Edmund turns to look at her. The man in black can tell that something has happened. This is quite obvious by the look on Edmund's face. The expression has disappeared from her face and her eyes have a lost look to them. She is looking straight ahead, but into nothing. Edmund turns his look to the man in black. He can see that he has noticed the change in Elizabeth. He nods his head ever so gently. Neither of them attempts to break up whatever she is in. Neither of them attempts to speak either; to her or each other.

The situation lasts for longer than the man in black thought it would. He had expected that maybe it would be short process, of less than a minute. Fifteen minutes later the situation is still the same. She is just standing there. The way Edmund is standing; is as if he is ready to catch her if she falls. There must have been a time when that has happened. She is giving no indication that the situation is going to change. She literally hasn't moved a muscle. The man in black has had to alter his position. He needed to change his stance. He is not in the habit of standing like this for such a long period.

Edmund notices this and with his eyes, the next time the man in black looks over at him, indicates that maybe he should sit down on his chair again. He does so as quietly as he can. His action doesn't disturb Elizabeth.

He has been sitting down for maybe five minutes or so, when Elizabeth starts to sway. It is only a small movement, but Edmund puts his arms out to catch her if she needs it.

His precautions aren't needed and Elizabeth comes back to them. They can both see that she is back in the room. She just turns round and starts walking towards the door. Edmund doesn't look at the man in black, but just follows her. For his part, the man in black watches them both go. He doesn't think he is supposed to follow them. They move into the room on the other side of the landing. The door closes as soon as they are in there, but it then swings open a second or two later. He can no longer see them.

He gets up from the chair and has a look out of the window. There is no one leaving the house and no one that he can see out on the street. He leaves the front room and then stands on the landing outside the other room. As far as he can see they are no longer in there. He steps in to make sure, but the room is totally empty. Somehow he is not surprised by that. He has no idea where they might have gone. There is nothing he can do about that. He makes his way down the stairs and pulls open the front door. Once he is out on the street again, he pulls the door shut behind him. He gives it a push to see if it will open again, but it does not. He tries the handle, but the door is now locked as it should be. The only thing that tells him; is that if he ever is to get in again to see them, he will have to wait until they are ready to see him and allow him in.

He is not a religious man, but he decides he needs a minute or two sitting down, to reflect on what has just happened. He crosses over the Bull Ring and walks the remaining twenty yards to the church doorway. He pushes the door open and steps inside. There is a wonderful comforting peace in there. He turns to his left and enters the main body of the church. He walks forward and selects a row of pews to take a seat in. He opens the door to the pews and sits in the end seat. He leaves the door open for now. He hasn't come in to pray and look for guidance, but he has come in for reflection, which in its own way can be looked at as a personal prayer. Usually the only time he has occasion to come in here, is when he is attending a funeral service. Matthew holds an excellent service. He has been a breath of fresh air to the town and the churches around this area.

He sits there for maybe as long as half an hour. He hasn't closed his eyes or looked down once. He has just taken in his surroundings, looking at the walls and the other pews; looking at the altar and the ceiling; looking at the windows and the doors; looking at nothing specific at all. Then all of a sudden, he feels he is ready to move. He stands up and steps out of the row and closes the door behind him. He makes his way towards the exit, stopping on the way to drop a couple of pounds into the collection. He goes out of the left hand door and enters the outside world again. He walks up past the Guildhall, but doesn't take a look at the cuffs hanging from the bars. About five minutes later he is home and in his kitchen, putting water in the kettle ready for a cup of coffee.

'We need to familiarise ourselves with this town as it stands now. I am struggling knowing where we are in relation to the times we have been in this area before.'

They have gone down the stairs and through to the kitchen. Once out in the back courtyard, they make their way through the gate in the wall and into the grounds beyond. From there they emerge onto Queen Street. They turn to the right and then after twenty paces or so, turn to their left into Back Lane. This twists and turns before they reach the end where it joins High Street. They walk along as far as the Fox Inn and then turn right into King Street. This is quite narrow. A few times they have to step aside, as a car is driven towards them, or from behind. They stand to the side, as they aren't sure what will happen if they don't. On reaching the bus station at the far end, they look to their right, before deciding to turn left. They cross the main road and then take the cut up through to Southfield Road. They follow that all the way to the end, coming out on a bend on the Shrewsbury Road. Taking their lives into their hands, they run across the road when there is a gap in the traffic. They know that no one will slow down for them, as they can't see them. They keep walking away from the town centre, but then take the next left turn into the Stretton Road.

They have walked maybe a hundred yards or so along there, when Elizabeth suddenly stops. She raises her eyes to the skies and then turns a full circle very slowly. For the first time in her walk she feels she is close to somewhere she has been before. But without a word to Edmund, she walks forward again before crossing over the road. She turns up a path and then after a couple of minutes she turns left onto another one. The ground is starting to rise under her feet. The feeling of familiarity, of a kind, is getting stronger every step that she takes. Edmund is walking behind her, maybe six or seven feet behind her. Suddenly she veers off the path they are on. There is no path to follow now. In places the undergrowth is quite thick. No one has been through this for years and years. She twists and turns for a few minutes and then she comes to a complete stop. She turns towards Edmund.

This is where you came to with your family. This is where you pitched your shelter, but you didn't stay here. But if you hadn't made that decision and persuaded your family to come, then you would not be here now.'

Edmund looks around the place where they are standing. He doesn't recognise what his eyes are showing him, but when he closes his eyes; his mind takes him back to the time when he had indeed been here in this spot.

Chapter 28 Elizabeth & Edmund

They stay there for several minutes. Elizabeth is feeling good. The thought that they should start to try to find this place and others, had come to her suddenly while she and Edmund were talking to the man in black. At first the sound had just been like a rustling breeze, but once she had locked out the sounds of the room around her, she realised that it had in fact turned to a whisper. The first words she heard were familiar to her. They were the ones others have heard too.

'It is time.' These words were repeated quite a few times, but she knew there would be more and in time other words came to her.

'You will find one place today, if you try to. But you will not find any more. Do not be concerned about this. It is not as straightforward as you and many would like. It is a complicated procedure and the only way I can describe it, is as a mish-mash that has to be unravelled slowly and patiently.'

Then the whispering had stopped. Elizabeth had no idea where it came from. But then she doesn't know why she is as she is. She doesn't waste any time trying to work it out. It is beyond her and she knows that. She has a role to play and she is quite happy to play it, as long as she can be with Edmund.

Elizabeth starts to move off in the direction they had been heading, prior to finding this place. As it stands this place has no meaning. After all it was only the place where Edmund and his family had come to evade the floods. Even though the whisperer had told her that she would only find this one place today, she is still determined to try to find the next place. Edmund guesses what she is going to be trying for next.

He has no recollection of where that cave is in relation to this place. Everywhere is so different. The changes over the centuries have been quite marked. They wander around for about half an hour, trying to see if they can get any clues, but by the end of that time they have no idea if they have come close, or whether they aren't even warm. It is perfectly clear that they are not intended, or not meant to find that place today, if they are ever to find it. In the league of important things and places, it is pretty low on the list anyway. But they both believe that at one stage they will have to find it, to make every other part drop into place.

They scramble up the side of the escarpment from the place they decided to stop searching anymore today. They make their way back past the first place and then follow the path they have created to get there, back onto the main path. From there they make their way back down and they are soon down on the Stretton Road again. They turn left and walk to the end of the road.

Not sure where they are actually making for, they decide that they need to keep walking around the town and to try to get their bearings in the town. To that end, they turn right onto the Shrewsbury to Bridgnorth Road. They have to cross the road, again a perilous journey, as the footpath is on the other side of the road. At least on there they don't have to worry about the motor vehicles that come in waves along that busy road. The only thing they have to watch out for; are the other pedestrians coming towards them from town. Neither of them wants to walk through them.

They cross the road again near the corner and walk round the corner at the Gaskell Arms. They take a walk around the cemetery out of interest, but the stones are all far too new to have any relevance to their original period. They continue walking up to the edge of town that way and then turn into Racecourse Lane. Walking past the primary school they take a right down the path between the primary school and Swan Meadow. Eventually they come out at the bottom, onto the end of Barrow Street. They know they are still near the edge of town. They are going to continue, but Elizabeth stops suddenly. It catches Edmund by surprise and he is several steps ahead of her before he realises she isn't walking with him.

She is standing there again with that far-away look. On this occasion, it is quite short, only a matter of a couple of minutes before she is back with him.

'There is a strong force near here. I believe it is near to where the man who wears black lives. I do not want to be seen by him, if we go too close to where he is. We need to go the other way and then we will not see him or anyone.'

She turns round and starts walking away from the centre of town. She turns the corner and when the footpath runs out, she walks along the bank at the edge of the road. The drivers of the few cars that come along have no idea that they are there, so don't make a space allowance for them. Elizabeth is not keen to test out whether at this stage they can cause them any damage.

A short time later, they turn left onto the public footpath and make their way slowly through the fields, skirting the edge of town. In some places there are sheep in these fields. Although she thinks they can't see her and Edmund, it is clear to her that they can feel their presence. Their path takes them relatively close to some of them, but as they near, the sheep turn and run away. It must be some kind of sixth sense that is doing this. They don't run far, but it is far enough to be away from whatever they can feel of Elizabeth and Edmund walking past them.

Eventually they find their way back into town and walk past the priory. When they turn the next corner, they find that they know where they are, almost in the Bull Ring. When they reach the junction, they can see the front of the house where they were earlier. There are two men, one of whom is dressed in uniform. The other one is the man who came with the man in black earlier. It looks as if they have managed to get a key from somewhere. They see the men open the front door of the house and step inside. They decide to wait and see what happens. Elizabeth instinctively knows that the man in black knows nothing of this. She is sure that he would not be happy if he knew this was going on.

Ten minutes later the two men reappear. There is nothing for them to see, so it is no surprise they come back out empty handed. The uniformed one goes to a police car parked in Queen Street. Andy walks up towards the town centre. He stops by the Guildhall and spends a couple of minutes inspecting the shackles that are hanging from the bars. A couple of people stop to talk to him while he is there, but it is only chit chat and town talk, about what has happened.

Elizabeth and Edmund have moved up past him and are now standing by the clock tower in the square. The place they are standing is well out of the way of passing pedestrians. They watch as Andy looks closely at the bars. They can also see that he would like to go the other side, but he can't do that now, as the market has closed for the day and they have locked the gates. Eventually Andy loses interest in this and moves towards them. He looks up High Street before moving off up there, wandering slowly. He stops every now and then to ask people something. From the shakes of the heads that they can see, he is not getting the answers he wants. They see him reach the last of the shops, the pharmacy. He then turns round and wanders back down the other side of the street. They see him pop into a couple of the shops, but he is soon out again, coming down towards them. When he is about half way down the street, he takes out his phone and stands still while he uses it. He looks at his watch and then finishes his call. He then walks down to where they are standing in the square and sits down on one of the benches. Elizabeth and Edmund think they are just too close for comfort. They take up position down past the Guildhall, at the furthest point where they still have a line of vision.

Less than five minutes later the man in black appears, from the Barrow Street direction. He sits down beside Andy and they are having a conversation. From where they are, they think the conversation is quite a heated one. Andy has taken the key out of his pocket and showed it to the man in black. It is easy to see even from where they are standing viewing all this, that the man in black is angry. Andy tries to calm him down and obviously manages to achieve that to some degree. They both get up from their bench and start to walk towards them. Just as they do that, Elizabeth sees a woman walk into the square, also from the Barrow Street direction. There is something about the woman that is different. She points her out to Edmund.

'Go after her, quickly. I think I have just seen the next person we will make an example out of. I need to be able to find out more about her. I am going to see where these two go now. I will meet you back by the clock tower or here, depending what happens. See where she goes and where she lives.'

They have to step back round the rear side of the Guildhall, as Andy and the man in black walk past on their way down the road. Edmund keeps going and comes out at the far end; in time to see the woman in question go into a shop in High Street.

Elizabeth watches as the two men approach the Bull Ring. As she had expected they would, they stop outside the house in Sheinton Street. Andy uses his key to unlock the door and both men enter. Elizabeth rushes over and through the doorway. She can hear that the men have gone upstairs. She risks climbing the stairs, so she can hear them a little better.

'We are not going to have this all going on again. I'm getting it from upstairs.'

'You are making it sound as if I am responsible for this happening. I am not. Given the choice with the people who live in this town, I would ideally not be involved, but I am. But if you think I have any influence or control on what happens, then you are misguided and to be frank a little more stupid than I took you for. Upstairs, as you call it, are worse. I'm surprised that you told them as much as you did. So why have you brought me here?'

'I need to see if they are here and you are the only one that can do that. Then if they are, then I want you to tell them certain things from me and my superiors.'

'That just isn't going to happen. I am not going to allow you to use me in this way.'

The man in black turns and comes towards the top of the stairs. Elizabeth just can't get out of his line of sight quick enough, so she doesn't even try. She just smiles at him.

Chapter 29 Elizabeth and Edmund

The man in black sees her the moment he turns at the top of the stairs. To be fair he does well not to let it show on his face, as Andy is now hard on his heels. Elizabeth stands to the side of the stairs, to let the man in black go past. He doesn't give her any eye contact. He does nothing with the movement of his head or his eyes to give Andy any sense of a clue that she has been listening to them.

The man in black reaches the bottom of the stairs and then stops. He turns round. Andy is halfway down the stairs. He has just passed the place where Elizabeth is standing. He stops as the man in black turns round.

'Let me make this quite clear. I don't know who they are. I don't know why they have come. I have no idea what their plans are. I think you will find that they will not do anyone any lasting harm, but there is no way I know that is true. If anyone complains then you can arrest them. If the people they expose have done something, then you can arrest them instead. I have done nothing and as such, unless you and your superiors back off, I am not even going to talk to you. So you have a choice. I can keep you in the loop as much as I know and can tell, or I can keep you out of it. Either way you will only have my word for it. The choice is yours!'

At that he turns round and opens the front door. He marches out and turns right. Andy has started to move after him. He stops to secure the front door once he has gone outside. Elizabeth goes out too, to see what he does next.

Andy has to run to catch up the man in black. They stop for a second. Andy says some words, but they are too far away for Elizabeth to be able to hear what is being said. The conversation doesn't last very long. The two men shake hands and part ways. The man in black continues up towards the square. Andy comes back down to the Bull Ring and gets into his car, which is parked there.

Elizabeth presumes that the man in black has got his way. Either way it has no great bearing on events. What will be will be. But she would prefer that the man in black was not going to be harassed by the authorities with what is going on, and going to be, in the town. That is not a desired result.

She watches Andy drive away and then walks up to the square, only to see the man in black walking away along Barrow Street. There is little doubt that he is on his way home. She then looks around, to see if she can see Edmund. She spies him standing by the Corn Exchange in High Street. She walks slowly up towards him. He sees her coming and smiles at her. He points at one of the shops over the road, indicating that she is in there. Elizabeth changes her course and makes for the shop instead. She enters the bookshop, but she can't see the woman. She turns left and then does a right. She is in line with the counter. There is a lady behind the counter and a gentleman customer is being served. She still can't see the woman she is looking for. She moves on past the counter, keeping an eye out. She might miss her, as the place is stacked with bookshelves. It doesn't matter if she does miss the woman though, as Edmund will follow her when she comes out anyway.

There is a passageway leading deeper into the premises. Elizabeth follows that through. By some book shelves in the far back corner, she see the woman. She has pulled a book from the shelves and is engrossed in reading something in it. Elizabeth moves, glides even, up to her and stands right beside her. She then turns until her mouth is very close to the woman's ear. She then whispers the familiar three words.

'It is time.'

The woman almost drops the book when she hears this. She looks this way and that, but she can't see anything but book shelves. Elizabeth wants to go back in and say the words again, but the woman is not settling. She is very jumpy for some reason. She keeps looking around her. Her eyes are darting everywhere. Elizabeth decides to whisper again, but from the place she is now standing, which is directly in between where the woman is and the passage she needs to use to get out of here. Elizabeth says the words twice in quick succession. She may only be whispering, but the woman can clearly hear what she is saying. She does drop the book on the floor this time and she makes no attempt to pick it up. She rushes towards where Elizabeth is, not that she can see her. Elizabeth moves swiftly out of her way. She passes her and dives down the passageway back towards the main shop. As she rushes past the counter, Lizzy says something to her.

'If you've damaged that book by dropping it like that you will have to pay for it.'

The woman only mumbles something in her direction, as she shows her her back and makes for the door. The customer Lizzy is serving tells Lizzy that some people can be so rude these days, something that Lizzy willingly agrees with.

She rushes out and crosses over the High Street, without even looking. Her face is as white as a sheet. She doesn't see the car coming down. It narrowly misses her, only because the driver slams on his brakes. The woman is oblivious to this. She steps into the Corn Exchange and sits down on one of the benches. Edmund stands there watching her, guessing what has happened in the bookshop. Elizabeth appears at the doorway just a few seconds later. She sees where the woman has gone, so she just stands by the doorway watching her.

After a few minutes the woman manages to gather her composure. She walks back over the road and goes back in the bookshop. She goes up to Lizzy, apologising, saying that she had suddenly felt unwell. She offers to pay for the book, but Lizzy has already picked it up and there has been no damage. The woman asks for the book and Lizzy reaches behind her and gives it to her. The woman pays for it and leaves. As she turns to walk down High Street, she is totally unaware that she has two people following her, only a matter of steps behind her.

She reaches the square and turns right along Barrow Street. She walks along there, walking quite quickly, until she gets to the corner by the Raven. This time she does look before crossing over. She crosses over on the diagonal, something that she has always done since she moved here. She is feeling much calmer now, but she knows she has been on edge for a time now, since certain things happened, which she was responsible for.

Elizabeth and Edmund are with her all the way, until she reaches her front door. She is still pre-occupied to a certain degree. She would normally go round and through the back door, but she isn't thinking really. She is working on auto pilot. As she enters the house with her unknown guests, her husband walks out of one of the side rooms.

'Not coming in the servants' entrance today then?'

'What?' she replies and then realises what she has done. 'Sorry, I was in the bookshop and felt a bit unwell. I wasn't thinking. I was just hurrying to get home and have a sit down.'

He comes over and fusses her, which she likes.

'Go into the living room and sit down. I'll go and put the kettle on, unless …' he stops to look at his watch 'is it time?'

'What did you say?' She snaps at him, all of a panic. She'd heard the words alright, even though they were coming out of his mouth and not being whispered at her. But even before he has a chance to answer her, she has recovered; as the order of words are realised. 'Sorry' she says 'I don't know what's wrong with me. I thought I heard someone whisper those words, but in a different order, to me while I was looking at a book. It frightened the daylights out of me. It made me feel so unwell in an instant.'

'To be honest sweetheart, you haven't been right for a while now. In fact it is ever since we had those murders in town and Martin & that other chap were murdered and Maggie killed herself. You've been a bit jumpy since then. I think maybe …..' he manages to stop himself saying the next three words "it is time". He continues but uses different words.

'I think that maybe you should go to the doctor and tell him that you have been affected by those murders. He will know what you should take and maybe who you should see, to get over it.'

'I'll see how I feel in the morning. Maybe I will feel better and it will all pass. Were you offering me something a bit stronger than tea? I think I could do with one, whatever the time is.'

'It's not that far short of when we have the first one normally.'

He goes out of the room to fetch their drinks. She is sitting on a single armchair. Her husband usually sits in the one opposite her. Elizabeth and Edmund can see that, as the cushion has the look of being regularly sat upon. They have sat down on the sofa. They are watching the woman. It is easy to see that she is still a bit on edge.

Her husband returns with two glasses, filled to the top. He hands one to the woman. She quickly takes a sip. He goes across and sits down on his chair and takes a sip of his.

'You can't beat a quality gin and tonic.'

'You're right darling. It does make one feel better. What have you been up to?'

'Just finishing off those returns I told you about. Do you fancy going out for a bite to eat tonight?'

'We could. I don't feel like cooking. Where do you fancy going?'

'I don't want anything too fancy. I'm not going to get dressed up or anything.'

'Well that cuts the choices down a bit. I take it we are walking?'

He nods back at her.

'We'll have to now we've had these.'

'Well that is us pretty much down to two choices then. It is either the George or the Bilash.'

'I doubt we'll get into the George without a booking. It's been ever so popular since it re-opened as a community pub.'

'Indian is fine with me. We can finish these and maybe have another and then we can take a stroll down and get ourselves a spicy curry.'

They sit and drink their drinks, unaware of their audience. They quickly finish their first drink and he goes off to get their refills. Elizabeth decides it is time to gently up the ante. From literally out of nowhere, there comes a distant wind sound; the sound of wind coming through a badly fitting window. It is not the sound of a strong wind, but more a breeze that has found its way through the cracks. The woman reacts immediately. She is on the edge of her seat and her eyes are out on storks.

Chapter 30 Lucy & Leonard

The sound of the breeze continues all the while he is away getting the refills. Lucy, that is her name, has stood up after the initial shock, and is trying to track down where the sound is coming from. She can't feel the draught that the sound her mind fully expects her to be able to find. Of course the first place she goes to is the window, but there is nothing there, including the sound. Now she is at the window, it is as if the sound is coming from the fireplace. But when she gets there, there is no breeze coming down the chimney and the sound isn't from there; it is from further over in the corner. She quickly scrambles round the chairs, but when she reaches the corner, there is nothing there, well not the sound.

It is at this moment that Leonard walks back in, holding the two refills. His eyes go to her chair, which is now empty. Only as he progresses further into the room, does he see Lucy in the corner, looking bewildered.

'Are you alright, sweetheart?'

'Can you hear that sound; it started almost as soon as you left the room to get the drinks.'

'What sound are you talking about, sweetheart?'

'It sounds like wind blowing through a crack in the window, or something like that.'

He puts the drinks down and stands still, trying to pick up the sound Lucy is hearing.

'Can you hear it?'

At first he cannot, but then after a few seconds, he picks it up too. To him it sounds as if it is coming from the window. He starts to edge over in that direction. Lucy looks at him oddly; that being because she thinks the sound is coming from the doorway he has just come through. Of course when he reaches the window, the sound isn't from there, as when Lucy had done the same thing. He starts to walk over to where Lucy is standing and as he reaches her, near the door, the sound seems to stop as suddenly as it had started.

'That was very odd!' he announces as he goes to sit down.

Lucy takes a bit longer to make it back to her chair. Even when she sits down, her eyes are still watching the rest of the room. They are about half way down their drink when something bangs from somewhere else in the house. Once again it is Lucy who reacts more markedly. She is up out of her chair, but she doesn't go to investigate; she leaves that to Leonard. As he makes for the doorway, the sound of the wind returns and this time it is a bit stronger. They can both tell it is coming from through the doorway.

Leonard gets to the door and steps into the hall. The noise is coming from the front door. He can see straight away that is where the bang came from too.

'The front door is open' he shouts over his shoulder to Lucy 'You can't have shut it properly when you came in that way.'

He closes the door and the sound stops, but not before he has noticed that the sound of the wind is definitely coming from outside. He hadn't seen that on the weather forecast, but they don't always get these things right. It is in a pocket is Wenlock; it has its own weather, so he has found out.

He makes his way back into the living room. Lucy has sat down and has her drink in her hand. Although the sound has stopped, she is still on edge. Leonard can clearly see that something is spooking her, but he has no idea what it is and why it would do that. She hasn't, up to this point, seemed the type of person who might be susceptible to things like that.

Elizabeth and Edmund have left the house. It was them who had caused the front door to bang. She had shut it properly, but they sprang it open and created not only the wind sounds, but also the wind outside, when Leonard had come to close the door.

Lucy and Leonard finish their drinks and get ready to go down to the Bilash. In the light of the breeze that has sprung up, they decide to take a jacket with them, in case it gets cooler. They leave by the front door.

As they leave, there is a swirling wind. It is not that strong, but it is around them, but then so are Elizabeth and Edmund. They aren't making it uncomfortable or frightening, yet. They are just surrounding the pair of them as they walk to the Bilash, with their own private wind show. As regards to anyone else who might be out walking in Wenlock, it is a still evening.

They pass a couple of other people on their five minute or so walk to the Bilash. They pass the normal greeting. Everyone they pass experiences a short burst of breeze as they do so, but they don't think anything of it, as a few steps on, all is still with them again.

The Bilash, when they get there, isn't particularly busy. There are maybe two or three other tables that are taken, with fellow eaters. Miah greets them in his usual enthusiastic manner. They choose where they want to sit, and Miah engages in a short conversation with them, as to how things are. He takes their drink order and leaves them looking at their menus.

Two hours later, they have had lovely meal, accompanied by probably more wine than they would usually have had to drink. That was down to Lucy, who was enjoying the meal and the wine, but she could not shake the whispering and wind sound out of her mind. She'd decided that maybe the extra drink might help her blot it all out. It doesn't work totally.

When they leave the Bilash, they are both pleasantly surprised to find that the wind they had walked here with has died down again, completely. They get as far as the George, when looking through the window as they pass; they see Brian and Jackie sitting in there, having a drink. Brian waves them in, the instant he sees them. They walk in to join them.

'We tried ringing you about an hour ago, but you weren't in. We thought you might have gone out for a bite to eat.'

'Yes, we have just been to the Bilash. It was very nice. I'm glad to say that wind has died down again.'

'I didn't notice any wind.'

'We came out over two hours ago. There was an annoying swirling breeze.'

'We only came out an hour ago. It must have dropped by then. David and Barbara say they might come down for a drink too. But they aren't sure. Barbara is waiting for something or other. They did say, but I can't remember. We'd decided to come out anyway. I'm glad we saw you walk past. What are you having?'

One drink turns into another and a third. By the time they leave at closing time, Lucy is well oiled and has forgotten about the events of earlier. By the time they have gone up to Brian and Jackie's house for coffees and another alcoholic drink, it is well past midnight when Leonard and Lucy are ready to make their way home. They have nothing pressing the next day, so it is of no matter what time they go to bed, or the state they are in after drinking a lot. To be fair, Leonard is not too bad, but Lucy has definitely had a few too many. Leonard has to guide her, to keep her on the pavement. To be fair, the pavement isn't that wide at the bottom of Racecourse Lane anyway. They lurch their way down to the bottom of St Mary's Lane and turn right at the Raven junction. It is just the matter of another couple of minutes for them to get home.

They go in the back door and in the kitchen, Lucy sits down on a chair by the table, while Leonard puts the kettle on, to make them a coffee before they go to bed. The kettle is about halfway to boiling, when there is a spark and a bang. It stops working. Leonard goes over to have a look at it. He lifts the kettle off its stand and sees a few drops of water on the stand.

'I must have slopped water on it. I've had one too many methinks.'

He grabs a towel and wipes the stand before putting the kettle back on it and pressing the button to switch it back on.

There is a big spark, a loud bang and the light in the kitchen goes out.

'Damn, I've made it worse somehow.' He says.

Before he gets the chance to do anything more about it, the back door flies open and a gust of wind blows through the doorway. It is much stronger and louder than the wind was earlier. Leonard fumbles his way in the dark, towards the back door. He manages to find it and closes the door. But the wind does not go. That is still in the room. It moves over towards the hall doorway and then separates, as it turns and blows straight at them. Lucy is sitting, gripping the edges of the table. She is paralysed in fear. Leonard is still by the door. His drink fuddled brain cannot understand what is happening. He can't see a thing in the dark and this noise is very strange.

Before he can think of doing anything the wind increases both in volume and ferocity. It blows straight at them and then swirls around them, before part of it dies down and changes to a whisper. Even before she can hear the words clearly, Lucy knows what the words are going to be. She is not to be disappointed in that.

'It is time Lucy' she wasn't quite expecting all of that. To her it is as if someone is floating round her all the time. She hears the words continuously for a couple of minutes. Leonard can hear the same words too. He shouts to Lucy. He does this because the noise of the wind is quite loud.

'What is this about Lucy? Why is the whispering about you?'

'I have no idea' she lies, as she shouts back to him. 'I have never experienced anything like this in my life before.'

It isn't Leonard who answers this; it is Elizabeth. She does so in the same whisper.'

'But you haven't come across me before. It is time Lucy; it is your time Lucy.'

Lucy can't help but let her bowels loosen a fraction. To hear her name in the whisper is one thing, but for the whisperer then to talk to her, brings this into a completely different dimension. This is bizarre, strange, and to be perfectly frank, frightening. As she feels a trickle of wee in her pants, the whisperer comes closer and whispers right in her ear, but the words are not just for her alone.

'You know what you have done, but I bet he doesn't, do you Leonard?'

It is Leonard's turn to feel more scared. He doesn't quite loosen his bowels, but it is a close call. Then the wind drops off completely and another voice comes over to whisper in Leonard's ear.

'But then you are not exactly the squeaky clean individual that everyone thinks you are. Admittedly no one really got hurt by your actions, but ….'

The whisperer drifts away and stops before finishing. Leonard and Lucy are in the dark, with voices by their ears telling them things. Then there is a tremendous bang. It is probably the biggest clap of thunder either of them has ever heard. But it is not outside the house; it is from the inside, in the room they are in. Boom and they both fall down.

Chapter 31 Lucy and Leonard

Well it is not a case of they both fall down. Leonard somehow falls against the worktop and gently slides down to the floor. Lucy slumps back in her chair and is lying like a rag doll, with her head flopped to one side.

The lights come back on in the kitchen, but not in their heads. Leonard and Lucy are still where they lie.

Outside the air is still. The clouds float harmlessly by in the night sky. It is not a warm night, but it isn't cool either. The night could not have been more different to the night that Mick and Nigel experienced when they were picked on by Elizabeth and Edmund.

Elizabeth knows that this is because things are changing for them already. To move Nigel and Mick was a simple mind over matter exercise. She has already found out that it is not going to be quite so simple with Leonard and Lucy. She knows that, because she has tried. Ideally she would have them moved by now. This is going to be so much more awkward than she would like. The easiest way to move them would be by using their car. But the problem is that neither she nor Edmund has any idea how they work. She has sent Edmund out to try to find something they can use to transport them to the Guildhall.

Edmund has a look around the garden, but it is quickly obvious that there won't be anything here he can use. Just as he is wondering where he might find something, he remembers watching Rod using a sack truck (he doesn't know that is what it is) to take the fruit and veg from his van, across to his stalls under the Guildhall. When he gives it more thought, he remembers watching Rod take the van back from where he unloaded at the bottom of High Street, along Barrow Street for maybe 50 yards and then turning down a track or something. Maybe he should look down there.

He walks along Barrow Street, past the Raven corner and carries on towards the town. He doesn't go far before he sees where Rod had turned his van into. It is dark down there, but he manages to still see where he is going. He walks down there slowly, trying to guess where he might have been taking the van. The nursery is off to the right, after he has walked down the track a bit. He goes in. There is a building there, but not a van. The building is locked, but not to Edmund. But he doesn't find what he is looking for in there. He looks around inside and out, but the sack truck isn't there, but there is something he can use. It is just going to be a bit more awkward.

The wheels are a bit small and it isn't the easiest to push and this is when it is empty. He knows already that it will be awkward with just one of them on, let alone both of them. But that is what he has to work with. He pushes it along Barrow Street towards Lucy and Leonard's house. It isn't exactly the quietest either. He worries that he might be heard as he trundles it along the edge of the road, let alone with any traffic that might come along.

Elizabeth is unfazed with the mode of transport, when he turns up in the drive with it. Together they go into the kitchen and lift Lucy. It actually takes no effort from them to do that. They move her outside onto the trolley. Elizabeth insists that they move Leonard at the same time. Edmund worries that they won't be able to manage the trolley with them both on it. Elizabeth knows that they will be alright.

They leave Lucy and Leonard's house secure. The sky darkens right over; any wind that might have been, dies away; anything that might happen around them stops, just long enough for them to make the journey to the Guildhall. They remove the pair from the trolley and while Edmund takes the trolley back to the Nursery, Elizabeth stages Lucy and Leonard by the bars of the Guildhall. She picks up a shackle and even though there is no opening, she slips it over Lucy's wrist and then makes sure that she can't slip it back off. She then does the same with Leonard. Edmund returns just in time to see Elizabeth change their clothes into rags.

They walk across the road and take their places behind the wall. The sky returns to its original state and a slight breeze springs up. It is a peaceful night as they wait for morning to come and a similar scenario to the last time. The man in black does not know, as he didn't before, that his presence will trigger something for the town to see.

They have only been there for a few minutes when someone walks by, on the other side of the road. It is dark in Wenlock at night, sometimes because some of the streetlights get switched off between midnight and five a.m. But even if the streetlights had been on, this individual would not have known that he almost trod on Leonard as he wandered by, probably on his way home. Elizabeth and Edmund have no concern that their captives might be discovered by this man stepping on them; after all there is nothing there to step on; for mere humans of the current time.

Just as the night sky starts to give way to the new day, there is the first stirring of life in the town. There have been a few vehicles driven past throughout the night hours, but no more pedestrians. Paddy Ryan and his sons walk along Barrow Street and turn up High Street, making for their shop. A couple of delivery vans arrive, one with bread and cakes for Catherine's bakery, another with papers for the Spar and Mrs P's. But none of these see anything out of the ordinary. They don't see Lucy and Leonard, who are still unconscious in their shackles. And they don't see Elizabeth and Edmund who are keeping their eyes on them.

A couple of early dog walkers come by; with not even the dogs, with their sensitive noses and hearing, being able to detect anything out of the ordinary. A few more cars come by, as people go off to their early starting jobs. A few cars come down High Street with early shoppers at Paddy Ryan the butcher. Someone comes along and unlocks the Guildhall, ready for Rod's fruit and veg market to prepare for the day. The trolley that Elizabeth and Edmund had used earlier is trundled along from the nursey with some bits and pieces on. In time Rod's van comes along, with the first load of goods to put on his tables. Still Lucy and Leonard are not visible, chained to the bars of the Guildhall.

Time ticks by and many people have passed them, but without being able to see them, before Elizabeth and Edmund know that the time for them to be revealed is coming soon. They have no control over the man in black, other than they know he will come along at some time. It does not really matter to them when that is, as long as he does; and they would not have been able to do what they had done with Lucy and Leonard if that hadn't been the case.

It is shortly before 9 o'clock. The town is starting to come more alive. The shops and the tea shops are starting to open. The bakery has been open for a while. Paddy Ryan's has been open for well over two hours. The Spar and Mrs P's have been open for nearly 2 hours. Rod and Viv's fruit and veg stall is almost fully stocked. Rod's van is back with the last of the veg to go out on sale. The trolley is on its final journey from the nursery with more plants for sale. The trolley will stop outside the market now for the duration of the day.

Elizabeth and Edmund have been watching the goings on intently from the time they got there. Time isn't greatly important to them as they are, so they have no trouble maintaining their position, watching and making sure that Lucy and Leonard are ready for the reveal.

Elizabeth looks to her right and sees the man in black walking towards them. She can see from his manner that he has already seen them. She can see that he isn't best pleased to see them standing there. She guesses that if he could, he would turn round and go back the way he had come and try to find a way to where he was going without having to come past here. What he can't see won't matter to him.

But that is not the way it is. He has walked this way into town. This is the way he virtually always walks into town and to be honest, he really wasn't expecting them to be standing where they are. As he approaches, he tries not to look anywhere else other than at Elizabeth and Edmund. He doesn't want to let his eyes wander to that place opposite them. He can already guess that there is a good chance he will find someone else there. He just knows there will be, but who will it be this time and why?

As he crosses the bottom of the square, he can't help but notice two people shackled to the bars of the Guildhall. One is a man and one is a woman. Like before, it is clear to him that no one else who is walking around, and there are quite a few people about, is able to see them, yet.

The man in black turns his attention back over to the two people standing opposite the Guildhall. They are dressed in the same clothes that they were in when he last saw them. He crosses over the bottom of High Street. He stops in front of them. They stand and look back at him.

'Why do you have to wait for me to arrive each time? You do know that you will be making it more awkward for me again. I had enough trouble with that detective over Mick and Nigel, let alone with the house you were in. I really don't need this.'

'All we know is that it has to be you.'

'Do I have a choice in this?'

'I know that we need you. That is all we know.'

'So what happens if I say no? What happens if I do not go over there and touch them? Will it change anything?'

There is a moment of quiet while Elizabeth thinks about what he has just said. This is an unexpected change in the process. It is a change that she has not predicted. She also believes it is a change that has not been accounted for. She waits to get the inspiration, so that she knows how to deal with this. Nothing is coming to her so far.

The man in black shrugs and turns away from them. He doesn't cross over the road as they expect him to. Instead he turns to walk up High Street. He goes into the Spar and a few minutes later he comes out again and walks across the road and the square. He then starts to walk away from them along Barrow Street.

Chapter 32 Lucy & Leonard

'What do we do about this?' Edmund asks Elizabeth.

'I do not know. I just do not know. But whatever it is, those two will remain as they are until it is resolved. They cannot go back. As far as I know, they can only move when they are touched by the man in black. Until such time they will be there, unseen. They will come to no harm. They will not know anything about it.'

They both turn and see the man in black is way along Barrow Street. He is past the Raven junction, almost at the place where Lucy and Leonard's house is. They wonder if he knows them. They wonder if he knows that is where they live. They watch as he passes the house, without even a glance across at their side of the road. That pretty much answers that question for them. What happens next? That is the question that they have no answer for as yet.

'You can stay here for a while and watch them. They will not move and no one will see them, but one of us does need to be here, in case he changes his mind and returns to do what he must do.'

'Where will you go?'

'I will go back to the house. I am hoping that if I go to a peaceful place and out of sight of them, then the answer may well be given to me.'

Edmund resumes his watch on Lucy and Leonard. Elizabeth walks round in front of him and walks down Wilmore Street towards the Bull Ring. She glances at the pair shackled to the railings of the Guildhall, as she passes them on the other side of the road. When she reaches the house, she pushes the door open. The feel of the house is as it should be. No one has been in here since they last left it. She climbs the stairs and goes into the front bedroom. She lies down on the bed and closes her eyes. Almost immediately she feels that she is floating. She is still awake, but her eyes are closed. She keeps them closed and resists the temptation to open them and see where she is floating.

She does not float for long. She soon feels that her feet have touched the ground. She is standing up now, rather than lying down. She decides that now is the time that she can open her eyes. She is in a room. The room is in a house, but she does not know where the house is and whose house it is.

She hears a door close somewhere below her. That must mean that she is not on the ground floor. She looks round the room. There is a big desk, with a machine in one corner and what her mind is telling her is a small laptop, at the front of the desk. The room is bright and airy. There are pictures on the wall, every wall. They are pictures of people, sports people; sports people and sports tops. There is a chair in front of the desk. The only other furniture in there is two bookcases. Neither is packed with books, although there are some books on both of them. But there are other bits there too.

She is still looking at the different things on there, trying to decide what kind of person this room belongs to, when she hears the sound of someone climbing the stairs. She is not afraid. She has no reason to be afraid any more.

That time has gone. She never feels afraid now. She knows that whoever it is cannot harm her, not that they necessarily will want to. She steps away from the desk and stands by the window, just to the left side of it. She notices there is a row of small teddy bears on the windowsill. She decides that this cannot be a bad person, whoever it is she is about to meet.

They reach the top of the stairs and then a second later they come into view. Immediately, they stop in the doorway. She can see him and he can see her.

'Why am I not surprised to see you here? I didn't notice you pass me on my way along the road coming back here. But then I guess that you don't have to travel the way I do. I don't walk so well these days and running is pretty much out of the question.'

The man in black is still standing in the doorway. Elizabeth hasn't said anything to him as yet. She is waiting for the right words to come to her. She knows they will and there won't be an awkward silence. That is what she had initially feared there would be.

'I think there will be a way that you can help us, without people knowing that you are the one who has touched them. They do need to be touched though, to make them visible. And I have been informed somehow that it is only you that can do that. I know it is not ideal, but it is the way it is.'

'You will need to convince me why I have to do this. You will also have to convince me why these people are being chained like this and exposed.'

Elizabeth has already guessed that he will ask something like this. She has been prepared for such a response.

'They will not be the last.'

She knows that this is not the wisest thing to declare, when she still has not overcome his resistance to helping with this couple. But she has been told, or she just knows, she has to tell him this. But there is more than just this.

'I told you how I came to be this way. I will also need your help to finish this for me and Edmund. I have things to find and places to find, once I have the people revealed to the others who live here. People are fed up of the way that some people talk about them. People are fed up with how some individuals are so negative about things. People are fed up with the pettiness of the town at times. People are fed up with how some people think who they are and what they do; makes them better than everyone else. Most people just want to live here in Wenlock, in a pleasant, without it being a bickering, environment.'

She suddenly stops as there is a noise downstairs. She wasn't expecting that.

'It's alright' the man in black says. I do not live here alone. Elizabeth wonders why she did not know that. It is not important, as long as she can do what she needs to get done.

'It would be better if we were not here when what happens next. I do not think it is a good idea that we are in the house with someone else.'

Surprisingly enough, the man in black does not object to this. She had thought for a minute that he might. Maybe it is the words that she can let him do this without people seeing it is him; that has made the difference. It would have been better if she had known that at the beginning. But that isn't the way it was meant to be, obviously.

'Come over here and stand beside me. We will go now. I will not allow you to be harmed.'

The man in black walks over to her and turns to stand beside her. She reaches over and gently closes his eyes with her fingers. Her touch is light and very gentle. He can feel her fingers as they do this. He didn't think he would have been able to. He is still awake and he knows he is still standing. Elizabeth takes a light hold of his arm and he feels himself start to float. He can still feel her hand on his arm. He knows they are moving, but he does not know how. Nor does he know which way they are going. He does not know if they have gone down the stairs and out or gone out some other way. He does know they are now outside. He can feel the breeze on his cheeks as they move along. All the time she has a hold on his arm. They float like this for a few minutes and then suddenly they stop and she is opening his eyes. They are in the house in Sheinton Street. They are in the front room upstairs, the one with the bed.

'Lie down beside me. I have something I need to show you. You asked me to convince you as to why those two people are there. I will show you. We will lie here with our eyes closed. I will be touching your arm once more with my hand. That will be the only contact. You will need this to be able to see what I am going to show you. You will see that what the man has done is not as bad as what the woman has done. In some ways it is not comparable.'

She closes his eyes once more and then lies beside him on the bed. She touches his arm with her hand. As soon as she does so, he sees pictures appear in his head. They are pictures of the man. He has seen him on occasion around the town, but he does not know him as such. He is part of a crowd who all moved to the town round about the same time. He thinks he can remember something about that group, but his mind will not allow his thoughts to go there. There is probably a reason for this, so he does not try to beat it.

He sees the man in an office. With what he can see behind the man through the window, he knows he is in London. The man is working at his desk. There is no one else in the room. The man in black knows he is now standing, as he feels able to walk in the room. He moves over to the desk and tries to see what the man is doing. He is just about close enough, when there is a knock at the door. The man suddenly acts very startled. It is clear that he wasn't expecting to be disturbed. He quickly changes the screen on the computer he was working on and then shuffles the papers in front of him and puts them away quickly in the top right hand draw of his desk. He then moves some other papers in front of him and picks up a pen. There is another knock on the door. This time he responds to it.

'Come in, I thought you just would.'

He makes that excuse for not having answered the first knock. In truth there are few people that this man works with who would have dared to open the door with just a knock. They always needed to be told to come in and not just knock and barge in.

The man in black watches as a lady walks in and gives him a few pieces of paper. She needs him to sign them for her. He doesn't just sign them as some people would, but he inspects each and every one, before signing each bit of paper with a great flourish. Once he has signed all of the papers, the lady informs him that she is now going to lunch. She will make sure that the door to the outer office is locked when she goes out, so he will not be disturbed. Does he have his key with him? Of course he has; he always has, but she needs to ask. God help her if she didn't and for some reason he had forgotten it.

Chapter 33 Leonard & Lucy

The lady walks out of the room again and closes the door. The man remains at his desk for maybe five minutes, before getting up and going over to the door. He opens it and looks out. There is no one in the other room. He closes his door again. He takes a key from his pocket and locks this door. No one is going to disturb him while he is doing this.

He flicks back to the screen he was working on on his computer. He also takes the papers he hid in the top drawer, out again. He resumes what he was doing before the interruption.

The man in black moves closer. He wants to try to see what he is up to with these papers and the computer screen. It is on first look just a list of numbers on the screen. The man starts checking them off with a set of numbers on the papers. Then he goes back to the screen and adjusts the numbers. The total of the list of numbers has changed, at the bottom of the screen. The difference is only a few pounds. That figure the man has put in a box at the top of the screen.

For the next forty minutes the man goes from screen to screen. All the time he is adjusting figures and taking the difference in the totals and adding it to his box at the top of his screen. He finishes that stage and then transfers the figure in that box to another page. That page reads: Pension Deductions. He puts a date by it. The figure is not huge on its own. But it is not the only figure on this page. The man in black sees that there is an entry for every week. Beside each figure is a tick, all except for the one he has just entered. Beside the tick it says transferred. The other thing that he notices is that the page he has entered this on is a document of multiple pages. The man in black decides that he wants to know how many, because he thinks it will be a lot.

Suddenly as if he is wishing it to happen, the screen starts scrolling down and down. It is quite amusing to watch the man while this is happening. Try as he might to stop the screen scrolling down, he just can't. It just keeps going and going. That doesn't stop him trying though. Eventually the screen reaches the last page, or as it turns out to be, the first page. The man in black can see the date that the first entry was made. It is about ten years ago. The figures on this page are smaller than the ones on the current page. No doubt he has got greedier as time has gone by. He hasn't quite worked out what the man is up to. He thinks that he needs to take a closer look at the pieces of paper the man is checking off. Maybe they will hold the answer.

While the screen is now allowing him to return to the page he was working on, the man in black takes the opportunity to look at the papers. He finds he can pick them up. The man at the desk appears to be unaware that he has done this. His eyes are locked to the screen. That is because Elizabeth is helping him.

The pieces of paper not only have figures on. They also have names and they also have a date beside the names. But it is the words by those dates that are interesting. "Died on" are the words by the date. The pension figures are about people who have died. Their payment is being adjusted by this man and he is siphoning off a portion from each one and transferring it. He puts the papers down again and watches the process continue. He transfers the sum for the week to a bank account and then he goes onto that bank account and the figure is there already. He notices that there are some transfers out of this account to another one. He can guess now why he is there and what is happening. The current figure for a week varies between £1400 and £1500. He does a quick calculation. £1400 by 50 weeks and that makes £70,000. 10 years of that would make a figure of £700,000. And it is probably £700,000 that he has taken away from money other people should have had. And that is without thinking whether he might have some other areas that he has been stealing from.

'Have you seen enough to understand why we are here and why he is chained to the railings?'

'I think so.'

'There will be an opportunity while he is chained for him to say what he has done, in public. But what he has done is nothing compared to the other one, the woman Lucy.'

Elizabeth takes hold of his arm and his eyes close again. He floats away for a time. The next time he opens his eyes, he is in for a real shock. It takes him a few seconds to see what is happening. He does not know where he is. He is in a house with a man and a woman. The man is not in the best of health, that is for sure, but he is still alive. What he sees next is in effect the murder of this man. He then sees Lucy, a much younger Lucy; an almost unrecognizable person that is Lucy all the same, disposing of the body in a cupboard.

Then Elizabeth leads him through to another scene. This time he knows this house well. He should, because this house belonged to the man in black at one time. But what he is seeing is a time before he owned this house. This is a time that will lead up to the reason why he found a body in the extension floor, when he did own the property. That is exactly what he witnesses. But this is something that has happened in the past. He is only a witness to the showing of the story, not at the actual time it is happening. In other words he can only see what happened, but not influence the outcome. It is a shocking scene that unfolds in front of his eyes.

Then the scene moves on to two or three doors along the same row. The man in black can guess where this is going. He is not to be disappointed with that guess. But of course the outcome he sees, is not the one that everyone has been led to believe to be what happened. He knows where they will be going next.

Sure enough his next and last visit to see what Lucy has been involved in doing; no it is more than that, the murders she has committed. He knows where this house is.

He sees Martin and Maggie. He can see that they are in a state of intoxication. He sees Lucy arrive and he sees Martin stagger upstairs. He sees them both have the last breath of their lives smothered out of them by Lucy. Lucy has thought that she has managed to get away with these murders, but now he has been shown how she did them, there may now be the opportunity for justice to be served on her.

He'd never in a million years expected anything like this to be revealed. He thinks that what these two have done is many times worse than what Mick and Nigel have done, although the crimes that have been committed are all crimes, just with different levels of severity.

He has seen enough. He hopes there is no more and there isn't. A short time and journey later, he is back in the room, his room.

'I can see what they have done. I think I can understand why they are there. But I still do not know why it has to be me to reveal them to the world. I also have no idea how to reveal what they have done to the world.'

'I do not know the answer to that one either. But it will happen somehow.'

'So what happens to them now?'

'I will go and leave you here. Edmund is keeping an eye on them, to make sure that they come to no harm. I will return when I know how this is going to proceed.'

Then she has gone and he is left alone. He goes downstairs to tell his wife what has happened. He knows that she knows things have been happening. Over a cup of coffee the narrative is completed. His long suffering wife at least is with him, that he really does not need to be the one in the firing line. People don't need any ammunition. But then that appears to be what Elizabeth and Edmund have come to the town for; to stop some of the issues that the town has, and of course find a new life for them.

It is late in the afternoon when he needs to go to get something from the town. His wife offers to go for him, but he says that he is not going to hide away. There is going to come a time, probably in the next few hours or so, when they will have worked out how he can help them, without being so obviously personally involved.

He only gets as far as the square, when he sees Elizabeth and Edmund over by the railings. They are bending down by Lucy and Leonard. At first they don't notice him approaching the centre of town. If he can help it, he does not want to cross over to where they are. But as it turns out he doesn't have to. Elizabeth turns and sees him and waves him away. She too does not want him to be seen at the spot.

He goes up to the pharmacy and picks up his prescription. The need for that to be done earlier had got lost in the events of the day. As he comes out of the pharmacy, he sees that Elizabeth has followed him up here. She is waiting for him to come out. She walks off as soon as he is out. He knows that he should follow her.

'It is good that you have come. I know what we will do. You will have to go home. I will come with you, but we must go by another way. Edmund is going to do something and the police will be alerted. At the time when they arrive, I will have to touch you. I have brought something from each of them. When you touch that and I touch you, then Edmund will touch them and they will appear to all that are there. You will be at home, so you will not be thought to be the one who is doing this. It would be good if you have someone else with you, to vouch for you. Then when the moment is with us, you go up to your room in your house and we will get this done. Is that what you need?'

'I can live with that' he replies.

He gets up from the bench he has been sitting on and walks to the end of High Street. He walks up the main road and then crosses over at the petrol station and keeps going.

At the top he takes a left into Racecourse Lane, by the school. He walks past the school and cuts down the footpath that leads into Hunter's Gate. He turns left as he reaches Barrow Street and in less than a minute he is home. He tells his wife what the plan is and they ring some friends and invite them round. Everything is ready now for the reveal.

Chapter 34 Reveal

It is maybe 40 minutes later that the police respond to a panic alarm, at the Spar Post Office. The alarm has gone off in the Spar, but no one in there knows why it has done so. There was no one at the post office counter at the time and very few customers in or around the area either, when it went off. But once the alarm has been triggered, then that sets in motion a police response. Two patrol cars turn up and most of the officers rush into the Spar, even though all of the members of staff are by the door, to tell them it is a false alarm. The alarm firm have arranged for an engineer to come out, to see what has happened.

One police officer has not gone in. He has just had to take a second look at something. His patrol car had come from Telford direction. So they'd come into town from the Buildwas direction and turned left into Sheinton Street (Shineton Street according to the sign at that end), over Bull Ring and into Wilmore Street. They passed the church on their left, then the Guildhall. At the junction of High Street they'd stopped. His fellow officer, who had been driving, hopped out and ran towards the Spar. He'd opened the passenger door and got out and was just about to follow his colleague across to the Spar, when he noticed two people, a man and a woman, chained to the railings in front of the Guildhall.

He'd had to take a second look, because he prides himself as being a vigilant officer. He is known for noticing things, for taking note of finer details. He doesn't miss much when taking in a scene, having arrived on the spot. The second take is because his brain is telling him that there was no one there a few seconds ago, when they drove past. But now there is! He walks over to where the two are standing. They appear to be somewhat out of it as they just stand there. Initially they don't respond when he talks to them. He knows about the other two men who were found chained to the railings; now it appears they have two more people.

The market is closed. The gates are shut. There is no one walking anywhere near when they pulled up. There is no else here now. The people who are about are outside the Spar, nosing around to see what is going on.

He talks to the man and the woman again. They look at him, but it is clear to the police officer that they are in a confused state. He decides that this needs to be radioed in and so that is what he does. He has no concerns that the couple might wake up properly and scarper. For one they are an older couple, and secondly there is no way they are going to escape from the shackles that are holding them to the railings, hand and foot. He seems to remember that previously the men were only shackled by their wrists.

He leaves them for a minute and goes over to the corner. A small crowd is now outside the Spar. His colleague is outside too.

'John, come here a minute. There is something else, if that one is under control.'

'It's a false alarm, or faulty alarm more like. What have you got?'

'Two people chained to the railings over here.'

'Like those others ones?'

'Come and have a look! It's an older man and woman this time. They are chained hand and foot this time. They are also well out of it, although they are starting to come round now. They look very confused.'

They walk over the road to where the couple are chained up. One or two of the crowd have now noticed them too. Attention is moving away from the Spar to the front of the Guildhall.

'I can't remember seeing them there when we drove past here.'

'No, I don't believe they were. It's easy enough to check though. I'll go and have a look at the camera and see if it picked them up.'

He goes off to do that. His colleague stands in the road and tells everyone else to keep back for now, until they have established what has occurred. It only takes a couple of minutes to check the camera. He is back right after that, shaking his head as he nears.

'There was no one there as we passed, according to the camera.'

'We saw no one either. What is going on?'

'I have no idea, but I guess we should see if they are ready to talk now. Maybe they can tell us how they got there.'

That thought is soon dispelled. They have no idea where they are, let alone be able to say who they are and why they are there. The police call for back-up. They also call for an ambulance. It is apparent that these two need looking over, to check for injuries. They then ask if anyone knows who they are. Not one person there knows their names. But there are maybe only twenty people there. Then someone else arrives and informs them that he thinks they live along Barrow Street, somewhere on the left. One of the other officers comes over to help. He takes a photo of the couple on his phone and then walks off, to see if he can find out whom they are and where they live.

The ambulance has arrived by the time he gets back with their names. It hadn't taken long before a neighbour identified them as Lucy and Leonard. But even armed with their names, they aren't getting any sense from either of them. The ambulance crew have been able to do a brief assessment. There is nothing visibly wrong with them physically. Whatever is up with them is down to something mental, in their opinion.

The fire brigade are now also on the scene, but as before, their cutting equipment is getting absolutely nowhere. This time they are unable to cut through the bars on the Guildhall either. They are resisting every effort on that front.

Then Andy the detective arrives. He takes a couple of minutes gathering what has occurred and who was where etc when they appeared. He thinks over the information for a minute. Something is different from last time and it isn't just the fact they are shackled hand and foot. Then the little light comes on in his head.

'Who was it who saw them first?'

'I did!'

'Tell me exactly what happened!'

'We drove up here from that direction' he points back down past the church 'we drove up and stopped where our patrol car still is. John got out of the driver's door and went over to the Spar. I got out and that's when I saw them. But John and I both agree they weren't there, or at least they weren't visible, when we drove past. John has checked the camera in the patrol car. It didn't pick them up either.'

'So you are saying nobody touched them?'

'I have and the ambulance crew have and the fire people have.'

'No, I don't mean that. Last time someone went up to them, apparently, and touched them. Did anyone do that? Who was around them when they appeared?'

'There was no one anywhere close when we passed and no one when I noticed them. At what precise second they appeared I don't know, but it can only have been maybe five seconds after we passed and I got out the patrol car and saw them. There just wasn't anyone there and no one could have got to them and back out of sight in that short time.'

'So there wasn't a man dressed in black there?'

'No, there was no one.'

'I want you to go along to this address.'

He gives the officer an address and sends him off, to see if the man in black is there. If he is, he wants him to bring him back with him. If he doesn't want to come, then he'll have to arrest him and bring him. He doesn't think that will be necessary though.

The man in black is expecting the visit. Edmund has informed Elizabeth that he has touched them and they have appeared. He has also told her that they appear to be confused, probably more so than they should be. When he is being sent for, he tells Elizabeth that they are on the way. The man in black is sitting in his living room with his wife and the two friends who have come round for a drink. One of them is an ex copper. That should add some weight to his alibi for not being there when Lucy and Leonard reappeared.

He doesn't have to wait long for the doorbell to ring. Elizabeth has left and is on her way down to join Edmund. No one else in the room was ever aware that she was with the man in black. The man in black's wife answers the door. She listens to the police officer, before inviting him in. He then explains again why he is there. Their guests, Paul and Ness, say that they will go with him. They walk along Barrow Street together with the police car driving slowly along with them. When they reach the square, they walk over to where Andy is standing, outside the museum.

It only takes a few minutes for Andy to have it confirmed by the man in black, his wife, Paul & Ness; that he was at home when all this has happened. But now he is here, he asks him if Elizabeth and Edmund are visible. This question has of course been predicted and it would have been a surprise if it hadn't been asked. There is no point in lying and that has never been his or their intention. The fact is that he wasn't there when the couple appeared, but he can see Elizabeth and Edmund. He relays this to Andy. Andy of course wants a bit more than just that bit of knowledge. That too is no surprise. But he is not going to get more with this crowd around them. It is not a big crowd, but there are enough people for it to be hard getting the man in black to ask Elizabeth and Edmund anything, without people speculating as to what is happening. On top of that anyway, it is doubtful that the man in black would agree to it. The problem is how they are going to achieve that without the crowd. Andy needs the man in black to go home again. He then needs to meet up with him again, to find out what is going on. He also of course wants Edmund and Elizabeth to be there too. The man in black relays this to Elizabeth. She replies to him.

'We will come to your house. I will come and Edmund will stay here. Andy can then come to the house by another route. Is that alright with you?'

'Yes, I need these people to see me walking away again.'

The man in black says to Andy what is going to happen. He readily agrees. He shakes hands with the man in black and the four of them turn away and start to walk back along Barrow Street. Andy waits for a few minutes before he does anything about following them. He tries to talk to Lucy and Leonard again, but they are either unable to talk back to him, or are staying silent. He suspects for some reason that it is the former reason. Even though he asks the on looking people to leave now, they are unwilling to do so. A white police van arrives and they put up a screen around the front of the Guildhall. That does the trick. All but the hardened one or two decide they are not going to be able to see any more for now, so go back to what they were doing before this all occurred.

Chapter 35 Reveal

Andy waits until the screen is up and most of the people have moved away. He leaves a couple of officers to watch over Lucy and Leonard. They have given up trying to get the shackles off them. They need to find out more from Elizabeth and Edmund before they decide on their next move. But Andy can't tell the others that is what he is waiting for. He just passes the problem upstairs in the meantime.

When everything is set, Andy says he is going off for a while. He leaves as if he is going back towards Telford. But at the end of the road he takes a left. He follows that road up to the Gaskell junction where he joins the Bridgnorth Road. He drives up past the petrol station and then out of the town. At the crossroads he takes a left turn and follows the lane down to the end where he turns left onto the Broseley Road into Wenlock. Two minutes later he is parking up on the man in black's drive. He parks as far in as he can get; to keep his car out of sight of anyone passing by.

With a cup of coffee in his hand, he asks the man in black what is happening and why these two people are there by the Guildhall.

'The problem is that they are not going to openly open up with it. As far as Leonard is concerned, I have no idea where exactly it was he worked.'

'That should be easy enough for me to find out.'

'Then can I suggest that is one of the first things you do. If you know that, you will at least have an opening lever with him, when he denies knowing anything about why he is as he is at the Guildhall. From what I have been shown and I don't really want to go into the how that happened area of things; he appeared to be creaming off money from pensions. It wasn't easy to make out, but it was something to do with what I presume was a final pay out after someone had died. Presumably he reckoned they wouldn't miss a few pounds. But he had been doing this for about ten years and at £1400 to £1500 a week that comes to a huge sum, probably over £700,000. I only say ten years as that was what paperwork was there when I saw it. So if you can find out whom he worked for and where that was, then you will be able to start getting more proof against him.'

'I'll do that in a minute. Tell me about Lucy now please.'

'This one is much closer to home, well some of it is. Some of it is definitely not around here, but I don't know where that one is. I can tell you what happened and you can ask other forces. But a lot of it will be familiar. You will find out that who you thought had committed these crimes, in fact wasn't guilty of them. It was Lucy who murdered the two people in St Mary's Lane. And it was Lucy who murdered the two people, Martin and Maggie, in the house off High Street.'

The man in black then spends the next few minutes telling Andy what he saw when Elizabeth took him on that "journey". At the end of it, he sits back in his chair and thinks.

'As you said it is going to be hard to break them without any hard facts. As you know I can't exactly explain how you, and then I, have come across this information. It is going to depend how hard they are. I suspect that Nigel will crack more easily. That Lucy sounds like she is quite clever. I don't think she is going to just admit her guilt.'

He starts to get up to leave, but he notices that the man in black has a strange look on his face. He is sitting in his chair staring ahead of him. His wife sees it too.

'He gets like this at times; ever since he wasn't well. He'll come out of it in a minute or two.'

But there is nothing wrong with the man in black. It is just that Elizabeth is talking to him. She has listened to the conversation so far. Mick and Nigel were quite simple ones to expose. Lucy and Leonard are much tougher. When she has finished, she leaves them to go down to where Edmund is watching over the couple shackled to the Guildhall.

'She says that she will do something that will help them reveal their crimes. I don't know exactly what she is going to do, but she says that you should not worry and you should not be scared. No one will get hurt. But you need to move the screen from in front of them. If you need to, you can put one up further away, to prevent people from seeing them, or getting too close. She suggests that one by the church, at the end of the Guildhall and maybe the other one from the square end of the Guildhall, across to the clock and then across to the wall of the Spar. She says you have an hour to organise this and then they will start. In the meantime, you can do your preliminary enquiries about Leonard and Lucy too, probably more about Leonard, as we know what Lucy has done round here.'

Andy thanks him and rushes out. He is on his radio by the time he is out of the door. He gets in his car and drives back round the way he had come. He blocks off the road with his car by the front of the church. He gets out of the car and walks up to the couple. They watch him approach. He can see they look much better now.

'Have you any idea why you have been selected to have this treatment?'

It is Lucy who answers first.

'Just get us undone and find the culprits. We must have been burgled. God knows why they have done this to us. Get these things off us.'

'We would if we could, but they can't be cut through. The fire people have tried. We have asked for another team that we used before, but to honest they couldn't get through it either.'

'Well however you got them off last time, you need to get these ones off us now too.'

'We don't know how they came off.'

'You must know!'

'Well we don't.'

'That's ridiculous. You must know how you got them off.'

'I wasn't there at the time. No one was there at the time. And when we asked the two individuals who were actually the ones chained up; they didn't know either.'

He almost starts to try to use the information he has obtained, but just in time he stops himself from using it. He has put out the calls for more information, but he has had nothing back yet. But he knows there will be people working on it. He needs to have a bit of patience. It may all be a bit weird and something that you can't quite explain to people, but he has little doubt that something will happen at the end of the hour. He also has little doubt that it will produce some sort of positive result. He wouldn't even attempt to speculate at this stage what level of result.

It is hard enough getting upstairs to understand he has to move the screens back. They haven't exactly got screens up yet, but they do have the police tape across the road in the places that have been suggested to them.

Once again there are a few more people who have gathered around. There is a police car blocking the bottom of High Street and the white van is parked across the end of Barrow St. It is obvious to everyone that they are waiting for something to happen, but of course no one knows what. Andy is back over by Lucy and Leonard, but nothing is being said at the moment. They keep trying to get their shackles off, but they have no chance.

'Have you checked our house?'

'As far as we can we have. It is all locked up and we have looked through the windows. Everything appears to be in order. If you have your keys and want us to go and take a look inside, then we will do that for you.'

'I don't know where our keys are. Leonard normally has one in his pocket, but we have been dressed in these ridiculous clothes and ours have obviously been stolen.'

'Would you like me to check to see if you have your keys on you?' he asks Leonard.

'Yes please' he replies.

Andy checks his pockets; well there is only one, which is full of holes. There are no keys. In fact there is nothing in there at all.

'Well I think it will be alright for now, but if you want us to get a locksmith in and then go and check the inside of the house over than we will.'

Leonard is about to agree to that, but Lucy suddenly lets her face cloud over.

'No, that won't be necessary. If it all looks alright, then it probably is. I wish I could remember how we got here. I can't even remember what we were doing before we blacked out.'

Andy finds this quite intriguing. Something in the way that Lucy has just reacted has told his detective's nose, that she suddenly realised that she didn't want them nosing around the house. That tells him that there might be something in there that might incriminate one or both of them. The fact it was her that reacted this way, suggests it might be something leading to her guilt. He has made a mental note of it, but that is for later.

He has a look at his watch. Most of the hour is up now. There are only a few minutes left before whatever Elizabeth is arranging will begin. The man in black is not with them. Andy actually wishes that he was. He rings him and asks if he will come here. He just will be happier if he is around. Thankfully he agrees to come down, but he wants to stand well back. He says he will look on from a distance.

The man in black arrives, but not from the direction of his house. He stands near to the church. There is only one other person standing there. The man in black has seen this person around town, but does not know his name. They discuss the situation in front of them briefly. It is briefly, but only because the hour is up.

Andy has just looked at his watch. The hour is up. Almost to the second; well it probably is exactly to the second, the situation starts to change. The end of the hour is heralded with a distant rumble of thunder. But the rumble continues for over a minute. Then as it dies away, there is a huge crack of thunder which lights up the sky. It is still daylight, but this lightning sends a silver streak all around. The sound of its crackle is right there, with them all. It has not gone away either. It arcs and sparks and continues to send streaks of lightning down. It is concentrated too, concentrated over this very part of town. In fact it is within the bounds that Elizabeth told Andy to screen off. The lightning stops and there is another crack of thunder. This time it is bang overhead.

Chapter 36 Reveal

The thunder booms on and on. If anything, the sound of it increases with every second that passes. It soon reaches the point when the decibels are causing some people to put their hands over their ears. Some are resorting to putting their fingers into their ears.

There are two people who cannot do this, Leonard and Lucy. For some reason, probably it is their vulnerability with being shackled to the railings; they are feeling the effects of the sound more than others. But then it really is bang overhead, over their heads. To them it really feels as if it is literally a few feet above their heads.

Then with the thunder still resounding in their ears; the lightning returns. Lightning forks strike the ground. They scorch the ground within several feet of where they are chained up. Even though Andy knows he has been told that no one will get hurt, this is something else. He'd not expected something like this to happen. He has to retreat to the relative safety of a patrol car. He is not the only one backing off. Every single pedestrian dives for cover. Some go into the Spar, others into the George. A few make a run for it towards their own houses. It is those people who are the first ones to find out just how localised these freak weather conditions are. As little as a quarter of a mile away makes a huge difference. They come out into a lighter world. They can still hear the thunder and see the lightning, but from even this little distance away, it sounds very tame. The thunder just sounds like a low rumble, albeit continuous. The lightning looks quite unassuming. If it could be viewed that way, it is like a gentle streak of lightning bolting to the ground, although they unable to see where it strikes.

Back in the centre of town, things have just changed again. The thunder is continuing, as is the lightning. But now the sky is darkening over even more. Darkening is not quite the correct word. Becoming blacker would be more precise now. It doesn't go all the way to be entirely black, but it has darkened significantly. Then the rain begins. It starts with a few heavy spots. The people who are indoors see this start with big spots hitting the windows. But this is not from the sky, this is from the spots of rain hitting the pavements and bouncing back up onto the glass. No sooner than the spots come, than the torrential rain follows merely seconds later, accompanied by a swirling wind. It is just possible to see through it, but that takes some effort.

Where Andy is sitting in the patrol car, he can just about make out Lucy and Leonard where they are still standing by the railings. He can see their faces and he can see that they are scared; scared at being exposed and unable to get away from where they are.

Then as the thunder relents a fraction, another sound comes to their ears. At first it sounds like wind whistling through a gap. It comes in waves, just like a wind would do, but this a wind of sound. The sound soon transforms from the whistling sound to words that can be defined. The first word that people hear quite clearly is "Leonard". At hearing his name, he looks even more frightened. He starts looking all around him, but there is no one that close. Then the whispering continues:

"Leonard takes a little bit here and a little bit there"

It repeats that phrase several times before moving on:

'Takes it from their pensions and puts it in his pot"

It repeats that several times on its own, before putting the two phrases together.

"Leonard takes a little bit here and a little bit there. Takes it from their pensions and puts it in his pot."

It repeats all this a few times and then moves on to the next bit.

"Every week many people die, so more for him to plunder from"

Again this part is repeated many times.

The words don't mean a lot to most of the people who can hear them. Everyone within the centre belt of the town is hearing these words. Only a few people understand where these words are targeted. Andy sitting in the patrol car; the man in black, who is now sheltering in the foyer of the church and of course Leonard, who has his eyes out on storks, as the whispering reveals more and more of what he thought only he knew he had done. Lucy is looking at his reaction. She quickly realises that she is not the only person to be holding a secret about their past. What she is really thinking about though, is what must surely be coming next; the revealing of her crimes; surely that is what will come next. But she has nowhere to go and until it actually happens, there may be a chance it won't.

"Ten years and more with just a little bit here and a little bit there. In time it becomes a lot; a lot that isn't yours"

The whisperer repeats the last bit, adding his name.

"In time it becomes a lot; a lot that isn't yours, Leonard"

The whisperer keeps repeating this phrase again and again for minutes. The whispering becomes louder in places and quieter in others. It isn't clear if the voice is that of a man or a woman; well not at first. It becomes louder where Lucy and Leonard are, but quieter in the buildings where people are sheltering.

Then the voice and the words quite clearly change. The words change to:

"For ten years and more I stole a little bit here and a little bit there. I stole from the pension fund payments of those recently deceased. I am guilty of this!"

Leonard hears the way the words have changed and then to his surprise, he realises that the whisperer has changed too. It is no longer the whisperer that started all this. The voice of the whisperer is now Leonard's.

Andy notices this too. The man in black notices the change, but is not aware whose the voice is. Andy has been recording as much as he can, but he suspects that with the sound of the thunder, the wind and the rain alongside the whispers, that nothing will be that clear. He doesn't want to stop to check it though.

Leonard's voice repeats his phrase, getting louder each time. It changes from a whisper to his own regular voice to, in the end, him shouting the words. Then as suddenly as it had all begun, everything stops. The thunder ceases, as does the lightning. The skies lighten some as the rain stops and the wind dies away.

Lucy is looking at Leonard with shock in her eyes. She had no idea he'd done this. Leonard for his part; is standing dejectedly. His eyes are to the ground and his shoulders are slumped. His general demeanour is of a defeated man, a man who has been found out. But he is still there and he is next to Lucy. He is also still chained to the railings.

All is peaceful for about a minute. Everything is still. Andy has ventured out of his patrol car, along with another officer. They stand beside the car and look over at Leonard and Lucy.

Then the whisper starts again. It is not Leonard's voice, but the voice of the whisperer.

'Leonard; it is time. Leonard; it is time.'

Again and again the whisperer repeats the words, until suddenly Leonard thrusts his hands out in front of him, as far as the shackles allow.

'Stop it, stop it! Stop these whispers. I did it; I stole all that money. Just stop it please!'

At that the shackles on his hands and his feet drop to the ground, but Leonard stands in the same position. He hasn't realised what has happened, but Lucy has. She knows for sure what is coming her way sometime soon.

'You're free of the shackles Leonard' she says to him. Step away, before it takes you back.

Andy and the police officer have seen him being freed and they quickly step forward.

'Is it true Leonard?'

His eyes are all around him. He is scared witless. He nods his head just a little bit.

'I stole from their pensions. I just did it because I could and then I couldn't stop. They didn't notice.'

From one set of shackles to another; the police officer reads him his rights and he then cuffs him. Andy radios in for a van to come and pick him up. There is still one person attached to the railings.

After the police officer has taken Leonard away, down towards the Bull Ring to wait for the van to come and collect him, Andy turns his attention to Lucy.

'Would you like to confess to something now too?'

He'd like to say what, but that would not help things. He can't reasonably explain how he knows what he knows. Lucy's face hardens and her eyes narrow. She is determined that she isn't going to admit to anything. After all how could they possibly have anything on her? Leonard has obviously somehow left a paper trail and someone has stumbled across it. Hers, she believes, has no such evident paper trail. People have been proved to have committed the murders of the people she'd killed; well that is what she believes. There is no way she is going to admit to anything, as they haven't got any proof. They have a confession from Maggie for the Wenlock deaths. That is what her head is telling her.

'I have no idea why I have been chosen. I had no idea that Leonard had committed those money thefts the whispers spoke about. He has never given any clue that he has committed a crime like that. I am only here like this, because he has done something.'

'Then why have you not been released like he has been?'

'I really don't know, but I have done nothing that I need to confess to.'

Andy has come across many people like Lucy in his time in the police force. They will deny everything, even it is blatantly clear that they have done something. These sorts of people have no conscience. Often they have no remorse either. They will stand there and stay calm, stay cold and remain in complete denial. It was worth a try in asking her, but she has looked like she would not be so easily got to as Leonard.

Then out of the blue a bolt of lightning strike the bars. The crackle of electricity sparkles in sound. It dances along the bars around where she is shackled, but it doesn't actually travel down her shackles. But it might just as well have done with her reaction. It makes her jump in surprise. It makes Andy take an involuntary step back too. Then another bolt of lightning strikes the bars by her feet. If she could have danced away she would have done. This time the sparks travel along the shackle and she feels a pulse of electricity coursing through her legs.

'For god's sake stop it. Can't you stop this? It's going to kill me. Set me free!'

'You know we have tried and can't. This is nothing to do with us.'

Before he can say another word to her; another bolt of lightning strikes the bars of the Guildhall.' This time the sparks go along the shackles and into her hands and arms. The tingle of it makes her jump in fright. Andy knows it is time he should move a little further away. It would appear that it is time for Elizabeth and Edmund to start their work on Lucy.

Chapter 37 Anne

But what happens next surprises him. As he steps away from her, she stands up straight and says to him:

'I have to have a sleep now.'

At that she closes her eyes and rests against the bars. All is as it was before the thunder, lightning, wind and rain had started, except that she is alone now, shackled to the railings of the Guildhall. Andy steps forward and speaks to her, but she does not respond. She is right out of it. He looks around him, but of course he cannot see anyone. He can't see Elizabeth and Edmund anyway, but there is no one else in view at this minute. He knows where the man in black was standing down by the church, but he can't see him either. In fact he hasn't seen him since he'd retreated to the patrol car, to get away from the weather.

The man in black is standing in the church doorway. The man he'd been standing with has gone inside the church and sat down on one of the pews. The man in black tries to see what is happening further up the road, but it isn't easy and from his position, he can't actually see Lucy and Leonard. He is pleased not to be directly in the firing line; being the one that people know is involved somehow.

Just before the sky lightens, a darkened figure walks in front of him and stops for a second. Instantly he knows who this is; he has seen them before. The black gown with the hood over her head is exactly the same as he'd seen her the first time. That time though, she had been a fleeting figure crossing his path. She hadn't stopped that time. It was only later that she let him find her and help her find herself, so to speak.

But today she has stopped in front of him. She has not turned towards him, but he knows it is her; he knows it is Anne. She knows she has his attention. It would be hard for him not to know she is standing there. She knows he can see her; he has always been able to.

As he steps out onto the path towards her, she turns briefly towards him and then away. That brief second is enough for him to be able to verify it is Anne. That is what she has done that for.

She walks quickly away; actually she glides more than she walks. He can already guess where she will be making for. The door opens to his touch and as he goes in and closes it behind him, he can see her climbing the stairs. He follows her up there and into the front room. She is already sitting on the bed, waiting for him to arrive. The chair is still there for him to sit on, so he does.

'It is very strange what is going on' she opens with.

The man in black agrees and then she continues.

'I have a feeling that I need to help you. Some paths appear to be crossing and I feel I can help you.'

'Can you see them?'

'Who do you mean?'

That pretty much answers his question. He spends the next few minutes explaining about what has happened so far, in this series of events. At the end of it all, she confirms that she cannot see Elizabeth and Edmund. Whatever it is that is going on in this town, it is apparent that they are from different sources. That is the only way he can label it. In a sense he thinks it is quite funny. With everything that they are able to do, Elizabeth and Edmund must have their limitations, as does Anne. What he wonders, but suspects he already knows the answer to, is whether they will be able to see Anne?

'I believe that she has an order of events that she must go through, to find herself and possibly Edmund. But I think it is just Elizabeth. Then she can be at rest. At least I hope she can then be at rest.'

Anne smiles at him. Other than it was the man in black who helped her, she also likes him a lot. That is why she is here, because she wants to help him. She has seen him a few times very recently and there has been something about him that appears to be stressed.

'She needs to find a cave.' Anne says 'I do not think it is my cave, but there are many up there. I have been there a lot since you found me. I have seen others. I think I know the one. She needs to find that one, to know where to go on to next, I believe.'

'Shall I go and find them and bring them back here?'

All the time they have been there, there has been nothing from outside. There has been no thunder to hear or lightning visible to them.

'It would be better for you if you were not seen looking for them. Do you know if there is a way of getting them to come, without you having to expose your position? I do not think it would be good for you to be seen in that part of town.'

'I do not know. It was the police detective who asked me if I would come down and observe. I have to admit I wasn't exactly keen. I will walk behind by the church and behind the Guildhall and see if I can see them standing on the other side of the road, where they usually stand.'

'Do not let others see you, if you can manage that.'

'I'll try not to.'

The man in black leaves her and goes down the stairs. The door opens again to his touch and as he leaves, it closes by itself. There is no one out on the street. Out here it is almost as if time has not moved on while he has been talking to Anne. He can see Andy standing on the road, roughly at the point where Lucy and Leonard are shackled. He thinks he can only see one of them. He thinks it is Lucy; Leonard appears to have gone.

He crosses over the Bull Ring and then cuts in towards the church entrance. Rather than walk across the front, he goes across the grass to the side and round the back of the church, and back down the other side, towards the back of the Guildhall. He carefully looks through the window and can see Lucy standing there. He can also see Andy a few paces away from her. Looking over a little, he can see Edmund standing behind the wall. He can't see Elizabeth. She could be anywhere.

He doesn't want to stay here too long. He is rather out in the open. He moves along the back of the Guildhall and then rather than go under the arch, he continues along Church Walk towards Barrow Street. There is still no one around when he reaches the end of Church walk. He looks left and right. The road is still blocked by the square, but other than that, everything is quiet. He decides to walk along towards his home. He has no idea where Elizabeth might be. She is probably doing something connected with Leonard and Lucy.

He has crossed over the road at The Raven corner, when he sees Elizabeth ahead of him. She is coming towards him. Even at this distance, he thinks he can see that she is relieved to see him.

He stops where he is and waits for her to approach him. She does so very quickly.

'Something has happened.' She has a concerned look on her face. 'I don't know why, but everything has just stopped. Lucy has said she wants to sleep and she has. She has just stopped. I don't know why. I do not know what is happening. Something else has taken over. I came to look for you, but you were not there.'

'I was there by the church, standing in the doorway. The policeman asked me to go
there. I think I may have the answer to why it has all stopped. May I ask you something?'

'Of course you can.'

'Have you seen anyone else while you have been here?'

'What do you mean? I am presuming you do not mean the people here in the town.'

'There is a girl who is dressed in a black cloak, with a hood over her head. Have you seen her?'

'No we have not. We would have known if we had, I am sure. Why who is this girl?'

The man in black gives her a brief resume.

'So you can see her, but she can't see us. And also we cannot see her either. That is most interesting.'

'She has come to me, as she wants to help me. I have told her what I know and she says you need to find a cave, so you can find your next move. She knows what it is like needing to be found. She wants to help me and she wants to help you.'

'Is she the one who whispers?'

'I don't think so, but I haven't asked her. I could understand if there was a certain type of person targeted. Anyway I think we need to go.'

'You are right. I will go and tell Edmund that we are going and that I have found you.'

'Are you sure you do not need Edmund with us?'

'I am sure of nothing I am afraid, but it would be wise to have someone looking over Lucy.'

The man in black looks at his watch. He stares at it for a few seconds and then looks at Elizabeth.

'Is it possible that time has stopped?'

'Anything is possible I suppose, why?'

'My watch has been at the same time for the last fifteen minutes I think. It is working, but just not moving on. I think we should hurry and I think we should have Edmund with us too. There is nothing going to happen while we are away.'

The man in black was going to walk back along Church Walk, but as they reach there, something inside of him tells him it is not necessary. As they reach the square they can see no one. There is not a soul in sight. Andy is no longer standing there. The only person either of them can see is Edmund and he has his eyes on Lucy. Lucy is just standing there with her eyes shut.

'Where is the Andy?' the man in black asks as he arrives.

'Those who were here just all turned suddenly and walked towards the George. They all filed in and the door closed behind them. It is as if they have been removed intentionally.'

'I believe they have. Come with us now. I have someone for you to meet, but you can't see them. Elizabeth will explain while we walk there. We will be going to the house. It is a place that she used too in her time. She is waiting there for us.'

'It must be time to look for and find the cave.'

'That is what she believes too. She says that you have to find it to be able to find the next place.'

The man in black walks quickly down Wilmore Street and when he reaches the door, he goes into the house. When he has climbed the stairs, he goes into the front room. Considering the fact that they can't see Anne and she can't see them, it is interesting that they are sitting side by side on the bed. What they have found out already, is that they can't hear each other either. This is going to be fun!

Chapter 38 Anne &

The man in black sits down on his chair. He finds it kind of amusing that he is sitting there with two sets of people from another time and he is the only one who can see everyone. But now isn't the time for those thoughts.

Thankfully everyone else can see him and hear him. Although they can't see each other, he does the introductions. He then goes through a brief resume with everyone. That way everyone knows what is what.

Anne then explains that she has been searching all the other caves that she can find. She says that she has done this, in case she might find other souls that needing releasing from their torment in time. The man in black has to relay all of this to Elizabeth and Edmund.

Then Anne says that she came across a cave not long ago. She had been sure that she had found all the caves that were to be found in this particular section, but then something drew her down the slope this day and after searching round a bit; she found a new entrance, or rather a very old one. She is almost certain it hadn't been there before when she'd searched this area.

The man in black has just relayed this information to Elizabeth and Edmund, when Edmund sits bolt upright. Even Anne can feel, if not see, the difference in the atmosphere of the room. She can also see by the way the man in black suddenly looks across beside her, that something has happened.

'I've remembered something' Edmund says 'It is about a cave.'

The man in black says to Anne that he will have to give her the information in catch ups as Edmund talks. And so with the relevant opportunities for the man in black to keep Anne up with them, Edmund tells his story.

"We were escaping from our settlement when we were going to be attacked. We'd gone up onto the escarpment, but I was told it wasn't safe even there. Elizabeth told me to go to the cave. We left the camp where we were. The others would not come with us. This is what I remember. Just as we started to make our descent, another sound came to our ears, the sounds of dogs barking. We are not talking about yappy dogs barking here; we are talking about serious barking, big dogs barking; big dogs with a serious agenda barking. That sound was far from welcome news.

I started down the slope. If, and it was still if, these dogs have picked up the scent from the settlement, they will easily be able to follow that scent up to where we had pitched the shelter. They will easily come across my uncle and the others still in the shelter. They no doubt will have heard what we have heard just now. I was guessing that they would now be panicking and wishing they had left when we did. But there was nothing I can do about that now. I had no way of changing that or helping them for that matter. They wouldn't know which way we had gone once out of their sight; that was why I didn't leave in the direction we were heading for.

Anyway, if these fighters have tracking dogs, then I and my parents were not much better off than my uncle and family. The dogs would soon track us down too. The scent leading away from the shelter they built would be just as easy to follow as the original scent from the settlement.

I knew there was no point in changing my plans at this stage, despite the dogs and the fighters being so close on our tails. And strangely enough I remember that I didn't feel panic, or the need to worry unduly about the outcome of our current dilemma. Part of the reason for that is that I hadn't heard a whisper. I knew that isn't something that I could be certain I would hear, but inside I was thinking that something would intervene to protect us.

The entrance to the cave is hard to find, if you don't know where it is. I also knew that the dogs would find it sure enough, but finding it and accessing the cave are two different tasks. I have been here before. I have played in this cave. I have experimented in this cave too, playing games. Planning a game in my head, a game where I am hiding from people. True, at the time I didn't think I would be hiding to save my life and the lives of my family, but nonetheless it would stand us in good stead for this threat, hopefully.

There was no doubt that the sounds were closer than they were. They were drifting over the top of the edge and down to where we were then, approaching the cave. If I was to guess where they were coming from, I would say the place where we left my uncle. But I really didn't have the time to think about that then.

I had to pull the moss away from in front of the cave. I'd matted a lot of it onto a set of sticks. Quickly I got Edith, followed by Edgar, to crawl in. The opening wasn't large, but they easily crawled through. I told them to keep going further in. They would have to crawl for about twelve feet before the cave opens up enough for them to at least sit and wait for me to guide them deeper. While they did that I busied myself with the task of covering the entrance up again.

Just before I pulled the moss cover up to put in place behind him, I felt something on my face. I looked up at the skies and was puzzled. The skies were clear. There were no clouds, at least none that I could see, but there were raindrops falling onto my face. Within a matter of seconds the drops had gone from the odd one or two that alerted me, to a constant volley of drops. In a few seconds more the heavens open and it started pouring with rain. It started battering down, with the drops bouncing off my face and the ground around me.

I realised that I had wasted more than enough time, precious seconds, looking up in the skies. I pulled the moss back into place as I crawled into the cave. I tied the corners onto the crude hooks I had made for this purpose when playing his game. I then crawled back a foot or so and started to grab the rocks I had stockpiled in the small alcove just inside the cave. I filled in the entrance to the cave quickly so that the gap was filled. I then pulled the bigger rocks out of the alcove and slotted them into place.

They have their own position in the entrance so that I could do it quickly. Maybe all along, this moment was what I had played his game for.

With the rocks in place, I moved backwards deeper into the cave towards my parents. The rocks I had just placed were tightly in place and slotted together in a way that is impossible to push out from within, or pull out from outside. I could hear the rain falling as I moved backwards. It sounded as if it was falling harder than before, harder than I can ever remember it falling. It has rained a couple of time while I had played in there before, but nothing like this hard.

I didn't think of it at that moment, it only came to me later, but this heavy rain would do a tremendous job of wiping out the trail of their scent. It was a shame that it hadn't started to fall just a few minutes earlier, but then it may not have changed things much.

I joined my parents and then squeezed past them. We could go deeper in the cave on our hands and knees. We didn't have to crawl now. We turned a corner a few yards further in. I whispered back to them that I was going to stop. It was pitch black in there and there was nothing that we could see. I was six feet beyond the corner when I stopped. I could feel my mother's hand on my foot. I stood up, feeling above me to make sure I had the right place. I did have. I knew that because my hands didn't have anything to stop them going up through the gap. I knew the gap is big enough for me to easily fit through as I had been through it before. I only hoped it would be big enough for Edgar and Edith too.

I told them I was going up as I did so. I told them to carefully follow me through. Once I was up, I moved to one side. Edith came up next. She was up with him with ease. I told her to go over, to make room for Edgar to come up too. It was harder for him to get through the gap, but he did it without too much difficulty. Once he was through, I got him to help me with my plug for the gap. Again I had used a frame made of wood tied together. To this frame I had fixed some thinnish flat rocks. The frame was wider than the gap we have come up through. In the dark we slotted the frame into place. I then took the stout wooden poles I had prepared and wedged them into place. One end slots over the edge of the frame, while the other end is wedged against the passage ceiling. The gap has been filled successfully and it wouldn't be easy to break through it, well I thought it was well plugged and not easy to find. When I fitted it originally, I just slotted it in from below. It fits snugly with the rest of the passage ceiling and without a strong light it wouldn't be easy to spot if you didn't know it was there.

Satisfied I had done what I needed to, I told Edgar to move over to where Edith was waiting. I carefully manoeuvred over the hatch and followed him. The space is about six feet across. It is nearly high enough to be able to stand up, but not quite. It goes no further than this.

I continued to talk in a whisper. The one thing I had no idea of, was how far our voices might carry. I told my concern about this and we talked in a very low whisper. We couldn't hear any noise carrying through to us from the outside. We couldn't hear the rain, if it was still raining; it was."

Edmund stops talking. I relay the last piece to Anne. Anne then tells me that this sounds like the cave that she came across. You had to crawl in and there was an alcove with some stones. But she said she hadn't found the hole in the ceiling like Edmund has just described, but she still thinks that this is the cave they are looking for. She admits that she didn't think to try the ceiling at all for a secondary hiding place.

When everyone is up to this point, the man in black says he thinks this time is for them to go to the cave. Edmund and Elizabeth have to go there, so this is all meant to be. He gets up from his chair and goes down the stairs. He looks to see if the others are following him; they are.

The street outside is quiet, but the light has gone some. It is not dark, but it isn't as light as it was; very strange

Chapter 39 Cave

'I think I am going to need a torch.'

The man in black can see they are puzzled by what he has just said. He explains to them.

'We are going into a cave, hopefully. I can't see in the dark. I don't know about the rest of you.'

'I can probably see more than you' Anne says. 'I am always in the dark.'

'It will be very dark in there. I am not sure how much we will be able to see in there.' Edmund has said this.

'I do not know either' Elizabeth says.

'So we'll go back to my house and pick up a couple of lights. I will hold both of them if you cannot.'

The man in black goes into his garage to retrieve a couple of lights from in there. He does not really want to go into the house to see what state his wife is in. It would be weird to see her, if time has stopped. He checks that both torches are working well. He grabs some spare batteries while he is at it. They are ready for the off.

They go right out of the drive and then up the footpath that leads to the primary school and the top end of Racecourse Lane. At the end of the path, they turn left and then out onto the main road. The man in black crosses over by the graveyard and they walk down the left hand side of the road. All is quiet and nothing passes them on the road. They don't see anyone on the pavements either.

At the Gaskell, corner they follow round to the left and over the Ludlow Road. They don't bother crossing over, even though there is no pavement on this side of the road after the Vet's entrance. There isn't any traffic, so it isn't a problem. They turn left onto the Stretton Road and then after a while take a right. Five minutes later they are on the Edge. Anne is now leading the way. She veers off the path after a while and makes her way through the undergrowth towards destination. She is having no trouble with the going and Elizabeth and Edmund are trouble free too. The man in black is struggling to make his way through. He is behind the other three and the gap widens between them. The light of his torch keeps them in his view. That is until Anne goes down the other side. The other two follow her down. The man in black is there about a minute after them.

It is not easy going down this slope. It wouldn't have been easy in daylight, let alone in the dark. By the time he gets down to where the others are; he is only just in time to see the last one of them crawling through a hole in the side of the slope. He presumes the other two are already in there.

With a bit more difficulty than they had done, the man in black crawls through the hole. On the other side he has to crawl for several feet. His light picks out the alcove where there are rocks stored. His light also picks out the others ahead of him. When he reaches them, he can get onto his hands and knees.

'We can't see very much here' Elizabeth says.

He shines his torch along and can see there is a corner. He makes for it and turns the corner. Edmunds tells him to stop soon after he has turned the corner and look above him. The man in black shines his light at the ceiling. There is an opening and so he stands up and manages to climb through the gap. It is a bit tight. Anne is already up here as soon as he turns to shine his light around him. Edmund comes up next followed by Elizabeth. Edmund moves furthest in and waits for the others to join him. Anne has stayed by the opening. This is as far as she wants to go. She has already seen that there are no souls to be found and saved up here. In fact she is finding it a bit uncomfortable in here. She doesn't know why that is.

'I have to go now' she says to man in black. 'There is no need for me to stay; now I have shown you where this is.'

'Thank you' he replies and relays the message to the other two. He knows it will be easier having a conversation now.

Anne disappears down the opening. Edmund is looking all around him and Elizabeth is watching him.

'There must be some reason why you have to come to this place first.' He says when Edmund doesn't say anything while he looks around.

'I agree, but I haven't a clue why that is. I just can't believe it is just a place I have to see.'

He continues to just keep looking round him. It is clear he is remembering his time there when they were escaping their attackers. The other two let him do this without asking any more questions. They don't want to disturb his concentration. There is nothing to rush for.

They have been there maybe five or ten minutes with nothing coming to mind for Edmund. The other two have sat down a little bit away from him, to give him room to look and think.

A whistling sound comes through from the outside. It is like the wind is blowing through the entrance of the cave. They can't feel anything, but they can hear it. All three of them look towards the opening. There is nothing to see. The whistling continues for a couple of minutes, before it changes into a whisper. At first the words are unintelligible. Then they become a little clearer.

'Lost in the dust and never found, lies a small disc, precious and round.'

It takes a few repetitions for it to become clear enough to understand fully. There is quite an echo in the cave and the whisper is distorted by this. But eventually they get it all and Edmund says it out loud.

'Lost in the dust and never found, lies a small disc, precious and round.'

As soon as he says it out loud, the whispering recedes and is gone completely a minute later.

'Does it mean anything to you?' Elizabeth asks him.

'I can't make any connection, but something somewhere says I should know. It was dark when we were here. We did not have any light. We wouldn't have used one anyway, in case it gave away our hiding place.'

Then his face brightens as a memory comes to him.

'Edgar said he couldn't remember where he lost it. He said that in the rush to get away, he might not have brought it with him. He said it was some time before he even realised that he didn't have it with him. We looked around our camp, but in the end gave up. It is small and we didn't know where to look.'

'Did you come back here to look?'

'No, he always said it was either he hadn't brought it with him, or he had lost it near the shepherd's hut.'

'The whisper suggests that we should look in here' the man in black says.

He shines his torch around the cave. The walls are smooth. The floor is quite smooth too. There certainly isn't any, or much, dust on the floor where Edmund is. They check the floor at that end of the cave anyway, but come up with absolutely nothing. Each one of them tries it in turn, but nothing is found.

'Can you remember anything about that day you came up here with Edgar?'

'He struggled to get through the opening. It was quite tight for him, but he made it through without too much difficulty. Then he helped me cover the opening. I had made a cover and he helped me put that in place. It was easier with two. He then joined Edith.'

'The cover has not survived the passage of time, but that is of no great surprise.'

The man in black moves over to the opening.

'The cover was over the other side. I was in there and Edgar stayed this side and helped me move it.'

'What did you do with the cover when you eventually left here?'

'We left it over there, the other side of the opening. We did that so it was ready for us to rush into here, if the need arose. But it didn't.'

The man in black is nearest, so he carefully goes over to the opening. On the far side the floor is quite dusty. He thinks about it and realises it is probably what is left of the cover Edmund had made. He feels through the dust with his hand, trying to do it methodically. After the first go he has nothing to show for his efforts.

'What size is this disc?' He had been thinking maybe a couple of inches round or something like that.

Edmund shows him by making a shape with his thumb and index finger. The size he is showing is about half an inch in diameter.

The man in black has another feel. This time he takes it more slowly. He very nearly misses it, but he doesn't. Something moves under the sweep of his fingers. He stops and marks the spot.

'You need to check this' he says to Edmund.

Edmund makes his way over and the man in black makes room for him to search. He shows him the spot on the floor. Edmund carefully takes up the search.

'It was on something. He used to wear it round his neck.'

'Was it a chain?'

'No, it was nothing as fancy as that. It was on a piece of cord we made from something.'

He stops talking as his fingers feel what the man in black had. It only takes him a few seconds to prize his item away from the floor, under the dust. He holds it up in front of him. It is dusty, so they can't see much.

The whisper returns very briefly with the words:

'It is time.'

It whispers those words just the one time and is gone again.

'I think we should go now' Elizabeth says. 'We have what we came for and we need to look at it more carefully and in better light. Can you remember anything special about it?'

'To be honest I can't. I never took a close look at it. It was just something he wore round his neck.'

The man in black goes down the opening followed by Elizabeth. Last down is Edmund. He is grasping the disc in one hand. He has one last look at the cave. He already knows he will not come here again. When all three of them are on the outside again, they hear something moving from within. Within seconds the hole they had crawled through has been filled with rocks. They see that they knit together perfectly. Then a few seconds after that, moss has covered those rocks. There is no evidence of the cave being there at all. Without looking at it any more, they make their way to the top of the escarpment. They walk back through the undergrowth onto the main path and then eventually they reach the Stretton Road. A few minutes later they are back in the house in Sheinton Street. As they close the front door, the man in black notices that it gets lighter again outside. He stands for a moment in the hallway, before climbing the stairs. It is only a few seconds before he hears a car drive by outside. The world is back on the move again.

He is confused, but he does not have an explanation for what has just happened. He climbs the stairs and goes into the front room. Edmund has a bowl of water and a cloth. He is busy cleaning the disk they found in the cave.

Chapter 40 Disc

Edmund is still sitting there with the bowl of water on his lap. Elizabeth is watching him with interest. They notice the man in black coming into the room and sit down on his chair. It is a few minutes later that Edmund stops. It is clear from the look on his face that he is not happy with what he has achieved.
'I just can't clean it up. It is like there is a coating on it.'
'What are you using in that bowl?'
'Just water, what did you think it would be?'
'Maybe a little detergent added to that might make a difference. Nothing too strong though and then after it has soaked for fifteen minutes, you can scrub it gently with a soft brush.'
'We can try that. Do you have some?'
'I'll go and get some.'
The man in black leaves them and intends to go home for it, but as the Spar shop is still open he goes in there. He buys some washing up liquid and a soft toothbrush. That should do the trick.
Back in the house he makes up a weak solution in the bowl and then Edmund drops the disc in. They sit there watching it for fifteen minutes. Nothing changes to the eye

though. When the time is up, Edmund takes it out. The man in black hands him the brush and he gently starts to brush the disk with it.

It certainly has done the trick. The detergent has loosened the coating and the brush is removing the bits of dust from the nooks and crannies of the markings on both sides. When he has finished, he wipes it carefully dry with another cloth. Who knows where they have appeared from?

He holds it in front of him and inspects the one side, before turning it over. The look on his face is totally different from the look on Elizabeth's face. His look is of wonder and relief on finding a very long lost family heirloom. Her face is one almost of shock. She was not expecting to see what she has seen.

Edmund notices the man in black looking at Elizabeth. He too turns to look at her.

'What is it?'

'I've seen that before?'

'My father used to wear it. Surely you remember him wearing it? Edmunds says.

'I don't remember him wearing it. If he was, then I think his clothes must have hidden it from view.'

'You are right, they would.'

The room is quiet for a few minutes while Elizabeth tries to recall where she has seen it.

'It is the side with the two figures on that I remember.'

And then the light comes on in her eyes.

'Where did your father get it from?'

'He dug it out of the ground one day. He was turning the ground, ready to plant some seeds. He saw it and wore it round his neck from that day.'

'There were two of them. My mother had one and my father had one. I don't suppose you know where your father found his?'

'It would be somewhere close to our settlement I guess' he replies.

'That would be my father's one.'

'I think I know what we have to do' the man in black says quietly 'but knowing it and doing it, are going to be two different challenges.'

'We need to find the other one, don't we?' Elizabeth says.

'Yes, the one your mother would have been wearing.'

'But I have no idea what happened to the rest of my family, after I was washed away. I have no idea where they would have gone and where they would have lived. Then I would need to know who she gave it to and where they went and so it goes on. We do not have any information to go on.'

'I know it sounds as if the task is impossible' the man in black says 'but it is obviously meant for you to be able to find it. So I think that it will be simpler than you think it will be to achieve. Saying all that, I have absolutely no idea where to begin.'

'We have to keep this one safe.'

'I have some fine cord at home which would be good for that. It should fit through the hole and you can wear it, like your father did.'

He realises as he says it, that they could both lay claim to their father wearing it. He leaves the conversation open. They don't appear to be bothered by it. They all relax into a comfortable silence, as they try to give it some thought about where the other disk might be.

Then the silence is broken by a scream coming from somewhere outside. The man in black looks out of the window, but can't see anything. He rushes back through the room and down the stairs. Elizabeth and Edmund have gone too. When he reaches the street, he can still hear the screaming. It is coming from the Guildhall direction. He runs as fast as he can towards there. As he approaches he can tell who the screaming is coming from. It is Lucy. She has come to again. She is thrashing around against the shackles, but obviously without any success.

'You all think you are so smart. But I was smarter than all of you put together. Yes I saw opportunity and took things that weren't mine. David Petrich was going to die anyway. He had it all and then suddenly he decides to go back to his roots. He had no family. I know, as I saw his will. It was delivered to my address by mistake. As soon as I opened the letter without thinking, I knew what I had to do. I couldn't let him just walk away with all that money. And then Mary fell into my lap in a supermarket car park. I saw it as a sign that I was meant to do it again. She was alone apart from her sister and her family here. But when she came here, they didn't want to know her. I knew then that no one would miss her. She was so easy to kill. I should have known it was only a matter of time before they dug up that floor and found her.'

She has been screaming all this at the top of her voice. She stops for a breather. The man in black can see Andy and another officer recording what she is saying, on their phones. They are making no effort to go and calm her down. Why would they? She is in the middle of her confession. She gathers herself again and then continues, shouting rather than screaming the words this time.

'I blame my mother. It was her who wouldn't have me live with her. My father wouldn't either. They both hated me. So I would have done the same to her when she wanted my half of the money my father left us. I was ready to, but she did it herself. Then years later, bloody Leonard falls in love with this place. I thought it would all be alright, because I look different. I am older and I have spent money changing things. But then there is always one person who notices things, just my luck. But then there were two people who were so horrible, that they made finding a solution to my problems so easy. They were so full of themselves and their own self-importance; they were so easy to get to. Setting it all up just fell into place. They thought they had something on me, but I turned that back onto them. How stupid they turned out to be in the end. And then all this happens. What is all this? Why am I in shackles and these dreadful clothes?'

Then suddenly with everyone looking on, waiting for the next bit of the tirade, things change in front of their eyes. But they don't actually see the change, as it is almost instantaneous. One second she has stopped talking, as if she is going to be taking another breather and the next she is standing there in her own clothes and more importantly, no shackles.

Lucy is the first by a mile to notice the difference. Importantly Andy and the other police officer have their eyes down at the vital second or two. The man in black is watching from opposite the church door.

It is almost as if Lucy knew it was going to happen, or maybe she always was ready for any circumstance; ready to take advantage whenever she could. She knows where everyone is standing. She's taken in everyone's position. She takes the only route of escape that is feasible, the one where she guessed there is no one there.

Lucy is off. For a woman of her age, she is agile and fast. Before hardly anyone realises she is free, she is already making for the archway beside the Guildhall. By the time anyone has started to move to chase her, she is through there and out the other side. In her head she is trying to plan her escape route. She reckons at best she only has a slim chance of escape, but a slim chance is much better than her other prospects; the rest of her life behind bars.

She darts to the left and then across the church green. The man in black watches her go. His days of running that fast are long gone. He moves to the left towards the Bull Ring. He might be able to see which way she goes, if she comes out by the Priory Hall. By this time Andy and the other police officer have started to chase her. The man in black sees her come out by the Priory Hall and take a right towards the Priory. She has a good start on her pursuers. The police officer is next to appear by the entrance to Priory hall. He looks left towards the man in black. He points away from him. The officer turns and starts running again, but he has lost even more vital seconds. Andy appears next, but he is not made for running. He too looks left and sees the man in black. He points again away from him, but Andy does not resume his chase. He is talking into his phone. He starts walking towards the man in black. He is not looking very amused by what has happened.

'Did you know that was going to happen?'

'What makes you think I know what is going to happen?'

'Your friends must have known.'

'I don't believe that they did. We were somewhere else when she started screaming. They came out with me, but I don't know where they went. I don't think they actually control things, they are just here.'

'Where are they now?'

'I don't know. I didn't see them when I came across the Bull Ring. I stopped opposite the church, because I could see you and your officer over the road from Lucy. Then as she ran off, I came down here and stood in the Bull Ring. That is all I know.'

'Come up with me and see if they are still where they were before.'

The man in black reluctantly goes with him, but when they reach the square they are nowhere to be seen. But Andy isn't going to give up on this so easily.

'Where were you when the screaming started?'

The man in black hesitates for a few seconds, but he knows he will have to say.

'We were in the house in Sheinton Street.'

'Let's go and take a look then.'

But when they get there the front door is locked. They can't gain access.

'I would say that means they are not in, or at least I am not allowed to go in. I think it is the former of those though.'

Andy turns away, as more police start to arrive.

Chapter 41 Lucy

Lucy knows the town better than the police officer who is chasing her. She is unaware of how many people will be after her, but she presumes that there will be the two policemen and possible some others.

Because of the Monday walks and other walks that she takes in and round about the town, Lucy probably knows these areas better than most people do too.

She knew when she made her escape that she needed to get off the main tracks as soon as she could. To go towards High Street would have been senseless. To try to go towards and along Barrow Street would have been pretty much the same scenario. That just left going to her right where that man was standing. Although he is probably a similar age to hers, she did not want to risk getting slowed down by someone when there was the chance to take a different route that should be people obstacle free.

So having taken this route, she turns her mind to thinking about where she should go. Of all ways, this direction is the least likely for her to come across someone, but that isn't enough. Give them a few minutes and they will get organised. She needs to be off the main tracks well before then.

As she turns the corner where the car park is for the Priory, she briefly thinks about cutting up the footpath to the left, by the field where they sometimes keep the Highland cows. That path splits after maybe thirty metres, with the left part going up towards the old station and the right hand path going along two sides of the field before it comes out on the old railway line. The problem with taking either of those tracks; is that she will be out in the open. She will be very visible to her pursuers and they could get people to cut her off.

She disregards taking that option and keeps going. The gates to the Priory are locked, as it is after closing time. Just after that there is a gate into the field on her left and a metal gate to the right. The left again will leave her in the open, unless she hides behind the hedge. That protection will not keep her from capture for long. She needs to keep going, so she clambers quickly over the metal gate. She hugs the right hand side as she runs along inside there. It doesn't take her long to know that she is out of sight from the road. She doesn't stop though, but she keeps going.

She could do with getting some things from the house, but there are a few problems associated with that. Firstly she doesn't have the key. Leonard normally carries a door key. Then there is also the point that they will keep a watch on the house, just in case she goes back there. The key issue she can get over. She has a spare back door key planted in a safe place, at the bottom of the garden. It would be so good if she could just have five minutes in the house, to gather a few things. She could get her wallet, her spare phone, some extra cash from the safe and some different clothes, more suitable for escaping in and keeping unnoticed. But that is not for this very moment. That is for later when they may think she has kept going and isn't still in the area.

She has a pretty good idea where she will go now. There is a place she found one day while wandering. She would often go out on her own when she needed to have some time on her own; some time to think things through. She wouldn't always stick to the paths and she has been here before. She has walked along the wall at the back of the Priory before. But in places that will leave her in the open, so she takes advantage of the cover the trees provide, just away from the wall. It is in the middle of the thicker set of trees that she has her place. She likes trees and always has done. They take her back to when she was young. She had her own special hiding place back in those days and she has her own one here.

She found it by chance, partly because she was remembering those bad old days. She just wondered if there could be a place like that here and so she looked. She was in no hurry that day and no one would have thought anything about her wandering around the trees again and again, trying to see if there was anywhere. And luckily for her, how that stands her in good stead today.

Something inside her told her there would be a place; a place for someone like her, who knew where to look. And so there was, not that she had ever thought she would need to use it like she had in the old days. If you didn't know it was there, then you would never know about it. She was sure when she first crawled in, that even the local kids hadn't found this place. There would have been signs and there weren't any.

Just before she reaches there the heavens open and the rain comes down really hard. Luck must be on her side, as that will make it harder for them to track her. She crawls in and covers the entrance with the stuff she'd put there on a previous visit. She had thought that she might come here some day for a place to think peacefully, so she had sort of prepared things ready for that day. She hadn't gone as far as putting any provisions in there, which for today turns out to be a shame, but not a serious shortcoming. She is pleased to find out that it is dry, but she already knew that really, because the ground was dry and hard when she found it. She reckons she should be safe for a while here, at least until it gets dark and maybe further into the night.

The only thing she can hear where she is; is the rain falling hard. There is a little breeze, but it is mainly the rain she can hear. What she doesn't want to hear are the sounds of human voices and the sounds of dogs. Neither of those would be good news.

It takes the police officer ages to finally admit that he has no idea which way she has gone. Her cause had been helped by him seeing someone on the footpath that goes along by the fields opposite the Priory. He had gone up that way, thinking it was Lucy, but by the time he got to the railway footpath, that person had long gone out of sight. He reckoned they had probably gone to the right towards Farley Halt and that is the way he went. But they could have gone straight over and up the steps by the cricket shed, or gone left back towards the station houses. Or they could have gone right and then left and into the Windmill Hill field, or taken either of the paths back onto the lane down to the mill. The options were almost endless the further he went. By the time he realised he was well and truly on the wrong path, Lucy had got clean away. The runner that he had seen had done a right and a left and was almost home again after their 5k run.

It is not deemed to warrant the use of the police helicopter. Another incident elsewhere has taken precedence for its usage anyway. The same incident has taken the dogs and their handlers in that direction too. Anyway the heavy downpour will have made it much harder to track her and as there isn't rain where the other incident is, they go in that direction.

Andy has several officers assisting him, but he already knows he has lost her for now. There is a chance she will try to get back to her house, but he thinks that is unlikely in the circumstances. He thinks she would be too smart to do that. Anyway, he has found out that Leonard has their door key. Thankfully for Lucy, he has forgotten about the key in the garden, if he ever knew about it. It was something Lucy did, as she had been locked out at times by her mother.

A police car is stationed on Barrow Street, just along from their house. The search is wound down for now at about midnight. Andy has been back to see the man in black. He asks him if he has seen Elizabeth and Edmund since Lucy escaped, but he says he has not. He had come home after talking to Andy and has been there since and no, they have not been to see him either. Andy calls it a day too and goes home; rather disgruntled with the way the day has ended. How could he let her get away like that? But they just hadn't been expecting the shackles to disappear like that, straight after she stopped talking. He is going to be in for a dressing down from upstairs probably for this. The only argument on his side; is that nothing that has happened in Wenlock recently would count as being normal.

Lucy waits until just after 3 o'clock. The rain has let up for a while, but now it is coming down again in sheets. She leaves the safety of her hidey hole and walks close to the wall, round to the back of the nursery. Over into the nursery poses not too much problem. Then she walks past the shed and onto the path leading to Barrow Street. She is careful when she gets to the top. As soon as she looks out to the left, she can see the light on in the car, further along the road. She knows immediately what that is. The question now is, whether it is going to be the only one watching her house. The answer is probably, but not definitely.

She turns round and makes her way back to the nursery and back over towards where her place in the trees is. But she doesn't go there. She keeps close to the back of the properties, going over whatever obstacles lie in her way, until she reaches the back garden of her property. She knows how to get over into her garden. She has done it before. It is dark and she is careful to make no noise as she approaches the place where her key is hidden. It takes her less than a minute to retrieve it and approach the back of the house. She can see with what little light there is; that there is no one watching the back. She opens the back door and quietly walks in. She can't switch on any lights, but she knows this house and she knows where the things she needs are. It is just a shame that the police car is outside. Otherwise she could take the car and drive to her special car hire place and get another car. But there are other ways of getting away.

She packs what she needs into the backpack she uses for long walks. She has a spare set of clothes, her passport, not that she will use it. She has her wallet and what cash was in the safe. She has everything she needs to help her evade capture for as long as possible. More importantly she has what she needs to gain access to more funds; funds that Leonard knows nothing about; funds that she has acquired from her criminal deeds over the years and that she keeps separate from her day to day monies.

Chapter 42 Lucy

Lucy has a look out of her bedroom window. She is very careful not to show herself to anyone who might be watching. But the only possibility in that direction; is the officer in the parked car. Where he is just along the road, he will have no chance of being able to see her. It is still raining very hard. It is much harder than when she came in. It will be hard to leave the warm and the dry to go back out into that weather again. Even with her waterproof on, it will be unpleasant to say the least. A very long time ago she spent several days out in the open, but it wasn't as wet as this is. She knows she needs to get away from here really and the further away the sooner the better. For every junction on the road she passes, the possible destinations increase and the chances of them tracking her reduce. Doing that on foot will be slow and have a high risk. If she could just get away in a car, then she would be much safer much sooner. Then of course if she were to get away in a car, she would be able to carry more; take more with her. But the policeman in the car would notice her pulling out of the drive and then the game would be up.

But the thought stays with her. She decides not to waste her time while she is there. She takes a small case down from on top of the wardrobe and starts to put more clothes out on top of the bed. All the time she is keeping her ears well pricked for the sound of someone coming into the house. She doesn't really count that as something that is going to happen. Her belief is that they think she has run off and is trying to put as much distance as she can between her and Wenlock. She packs it all in the case and then takes the backpack and the case downstairs. She puts the backpack on, so that if she has to run she has it with her. The small case she puts in the hall by the cupboard door.

She needs something to drink and some food would go down well too. She does two things with that in mind. She makes a sandwich to eat now and then she also prepares some to take with her. That will mean she won't have to find food on the way, whichever way she departs.

With all that done, she looks out to see what the weather is doing. It is just the same, maybe even worse. The wind has sprung up again too. She is in two minds what to do. Getting this wet with no place to get dry again is not a good thought. She doesn't really want to go back to her hiding place; her need is to move away from here. If she doesn't, there is a good chance they will find her in the morning. On top of that she is tired and she needs some sleep. None of this is ideal. Does she dare risk taking a couple of hours sleep in the house before leaving?

She goes and has another look at the car out on the street. It hasn't moved and then it is only speculation on their part that she might as an outside chance come here; not something they really think she will do.

She decides to risk it. She doesn't go upstairs, but goes into the dining room, which is at the back of the house. She draws the curtains and lies down on the carpet. She is asleep before she even gets a chance to set an alarm on her phone. When she opens her eyes three hours later, she is in a bit of a panic. It has started to get light outside. It is still early though, but not ideal, as she could be seen easily in this light and more so when full daylight comes. One good thing is that it has stopped raining and the wind has died down. She is annoyed that she has overslept, but at the moment it hasn't cost her freedom. She goes to check on the police car; it is still there. Surely it won't be long before he gets relieved. But then maybe they did that while she was asleep. She really needs to get away from here fast and fast means by car. Then an idea strikes her. It might work, it might not. It might backfire terribly, but she decides it is worth a go. Now the question is; which phone should she use for this? She decides against using the house phone and she doesn't want to use her spare mobile, so she risks using her ordinary mobile.

She dials 999 and asks for the police. She says she has been woken by a woman screaming. She thinks it is the same woman that was screaming last evening by the Guildhall. She gives her name as Mary Horner in Southfield Road. She then cuts the call and runs through to the front of the house to see if what she thinks might happen; does.

It takes less than a minute for the car to move. It does a quick U-turn and races off, away towards town. She doesn't waste a second. She has the car keys already in her hand. She grabs her case and goes out the back door. She doesn't waste time locking it. She opens the driver's door of the car and throws her case and backpack over to the passenger side, before she scrambles in as quickly as she can. She fumbles with the key, trying to get it into the ignition, but manages it soon enough. The engine fires on the first turn. It is a new car, so that is not a surprise. She reckons she has already taken a minute to get this far. She needs to be out of the drive and on the road. The police car could return any second. It probably won't, but it could and she doesn't need that.

She doesn't rev the engine, but pulls forward until she is at the roadside. She is out onto the road in a second and has turned to the left. The car picks up speed steadily so as not to attract attention, but there isn't anyone out walking yet. She turns the corner at the end of Barrow Street and puts her foot down some more. So far so good, is all she is thinking?

One part of her wants to drive as fast as she can, but she manages to keep her eagerness to put distance between her and Wenlock to the back of her mind. Escaping is the most important thing. How long has she got before they realise she rang the police and how long before they realise her car has gone? She doesn't know the answer to either of those.

She makes it to Broseley alright. She had taken the Barrow Road. She turns right at the cross and then down over the Severn and up the other side. She's driven this route before, some time ago. In her head she knows where she is heading for and the route she is going to take to get there. It is a route that avoids the main roads. On the negative side, it will take her longer to get there. On the positive side, it will be much safer and she will be less likely to be noticed, particularly by road cameras.

She stops after an hour, to make a phone call. She'd switched her normal mobile off after making the 999 call. There is a good chance they would be ringing her back on that number when they don't find the woman. And also if she has it on, they will be able to track her movements. She still has the phone, but that is all. She makes this call on her spare mobile. She has used this car hire service before. There are no awkward questions to be answered. At a price, she will have some new wheels in less than an hour. Then she can really turn her mind onto a new destination. If she is lucky, she might even be able to change her identity.

The changeover goes smoothly. Her car is now parked up in a garage where she has retrieved her rental car. It is legal, but pretty much untraceable. She has paid the fee for the one week hire in cash. It isn't cheap, but she already knew that. Anonymity comes at a price.

She remembers something as she is planning where to go, half an hour after picking up the car. In films; when people are running away, they always seem to run up. They run up in a building, or they make for the top. But when they get there; there is nowhere for them to go. She has that conscious thought, as she sits eating a sandwich in a lay-by. She sips on her soft drink in between bites of sandwich. The question currently running through her mind is: are you better going to a big town or city? Or are you better going to a small town in the country? The bigger place is probably better, as you are less likely to be noticed. Someone new would stand out in a small town or village. That makes up her mind. She decides that she might as well go for the biggest in the country.

She hasn't got a map book and she doesn't want to use the motorway, or even the dual carriageways. She still wants to use smaller roads. Her geography isn't too bad and so when she starts off, she takes decisions at junctions, based on her limited knowledge. She knows it won't be the most direct route, but in general she is making for the capital. She wonders as she drives steadily along in her car, whether they have discovered she has hoodwinked them. Someone will be in for a dressing down, but she doesn't care about that. At the moment she is still free and evading capture. She will stay somewhere quiet for two or three days and then make her way to where she has her safety deposit box, with everything she needs to make another life. She has done it before and she will do it again.

Back in Wenlock, there is no one around when the police car arrives in Southfield Road. He drives around for a few minutes, before being joined by another two cars. It is probably ten or fifteen minutes after that when they find out the address given by the caller is not occupied by someone of that name. There is no Mary Horner at this address. The cars race back round to the house in Barrow Street. At first they notice nothing different. That officer had not been round the back of the house. Lucy's car had been round the back. Leonard's car is in the garage. They see the car in the garage, through the window and they don't realise there was another car. It is only an hour and a half later when Andy arrives on the scene, that the car is missed. By that time she has long gone and in truth she is not far away from having swopped it for her rental car.

The trail is properly cold now. When they find the back door unlocked and obvious signs that she has been there, then things go from bad to worse for the officer and Andy. She could literally be anywhere. They question Leonard as to where she is likely to have gone, but he really doesn't know. He tells them that she has always been in the habit of going off for a few days. She doesn't tell him where and he doesn't ask.

Chapter 43 The man in black

He knows something has not gone to plan when he walks along Barrow Street towards town in the morning. There is quite a bit of activity at the house where Lucy and Leonard live. Thankfully he doesn't see Andy. He really doesn't want another session of his questions. He makes a mental note to walk the long way home, to avoid any possible meeting. That isn't to say that Andy won't be in the town anyway.

It would also be good if Elizabeth and Edmund aren't around too. He is slightly curious about where they have gone and what they might be doing. It has seemed so far as if he has had to be involved in everything, so it is probably only going to be a matter of time before his services are required again. He does what he has come down town to do and is ready to go back. Something nags at him, that maybe he should just make a check on the house in Sheinton Street, but when he does, he finds that the door is still locked. He makes his way home.

The rain starts again early that evening. The police presence has been reduced in the town, after a day of hunting locally. They have now realised that Lucy and Leonard had two cars and that she has driven away. They are checking with other police forces for sightings, but nothing has come up so far.

The man in black is woken at about 2 o'clock. The wind is blowing a gale and the rain is lashing down. It has been for hours and appears to be getting heavier and heavier. Those around in 2007 will remember the rain that came that summer. It caused serious flooding in places. As he lies there wondering what has woken him, he listens to the wind and the rain. It is possible it was an extra strong gust of wind that woke him, but something inside of him tells him it is not. He has no intention of going out in this, unless it is something like the side gate banging. But he hasn't heard anything like that since he has been awake.

'Would you like a cup of coffee?' the voice beside him makes him jump. He thought she was still asleep.

'Did I wake you, or was it the wind and the rain?'

'I don't know for sure, but something did. It was probably the same thing that woke you.'

'I'll go and make us a drink.'

'Thanks, because I don't think I will get back to sleep easily with this racket going on. I can't remember the rain hitting the windows so hard.'

'I think it is more the direction and strength of the wind, rather than the heaviness of the rain.'

He puts on his dressing gown and sets off to go down to make their drinks. One of the dogs is fast asleep on the landing. He has to step over it to make it down the stairs. The other dog is fast asleep in the hall downstairs. It is stretched out across the hall, sleeping deeply and undisturbed by the weather. If it had been something else, they would have been awake and barking. That does something to settle the man in black.

He switches on the kitchen light and puts the kettle on. Just before it comes to the boil, he hears a now familiar sound. It is a familiar sound which then will become something else, if the pattern is to continue.

He makes their drinks and then takes them upstairs. He just makes it into the bedroom when the power goes off.

'I was wondering when that would happen' he says as he walks round the end of the bed, his way being lit by the light of her Ipad. He gets into bed on his side and they wait.

The whistling sound seems to go on for much longer than usual, but sure enough, in the end it changes into a whisper. They can hear it is a whisper, but they can't interpret any of the words. They just don't become clear enough to distinguish the words. And that is the way they stay. They just don't become clear.

'Have you checked that it isn't just our fuse box that has tripped?'

'No, I haven't. I'll go and see.'

He grabs the torch that he keeps at his bedside and goes down to check. He is back less than a minute later.

'No, it is all dark. Even the road sign light is off. And you can just hear an alarm somewhere.'

He gets back into bed and finishes his drink. As the whispers came, the noise of the wind and the rain diminished significantly. It is quite evident to the man in black that this is something connected to Elizabeth and Edmund. Other than that, he has no clue. He presumes that someone will have contacted Western Power to advise of the outage. You shouldn't do that, because if everyone assumes so, then it might never get reported. He decides he will.

The landline isn't working, but he gets through on his mobile. Yes it has been reported. But no they have no idea when it will be fixed. And no, they don't know what it is. Their system isn't showing up the outage. They have sent someone to try to investigate the issue. They haven't heard back as yet from them.

The engineer, who has been sent, is having no luck in reaching Wenlock. There is a tree down on the Buildwas Road. He has reported that in. In the meantime he has turned round and is trying another route into Wenlock. He gets through Cressage and onto the main road, but when he reaches the bottom Harley turn, the road is blocked there too. He reports that in too, but someone has beaten him to it this time.

It is a longer detour this time, but what he finds out in effect is that all roads into Wenlock are blocked, one way or another. There is no point trying to make it in on foot, as all his tools are in the back of his truck. He reports in and is told to wait for police help.

Back in the house, the man in black is still sitting up in bed, waiting for something to happen. Neither of them can get back to sleep, not that they are trying. It is really hard to ignore the whispers. It is harder still, as they seem to be moving round the room, whichever room you go into, they follow you. But still they cannot make out what the whispers are.

That isn't the case in all of the houses in Wenlock. Pretty much every resident has been woken by the storm and then subsequently kept awake by the whispers. Most of the residents can only hear the sound of the whispering, but can't make out a single word of what they say. But there are others, not that many, who are able to hear exactly what the whispers are.

Some of these people either heard what the whispers said to Leonard and Lucy earlier when they were shackled to the railings of the Guildhall, or they had been told about them by friends or neighbours. Wenlock is a small place and word has a habit of spreading fast, particularly about things that are bad.

For those who can hear the whispers, they know instantly they are aimed at them, personally. Each and every one of them is guilty of the thing the whisperer is telling them. Some of them, who think they are hard people, are extremely unsettled by the whispers. In some cases they are really puzzled as to how the whisperer might know what they are telling them. They think they are the only ones who know what they have been doing or are doing. That is clearly now not the case.

Their initial concern is that the whisperer might be publicising what they have done and who they are, to everyone in the town. But that is not the course of action that the whisperer takes on this occasion. When the whisperer has finished repeating the whisper several times to each of the chosen individuals, they are then whispered a choice. In some cases it is a number of choices. In essence, the whisperer is giving them the opportunity to stop in some cases, to rectify and come clean in others, and in the case of a few, to turn themselves in, along with their ill-gotten gains. Those who are asked to stop; are mostly those who just can't resist saying things about others. Those who are asked to rectify and come clean; are mostly those who have stolen or a similar crime. The others are of a serious nature which are just totally unacceptable and need to be put through the courts.

They are all told what to do and how long they have to do it. The whisperer promises that no one will escape doing what has been asked. It is their choice how they do things. The easiest cause will be to do what the whisperer has told them individually to do. If not, the whisperer will make something happen. It is not specified, but only a few dare to poo-poo what the whispers are warning.

The whispers continue for the best part of an hour and then they are gone. The whistling sound comes back and then that too disappears, only to be replaced by the wind and the rain picking up again. That continues for another hour or so and then that too starts to relent.

It is just before the rain stops that they both fall asleep again, but not before the dogs have been out in the garden. The ground is soft after all the rain, but there isn't the standing water that you might think there would be after this amount of rain.

The man in black is sure that he is asleep, when his eyes close. But what happens when they do; is that he sees Elizabeth and Edmund there in front of his eyes. They are looking directly at him. And they know the very second that he realises they are there.

'We thought this might be an easier way.' Those are the words Elizabeth says to him as he lies there in his bedroom.

The man in black does not answer them, but just watches them. He is trying to work out where they are. It doesn't take him long to know that they are in the house in Sheinton Street, in the front bedroom. They sit down and beckon for him to come.

Without really knowing how he gets there, he finds that he is sitting in the chair in that bedroom, opposite them. He also notices that somehow he is now dressed.

'What happened to Lucy?'

'She will not get far. But that is not our concern at the moment. You have the cord for the disk with you.'

'I don't think so.' He replies.

'Feel in your pocket. You will find that you picked it up.'

He does and he indeed finds it in there. He hands it over and Edmund strings the disk and then hands it to Elizabeth to put round her neck.

'We have been thinking and we agree that you are right. It will be easier to find the other disk than we thought. It will be somewhere near here.'

'So it has to be in or around a settlement, this settlement. Otherwise why have we been brought back here?'

'You have been brought back, because it is time. That is what the whisper says. And the whisper seems to know most things. It is time for both of the discs to be recovered. I would say that something is going to happen that leads to the second disc coming to the surface, so to speak.'

Chapter 44 Disc

'I have a feeling that it has to be here' Edmund says, as they wonder where to start their search. 'There has to be some connection to this town. Why else have we come here and are the forces shackling these people to the railings?'

No one knows if he is right or wrong. There are literally no clues to go on. Always assuming that this is the place where the disc has ended up. The one disc being found in the cave is easy to understand. There is a path to follow for that one. Edmund's history is more catalogued. On the other hand, Elizabeth's is very vague. But there is little doubt now that it is that disc which they have to locate. They have no clues and who knows how many hundreds of years since its last known location, and even that location isn't known precisely. If only they had some information about what happened to Elizabeth's family after she died. But they haven't unfortunately.

'It's all here' a voice says behind them.

But the only one to hear the voice is the man in black. He turns to find that Anne is standing in the doorway. He tells Elizabeth and Edmund that she is there and has spoken.

'What do you mean by that?'

'It is all here in the town, or close by. There are burial grounds in and around the town. I do not know for what years they were used, but some of them go back to Roman times.'

'I'm not getting the feeling that the disc is in a burial ground. Anyway if they are in the town as it is today, then it may have a building on it and I don't think that is the case.'

The conversations are long, as only the man in black can hear and see everyone.

'Can you possibly ask?'

No one is sure who this question is aimed at. It is the man in black who has asked it. Even he is surprised by the words that have just come out of his mouth. It takes a few second before anyone responds, but it is Elizabeth who does so first.

'Can we possibly ask what?'

'I meant can you possibly ask whoever brought you here, if they know something that might help us.'

'I don't know if I can ask anything.'

'You won't know if you don't try, anyway. At the moment you have nothing. Maybe you should go into the other room and ask them out loud.'

'Do you think I will get an answer?'

'I have no idea. But surely it is worth a try.'

Elizabeth doesn't say any more, but gets up and walks through to the other room. The three others stay in the front room. She is back less than a minute later.

'I need to be in here. You will have to go downstairs, to the room down there.'

No one asks how she knows this, but the man in black takes it to be a good sign. It is either that, or Elizabeth has decided she needs to lie down to ask and the bed is in this room. With the message relayed so everyone knows what is going on, the three retire down the stairs into the living room.

Elizabeth waits until she hears that they have reached the bottom of the stairs. She stands waiting, as she thinks she should know what to do next.

Everyone upstairs and downstairs hears the arrival of the whistling sound. It whizzes in through the front of the house and seems to permeate every part of every room. It swirls and dives, almost as if it is making sure of something. It soon changes into a whisper, but then that is upstairs. Downstairs the whistling fades to a distant sound, but is still there nevertheless.

As is the norm by now, the whispering that Elizabeth hears at first is unintelligible. The sounds all seem to be joined and they make no sense. She concentrates even more, but still she can't distinguish one word from the next one. She lies down on the bed and closes her eyes, in the hope that will help concentrate her thoughts even more. She is rewarded for this action, by the whisper becoming clearer. She starts to be able to hear the words being whispered.

'It is time for all this to end.'

This is repeated several times, before she does see, yet she doesn't see, a picture in her mind. She tries not to question anything. She tries to go with the flow. Again she is rewarded by the whisper. She feels that she is falling asleep and in many ways that is what she is doing. She is being removed further from her conscious thoughts. Everything goes quiet around her. She can't hear any noise, other than the rustling of the whispers, as she sinks deeper and deeper. Then in an instant, she is transported in her mind to another place. She doesn't recognize the place, but she does recognize the person she can see. This person is not alone. There are a few others, but she can't make out who they are. They are all standing together around a hole in the ground. Elizabeth tries to move so that she can see some more. It takes her a while to master it, but she does it in the end. What she sees when she looks into the hole in the ground, makes her shudder? There are two bodies in there. They are lying side by side. One is a man and one is a child. She knows both of them. The adult is her father and the child is herself. As she realises who they are, someone starts to fill the hole in the ground with the earth they have dug out of it. She stands back and waits for the next progression. She knows there will be more to come.

She also thinks it is unlikely she will follow this step by step. She blinks and her world goes black for a few seconds. She is right about that. The next thing she sees; is her mother in a settlement. She is busy cooking something, probably a meal. A young child is running around near her. Elizabeth does not know this child. A short time later, a man comes into the scene. Elizabeth does not recognize him either. She gets the feeling that it is alright. She doesn't need to know who they are. She makes a note of their features.

She blinks again and once more she has moved on. By the way her mother looks now, she has moved on by quite a lot of years. A man comes to her side. It is not the man she saw before, but then she recognizes something in him. She knows it is the child she saw before. Her mother bends over and she sees the disc around her neck, on a cord. She knows she is on the right track here. The other man does not appear this time. She blinks again.

This time there is another hole in the ground. This time it is a woman in the ground. It is her mother. The man in this scene is older, but it is still her son. He has a woman at his side and there is a boy and a girl. Elizabeth notices that the girl is wearing something round her neck. She thinks she knows what that is. She tries to move to get a better view. They start to fill in the hole. A bit of dirt flicks towards where Elizabeth is standing and she blinks. She is no longer there. Time has moved on once more.

The man and the woman aren't in this scene, but the girl and the boy are. The girl is lying in a bed. She does not look very well. As she lies there, the boy is mopping her brow with a wet cloth. They can only be in their teens. The girl then suddenly reaches for something. She takes something from her neck and gives it to the boy. Elizabeth can clearly see what it is she has given him; the disc. She tries to get closer, but on the way there she blinks again. This time she is outside in the country. She still has no idea where she is. The man is the same person, but yet again some years have gone by. The man is sitting on a rock and looking at something. She goes over and stands beside him and then she can see what he is looking at. He is looking at a flock of sheep. Elizabeth starts to get excited. She thinks there is a connection.

The man stands up and shepherds his flock closer to where he lives. It is a crude hut by a hill. Inside she is fractionally disappointed, as she thought the hut would be a different one to this. She blinks again, but she is surprised to find she is still here with him. When his sheep are safe, he turns and goes into the hut. Inside it is very basic. It is hard to know if she has seen this before or not, but she knows there must be some significance in all this. She watches intently as she thinks something important is about to happen. Why else would she still be here. He has a fire in the hut and he goes to stand beside it. He then removes something from round his neck. It is the disc. It is at this moment he turns round, as if he has heard something. He goes over to check the door is shut; it is. He then goes behind the fire to the rock that is there. There is a stout bit of wood leaning against the side of it. He lifts it up and then manoeuvres it under one corner of the rock. With great effort he levers the rock off the ground, enough for him to stand on the wood and lean in with his hand for something. It is a small leather pouch. He quickly puts the disc in the pouch and then places it back under the rock. Then he lets the rock down on top of it again.

Elizabeth sees all this and wonders why the pouch was not already out, ready for the disc to go in. Then the reason comes to her. The pouch has something else in too. She blinks again and when she returns she is still in a hut. It looks different to her as things have changed. Then as she is still trying to work it out, he comes in through the door. It is morning. The sun is shining through the doorway. She knows it is him, but he is much older. He goes to the fire and then she sees him walk and pick up a stout piece of wood. He goes behind the fire and she sees it is the same rock. She knows it is, because there is a crack half way down on the left hand side. It makes it kind of look like the letter E.

He puts the end of the rock under the rock, but he does not have the strength to lift the rock. She moves in closer. He gives up with a big sigh and then takes his top off and starts to have a wash. Elizabeth notices that he is not wearing anything around his neck. In fact, being more specific than that, he is not wearing the disk. It must be in the pouch, under the rock. She blinks and to her surprise she finds she is back in the room; the room in Sheinton Street.

She gets up from the bed and goes downstairs to see the others.

'I have a clue' is all she says to them.

Chapter 45 Disc

Elizabeth relates everything she has seen to the others. Yes, it is true it is a clue, but there is still the problem of where. Yes it does confirm, sort of, that the area it is to be found is here or close to here. But that is still a large area to look for such a small item.

No one can come up with any idea of which direction it may be. No one has anything to go on from that long ago. No one believes the hut could possibly still be standing after all these years, even if it is the same hut and they aren't even sure of that. So it is not as if you could even ask around, to see if anyone locally knows of an old hut or such like.

The only person who can really help them with distance is Edmund, but he says he has no idea. There were other priorities at the time and he just can't remember the route they took, or how long it had taken them. He says that for all he knows they could have travelled in a big circle as they tried to get over flood waters.

They also discuss where Elizabeth may have stood when she originally saw disaster looming. The scenery will have changed massively over the intervening years. It is possible that parts of the town could be standing on land that she had looked over.

The man in black decides he needs his ipad and that is back at home. Maybe a bit of help from internet search sites will help them to narrow down things. Half an hour later he is back. He has done a quick search. If anything the opposite has happened and things are even less clear.

The monastery had been founded in 680AD and more or less there was little other than a small settlement there, until you get into four figures. Then the town was centred on the three main streets. They looked, well he did, for maybe half an hour or so, but there is precious little before the year 1000AD. It becomes clear that whatever people there were before that, were small individual, possibly farming settlements. They found nothing whatsoever that gave them any clue as to the direction they are searching for.

But something does come out of it; The Wrekin. The man in black had not given it any consideration before, but he sees it mentioned in part of what he is reading.

'Could you see The Wrekin?'

All he gets is a blank look for that. He shows them a picture of the hill. He explains how it stands out in the vicinity of Wenlock. He shows them another picture of it and although that helps, it doesn't give it placement in context with this area. There is nothing for it, but to go to a point where the Wrekin will be visible. Hopefully that will give them some bearings and then a lead on the clue. That is the hope as they walk along the road towards the school. He walks into the small car park and then into the fields. At the far end he finds a place where you can see across to the

Wrekin. At last there is recognition; well from Elizabeth and Edmund, but not from Anne.

The man in black asks them to hold their thoughts, while he takes them to another point. They walk along the top of the edge and at some point cross over the main road. They keep going to a place further along, somewhere in the region of where the cave is. When they reach the point he has been aiming for, then he stops and shows them the Wrekin from this angle.

'It is not in this direction' Edmund says. 'We did not see this on a daily basis. In fact I only saw it when I came up here for the cave.'

On reflection the man in black had worked that one out, but he needed it to be confirmed. Elizabeth is less sure, but then she and he are from different times. It is Edmund in truth he needs to recognise where it stands, in relation to his life here.

Edmund stops and stares at it. It is easy for them to see that he is trying to work out some kind of direction in his head. Suddenly he turns away from looking at it and starts to walk along the edge. He goes down an old path that you wouldn't really have known was there. In fact it isn't even as visible as an animal track, but Edmund knows where to walk.

'It wasn't anything like this when I was here. There were trees everywhere in this part. That is what has been making this so hard. The landscape has changed dramatically since my days here. It is definitely not in that direction.'

He stops again after a while and smells the air. His eyes are closed too.

'I was trying to smell water' he explains after a minute or so. 'There were streams around here. But they were all swollen and so apart from what may have changed in the intervening years; I would not be likely to recognise anything about them now. But I know we have to cross a stream and we could not go straight across when we wanted to.'

He starts walking again and they follow the contours of the land. Anne is starting to trail behind them. The man in black goes back to see what is wrong.

'I do not want to go any further. I don't think I can be of much assistance to you. Anyway I am uncomfortable in this light.'

'That's fine' he says 'I am sure you will know if we are successful.'

At that she turns round and starts to make her way back the way they have come. The man in black can see they have walked quite a distance already. He is thinking that at some point they will make a turn. Surely it can't be much further than this from the town?

He explains why Anne is not with them anymore. It is not a problem to them. They resume their path, with Edmund still leading the way. An hour later, even though the progress has been stop and start, they have still moved a fair distance from Wenlock. The man in black is concerned that they have moved too far. He has asked Edmund a couple of times, but his reply each time is that he thinks they are still going in the right direction. Elizabeth is very quiet at the moment. In fact the further they have gone, the more withdrawn she has become. She will not answer his questions about this though. There is nothing he can do but carry on, for now.

'We have come too far' Edmund realises that this is not right; at last. 'We came this way I am sure, but the shepherd's hut is not this far out of the town of Wenlock as it is now called. We have missed the stream and the place to cross it.'

The man in black thinks it is quite amusing how he is using the collective we, now that he hasn't found their destination, while all the way so far it has been I. It is true though that they have all been looking for anything that might point them in the correct direction.

They make their way back, more or less on the same route they came on. No one sees anything that helps at all.

'I think we must be too far over' the man in black says. Of the three of them, he hasn't been where they are looking for. Where they know will be different too. It all makes it really hard to locate where the shepherd's hut would have been, if indeed that is where they should be looking for. He continues:

'I think we should go back to the town and start from there. I think we can safely say we should be looking on this side of the town though.'

The others agree.

'So I think we should search in an arc, starting close to the town and then steadily moving out a bit further. It is going to take time.'

'I think we should start that tomorrow' Elizabeth says. 'I have something that I need to get done. I think the reason we are finding nothing, is because we do not have things in the right order.'

'You are talking about Lucy, aren't you?'

'I think that is possible. It is just as we went further from the town I got worse. Now I am returning; I know there is something I have to do.'

They make it back to the house in Sheinton Street, where they part company. Elizabeth and Edmund go inside the house, while the man in black walks along into town and then along Barrow Street to his house. There is someone there waiting for him when he gets there. It is Andy.

'Don't even ask' the man in black says to him, when he sees him waiting for him.

'I wasn't going to' he replies.

'You also want to know about Lucy?'

'I was thinking about asking for help.'

'I don't think you will need to. I have a feeling that will be dealt with. I don't know of course, but I believe they will have to find her if they are to move on, so to speak.'

'Normally I would get you to explain that, but I don't think I would understand the answer.'

That's good, because I don't understand it either.'

Chapter 46 Lucy

Lucy finds somewhere where she can rest her head for a couple of days and nights. They weren't particularly happy when she couldn't produce a credit card to pay for her stay, but she has cash and leaves a deposit too, which makes it acceptable. The car is parked in a street around the corner. It should be safe enough there. It is a non-descript vehicle that doesn't attract too much of the wrong attention. She has her backpack and small bag with her.

She sleeps fitfully the first night. She keeps waking up, thinking that the police are going to burst through her door any minute and arrest her. The thought unsettles her so much, that she decides that she needs to move on more quickly than she initially intended. So in the morning, she removes her things from the room and puts them back in her car. She may or may not come back to stay for the second night she has paid for. She is not certain at this point.

She knows she cannot use the phone to direct her to her next destination, so she walks to the shops and buys a small road map. The address she needs is in her purse, but she knows it anyway. The storage unit is in Watford. She doesn't need to call in advance. When you pay for the premium service, you can pretty much call in whenever you need to. There is always someone on duty there.

She is finding that for some reason she is nervous this morning. Several times in the night she thought she heard things. She thought he heard a whistling sound, but when she went to the window, it turned out to be just the wind outside. The sound was coming through the small vent in the window. Then she heard people talking, but it was faint. That turned out to be people in the corridor, when she looked out there.

Now that she is on her way to Watford, the car is being gently buffeted by a side wind, or so she thinks it is. It is making a whistling noise as she drives along. It hadn't been doing that yesterday. She keeps thinking that she will hear a whisper next, but that doesn't come while she is driving to the storage company.

She makes it there well before lunch time. She pulls into the entrance and presses the buzzer by the gate. She gives her member number and a minute later, she is allowed to drive in. She parks up and walks into reception. It has become quite breezy out there and she is almost blown in. She shows her card and is asked to sit in the waiting room while they access her things.

Fifteen minutes later she is taken through to one of the back areas. She is shown into a large room. The number of her unit is easily visible on the front by the door. Once it is checked and agreed, they put their key in one lock and then she puts hers in the other. Once they have made sure the door opens, they leave the room. She locks the door behind them.

Twenty minutes later she has finished transferring what she needs into the large holdall that was kept in there. She has cleared it out completely. It will probably not be a good idea to come back here again. That is particularly as she will be changing her identity and her looks. Even though the service is supposed to be guaranteed, there is still the possibility that someone could let the cat out of the bag, so to speak.

The service is paid for a year in advance. She will wait for a month or two before she contacts them, to tell them she will not be renewing it. There are other places she can use in the future; other places who will only see her and know her as the new Lucy, or whatever she will be called then.

A change of vehicle is now required too, she thinks. Now that she has her alternative papers, she can ditch her car. She stops to contact the place she hired her car from. She arranges for her car to be taken to East Midlands Airport. She tells them it will need to be done on trade plates. She will get their car there for them to collect.

Later in the day, she has been to the airport and dropped off the hire car in long stay. She has left the key on the back offside tyre. They have done the same with hers, but she doesn't go to it. She goes to the terminal and grabs a cab to take her to Nottingham. When she gets there, she finds a car hire office and rents another car. She finds a small hotel to stay the night in. This time she has been able to use her card, her new card. The hotel is not part of a group.

She takes all of her bags into her room. What she could do with now, is somewhere to rent short term, so she can get things sorted. A quick hunt online allows her to find somewhere in the peak district. She pays for it online and is told where she can pick up the key and directions to the cottage she has rented. After another restless night with more whistling noises disturbing her sleep and more sounds of people talking, she leaves early in the morning before breakfast time.

The day is an overcast one and the rain has already started to fall before she leaves. The wind soon picks up too and she struggles to go at any speed, as what traffic is on the roads is being forced to drive slowly too. Just as she is nearing her destination, a thunderstorm breaks around her. She has heard the boom of the thunder for the past few miles. The lightning has been lighting up the dark daytime skies too, for just as long.

With difficulty, she follows the instructions and directions she has been given and she finds the cottage she has rented, and the key box where she will get access to the door keys. She dives into the house, but leaves her bags in the car. She has not got the inclination to brave the storm to bring them in with her. If anything the storm has intensified since she arrived.

She turns on all of the lights and puts the kettle on. There is a welcome pack waiting for her in the kitchen. It has just a few of the basic essentials: milk, coffee, tea, sugar, bread and butter. It is more than she has brought with her. Her intention had been to unpack and then go out and do a food shop, to last her for a few days. That isn't going to happen in this weather. She will just have to manage on what there is in this welcome pack. It could be worse she thinks.

With no let-up in the weather an hour later, she decides that she needs her bags in with her. She is not happy leaving the big holdall in the car. It is too important to her. It has everything she needs. It also has a bit of her history in there too. In fact there is enough to incriminate her for some of her dreadful deeds. She needs to keep it close while she changes things and then it can be safely locked away again somewhere else.

Everything is in with her and she has just turned on the television to watch the news, when the power goes off. It leaves her more or less in darkness, as the day is still very overcast outside. Before she can move to look for something to illuminate the room, she hears the whistling sound again. This time she knows for sure that it is the same one. There is just something about it. It moves around her, twisting and turning, as it races round the room. She can feel it as it rushes by her and then gathers in one place, ready to make another pass of her. She experiences that for a full five minutes, in the dark. She is rooted to the spot and there is more than just a small pang of fear in her heart. That is because she knows that the whispers will start soon enough and they surely do.

'It is time now for you Lucy. You are ready to reveal.'

Surprising it only whispers this once. There is no unintelligible bit. It just says those few words and then stops. The whispering stops and the whistling does not make its return. She is still rooted to the spot. She is expecting something else to happen. She has no idea what that might be, but she is sure something is coming. It is, but it is not what she is expecting, I am sure.

Her eyes are wide open and as best she can, she tries to keep looking all around her, trying to be prepared for what comes next. She doesn't want to close her eyes and she doesn't even want to blink, as that might give it a start on her. Inevitably though something has to give and it is Lucy who gives first; she blinks.

The car is parked in the middle of the road. I say the middle of the road, but it is actually only wide enough at this point for one car. The doors are all wide open. The engine is switched off. The lights are all on full. Even the bonnet is up. Then the horn starts to sound. Lucy never knew that a car horn could be so loud.

She thinks she must be dreaming; having another restless night, like the two previous ones. But unlike those two nights, she feels that she is cold. She knows she should open her eyes and then that dreadful noise will stop. She does so and then the dream becomes a nightmare.

She knows immediately where she is. She has no idea how she got there. She is shackled to the railings of the Guildhall. In front of her is her car. It is not either of the rental cars; it is her car. She can see her bags on the seats of the car. She starts to scream, but it makes no difference. This is no longer a dream. This is no longer a nightmare. This is reality.

People come out and look. People call the police and they come. Andy comes too. It doesn't take long to find what they need in her things, to incriminate her completely. This time they take no chances. They handcuff Lucy while she is still shackled to the bars. On the other side of the road now are three people. Most people will only see one. But Elizabeth, Edmund and the man in black are watching.

The shackles just disappear and Lucy is still held by the police handcuffs. Andy looks over at them as he leads her towards the police van. He can't see them all, but he knows three people are watching him lead her away. He nods at the man in black and he just smiles back at him.

Chapter 47 Disc

They start off fairly close to the town the next morning. It is slow and laborious, but they stick with it. As nearly as they can make it, they only have a couple of hundred yards between the first sweep and the next one, going back the other way.

It is interesting doing the search this way, because they find out things. They find out just how many streams there are and where they run. They also find that you cannot always cross them where you want to. All this is familiar to Edmund. They all have a good feeling. Elizabeth is much more settled, now that Lucy is back and in police custody. As soon as that happened, she knew that she could move on.

'I can't say for sure, but something about this stream and it being here is right. It almost feels familiar.' Edmund says as they cross one of the streams.

'I can feel it too' Elizabeth cannot keep the excitement out of her voice.

'I'm remembering things' Edmund says and closes his eyes.

Elizabeth and the man in black stand back a step, to give him room.

'By the end of the next day, it was more the lack of food than anything else that made up our minds to leave the safety of the cave. There was that and the fact that at last the rain had stopped falling. Initially it let up a little, but after a few more hours it relented and finally stopped. We waited a further hour or so, in case our attackers were just waiting for this time to resume their hunt. There wasn't a single sound that came to our ears that spelled out any danger. The sounds we were hoping not to hear, being dogs and men roaring.

We had to move now, while there was still going to be light for another couple of hours. Who knows how long it would take to get food and what state the settlement would be in. We feared the worst of course. We were right to as well.

We made our way out of the cave and slowly up to the top of the slope. The ground was wet, very wet. On the flat it would have been soft, but there wasn't much soil between the surface and the rock underneath. Even so it was slippery in places. When we reached the top, the ground was about the same there, except there was water lying on the ground everywhere. Edgar walked ahead as we made our way to where we had pitched our temporary shelter. When we found it, there was little left, except the makings on the ground, swishing around in puddles.

We quickly moved on from there and made our way by an indirect route back to the settlement. Our huts had been wilfully destroyed by force and then by fire. There was little left, other than the charred remains of the few huts that had stood proudly there before. There were other charred remains too. There was little evidence of any possessions left there in our own huts or the others. There was also plenty of surface water around here. It was about six inches deep as we sloshed around, inspecting the remnants of our former abode.

Edgar decided that catching fish is more likely to be possible in the current conditions. The need to find food overruled the need to bury the dead, or what was left of them. Their charred bodies weren't going anywhere soon, so he would leave it until he had caught something to keep the hunger at bay, before he came back to give them a decent burial.

We left the settlement and made for the stream, except when we came into view of it, there was far more than a stream rushing down towards the river a few miles away. The stream that had been maybe six feet across most of the time; was now ten times wider than that and who knows how deep. Despite the waters being so high and what would appear to be a lot of the lower ground flooded by flood waters, we had not seen a single piece of wildlife since we had left the cave, not one.

It was after we had moved off from the settlement and rather than follow the flow of the stream down to the river, we had decided to move to higher ground. Part of the reasoning for this was that we didn't know how much more water was yet to come down the stream. Often the stream would swell more than a day after any rain had stopped. What we needed to do is to go up; back up to the level we were at before.

We decided not to go to exactly the same place though. Although it was unlikely to get more flooded than it is already up there, there was also nothing there for us to forage or hunt. Food was a priority, well after our safety of course.

We kept our eyes peeled for any movement that caught our attention. Initially there was nothing, but then we soon began to spot evidence of where the wildlife had gone.

It was I who came up with a potential place to go. I wasn't at all sure that there would be anything there we could use, but if there was, then the place would be ideal for us to have a fire, after it got dark. Even though the rain has stopped, the sky was still very overcast.

It was tricky making our way across the valley. We had to turn back a couple of times, when we couldn't get across the streams we came across in our way. None of them were swollen in the way our stream was, but they were still too wide and possibly too deep to cross safely.

Eventually we found a place where it was relatively safe to cross. Someone at one time had placed a fallen tree across the stream. Although the water was lapping almost at the top edge of it, it was possible to cross over safely. What puzzled us all was that there wasn't that much water at this point in the stream. What water was in it further down must have been joining it from some other source. Don't get me wrong; the level is higher than it normally would be, but it wasn't anything like as swollen as the other streams they had seen. I think that is this stream.

He stops for a few seconds.

'I think we should walk as I talk. I think I know which way to go.'

He continues, with Elizabeth guiding him, as he has his eyes closed.

'As we moved over, it became apparent also that this side of the stream and the area in this this direction had not experienced nearly as much rain as we had done.

As we neared our destination, we came across some sheep. There was just the odd one or two at first, but then a big flock of them. They seemed to be unharmed by any rain that had come down, though looking at the ground here it wasn't very wet at all. In fact it was quite dry.

I knew where I was and although we were unable to see it yet, I was leading them to the shepherd's hut. The shepherd always kept a good store of wood, ready for the nights he would have to spend up here looking after his sheep. I could only hope that the fighters had not come this way. That hope was soon dashed when we came across the body of the shepherd. He had been killed quite savagely and then left for the elements. It didn't seem right to leave him out in the open, even though we needed to get where we were going, as the light was all but failing us. A crude covering of stones was enough to keep the carrion at bay for now. We were worried that as the shepherd had been found, then maybe his hut would have been too and then destroyed.

We moved quickly on, as the last of the light was on the verge of disappearing. We still couldn't see his hut.'

Edmund stops.

'It's here'.

'How do you know that? Where is it?'

'Well the hut isn't here anymore, but we didn't expect that to be still standing. But this is the place.'

As if to confirm that, a flock of sheep wander into view round the end of the hill. There are maybe twenty of them and when they see them, they stop.

'So the hut would have been here back against the side of the hill. It was behind bushes and there was a moss wall.'

He steps forward and moves this way and that, seeing a picture in his mind. He closes his eyes and then feels in front of him, more so that he doesn't walk into the wall. Then he stops again.

'The fire would have been here and the rock behind it.'

All they can see is a mossy bank.

'I hope no one minds what we have to do now.' The man in black says.

He takes off his backpack and takes out some tools. He starts to scrape away at the moss. It is thick and there is earth beneath it in places.

'You are sure this is the spot Edmund?'

'Yes it is there.'

It takes ten more minutes before the man in black has uncovered a large rock. They knew a few minutes ago it was the right one. The crack showed the shape of the letter E. It takes another ten minutes to get his lever in place with the block of wood. It takes fifteen seconds to lever the rock. It moves far more easily than he thought it would. The bottom side where he is standing lifts up; lifts up enough for Edmund to feel under it.

His hand comes away quickly and he says.

'Let it down now.'

He hands the pouch to Elizabeth while he and the man in black repair the damage they have done. Twenty minutes later, they start the walk home. They will always know, but they don't think anyone else will be able to notice, if anyone ever comes this way anyway.

They walk back to the house in Sheinton Street where, with the three of them looking on, Elizabeth pulls the top of the pouch open. She shakes the contents out onto her hand. Two things fall out. One is the disk and the other is a gold ring.

The man in black leans forward to take a closer look and then he blinks.

Chapter 48 The last chapter

The house in Sheinton Street becomes occupied early in the spring. The young couple, who move into it, were notified that it had been left to them. The man in black meets them one morning while he is walking in the town. He notices they are both wearing something around their necks that glistens in the morning sun. As he passes them, he can't help but notice the gold ring on her finger. He can't help thinking that they look a nice young couple and how relaxed and comfortable they appear to be. But what he remembers most about that meeting; is that as he approached them, there was a whistling sound in the air and when he passed them, it turned into a whisper; a Wenlock whisper that said "Thank you."

The end

Wenlock Whispers Copyright © 2019 William (Bill) Stenlake

Wenlock Whispers by Bill Stenlake

All rights reserved. No part of this book may be reproduced, distributed or transmitted in any form, by any means without the prior consent of the author.

All characters in this publication are fictitious and any resemblance to persons, living or dead is purely coincidental. Some places named in the book exist and are real and some do not exist and are not real. The placement of all things geographical is relevant to this story only and as such should be deemed fictional.

Book Cover Photo: © FlairImages/Dreamstime.com

Other books by Bill Stenlake:
HOLLOW MILL
THE KEEPER
KENAN'S LEGACY
CORNERSTONE
THE GRAND MASTER
DETECTIVE BRAMLEY BOOK 1
RANDOLPH
VOICES IN MY HEAD
LOWARTH TOLL
THE CORIDAE KEY
BRAMLEY BOOK 2
THE MANNACHS
DIMENSIONS
THE ROOTS
A PAIR OF SHORTS
THE WATCHER
THE KEEPER TRILOGY
IT'S DARK IN WENLOCK
RODDY JOHNSTONE
IT'S MURDER IN WENLOCK

Printed in Poland
by Amazon Fulfillment
Poland Sp. z o.o., Wrocław